Kingston

M. Monique

Published by M. Monique Presents

Contents

To my family...

Prologue

KINGSTON

"If nothing else, I can count on my sons to come see me."

Nathaniel Wells' guttural laugh was louder than it should've been. He made light of the fact that we were separated by the glass partition as if him being here was a joke. I shook my head, annoyed by the fact that I drove here to share some good news with him.

"We'll always come visit you, Dad." My baby brother, August, was only fourteen and didn't understand visiting your father in prison could scar you for life if you let it.

"I just came to tell you that I did it. I'm a college graduate," I informed him.

His smile was wide, and his boisterous laughter seemed to shakc the glass.

"My son!" he exalted.

While I appreciated my father's congratulatory response, deep down, I wasn't happy. The one person that should've been there celebrating this time with us was gone.

"Your mother would be proud," he stated, still smiling.

And here was my issue with Nathaniel Wells. Because of him, our mother was dead. Or should I say because of his lifestyle our mother was dead. Either way, Nate was responsible for taking away the best part of me.

"Yeah, she would," I conceded.

"King's gon' be a federal agent, Dad! Ain't that cool?"

Nate chortled. "Hell, yeah it is! My boy gon' be some-muthafuckin'-body!"

August beamed with pride and so did my dad.

"That's what I wanna hear, Son. Get outchea and do better than I did," he encouraged. "Ain't no hope for me. But it's hope for you and August. I wanna see my boys succeed more than anything."

"We wanna see you get out of here, Dad," August said, his voice cracking.

I hated bringing him here. Every time it was the same. He wouldn't cry in front of our father, but he'd cry on the way home. I never stopped him from grieving the man that procreated us. Hell, I still grieved him too.

"One day, baby," Nate answered.

Why he chose to fill my brother's head with that bullshit irked me. Not that my father was given life in prison, but he was given forty years, with thirty-four left to serve. The state of Georgia was making him serve it day for day, too. At forty-two years old, he'd be into his seventies by the time it was said and done. That was providing he didn't get into any trouble here and add time to his already healthy sentence. Prayerfully, death wouldn't take him first. Still, he needed to stop pumping August's head up like he'd be getting out next month.

"How's Miss Lily doin'?"

"She's maintaining," I replied.

If she knew he was asking about her, she'd find a way to call up here and cuss him out. My grandmother couldn't stand the ground Nate walked on. She blamed him for her only daughter's death. After losing my mother, my grandmother never recovered. Her two sons dealt with my mother's death just the same. The family was still grieving, even six years later.

"Tell her I said hello," he requested.

August sighed. "That's not a good idea, Dad."

"Yeah," I seconded. "Give her time. She's not ready to forgive you yet."

My father's brown eyes met mine. He stared at me, seeing our similarities, as well as our differences.

"What about you, Kingston? Have you forgiven me?"

Chapter One

KINGSTON

Present day…

"I need a ride to class."

I glanced up from the file I was perusing to see my brother, August, standing at my office door.

"There're two cars in the garage," I stated, going back to my file.

"Yeah, but if I put a dent in either one of 'em you gon' kill my ass. I'd rather you take me to school."

Flicking my gaze back towards the younger version of me, I felt my temper rising. Only August was bold enough to try me. I figured it was because I was his older brother, and I loved him so much that I let him get away with entirely too much shit.

"I wouldn't kill you if you didn't crash everything you get behind the wheel of."

"Mane, that wasn't my fault this time. The repairs will be done by Monday. You gon' take me or what?"

Immaturity wasn't something I knew anything about. When I was twenty, I was nothing like August. He had everything that I didn't growing up—a stable home, money, and nice clothes. He had love, too.

Our father currently resided at the Georgia State Penitentiary. He'd been there since I was sixteen and August eight. Nate was one of the biggest drug kingpins in Florida, and by the time the law caught up with him, they weren't too keen on letting him go.

Our mother, rest her beautiful soul, died shortly before my father went to prison. One night, she was out with my father and his crew when a rival crew shot up the spot. Three people died that night, one being my mother. Marie was beautiful, pure, and loving as fuck. She didn't deserve what happened to her.

It was my father's ways that got her caught up in a street war that left her dead. Thank God those responsible for her murder were either behind bars or dead. The man in me still sought revenge because I couldn't let her death go.

Granny Lily, our mother's mother, had been raising us since our father went to prison. She'd done a great job, giving us the discipline and structure we needed to become adults. I was already sixteen and had experienced too much in my life that caused me to grow up early. All Granny did was provide me shelter and give me the love I'd lacked. Otherwise, she had a grown ass man on her hands dealing with me. August, on the other hand, was a slow learner and took the love we gave him and turned it into him being a spoiled fucking brat. Still, I loved him to death.

"Yeah, I got you." I sighed, closing the file and rubbing my tired eyes. I had too much work to do and didn't have time to run him clear across town. I got up, stretched my back, and left my office, closing the door behind me.

Granny came shuffling inside from the deck with me mugging her.

"Granny," I fussed. "You weren't on those stairs were you?"

She smacked her teeth. "Boy, who daddy is you? I had to check my garden."

"Granny, I told you to stay outta that garden unless one of us is with you. You'on need to be comin' up or down those deck steps by yaself."

At seventy-six, Granny thought she was twenty-six. Her mind was sharp as hell, but her body was teetering along by a string. She'd fallen twice already this year and despite getting her a walker and a cane, she refused to use either. I threatened her that I'd put her in one of those mobile wheelchairs. She cussed me out so bad I was depressed for a couple of days.

Granny stood maybe five feet tall and was slim. My granny's hair was long, natural, and gray. Her deep brown skin was flawless with a reddish undertone. My mother looked and was built just like my granny. Every time I looked at her, I saw what we'd all lost. I was sure that's how my granny felt every time she looked in the mirror.

"Granny, please listen, aight? I'm tryna keep you here with me a lil' longer. Don't you wanna see me get married? Have some kids?"

She guffawed. "Yes, I do!"

"Aight then, stop being hard-headed and stay off those steps. The garden ain't goin' nowhere."

August passed us, shaking his head. "You know she's hard-headed. Where you think I get it from?" he quipped.

Granny and I both smacked him upside his head.

"Go get in the car, mane. I'm comin'."

August clicked his teeth, then laughed as he headed out of the front door.

"I'ma drop him off at school, then I'll be back, Granny." I kissed her forehead. "You need anything back?"

"No, but I thought you had a full plate this week," she stated.

"I do," I confirmed. "Closing out this case, and there's several more that need my attention."

She made a face and said, "You're up here talkin' about marriage and kids... How you figure when you work all the time?"

"It'll happen when it's supposed to, Granny. Don't you fret over it. I'll make you proud of me, don't worry."

She smiled then and her weird brown eyes softened. "I am proud of you, Kingston—very. Marie is too."

Hearing my mother's name brought an instant smile to my face. Although the pain was still there, slowly I was accepting her not being here.

"I do what I can for y'all, Gran." I hugged her to my chest. "Now go sit down 'til I get back."

Grumbling, she shuffled off to her room which was just off the kitchen. I chuckled, shaking my head as I went the opposite way towards my room. This house we lived in was one I bought two years ago. Unlike most men my age, I didn't mind my granny living with me. Once I moved out of her house, it wasn't a few weeks before I was moving her into my house.

My uncles kept trying to get her to move North with them, but my granny would never leave her daughter's side. Staying in Pensacola made her feel closer to my mother. As long as I was alive, my granny wouldn't ever want for shit.

In my room, I grabbed my keys and wallet off the nightstand, then backtracked to the garage. August was sitting in the passenger seat of my Charger with the door cocked open.

"Mane, it's early but you know it's hot as hell outchea. Took you so long?"

I slid into the driver's seat and cranked the engine.

"You need a ride," I reminded him. "If you had ya own shit you wouldn't be outchea sweatin' and complainin'."

He closed his door and gave me a look. "Why you so damn hard on me, bruh? Like I'ain got enough shit on my plate."

I couldn't help but chuckle. "What shit, baby? You're in college, got a roof over ya head, food to eat. Ya pockets stay swole 'cause I won't see it any other way. I'd rather you go to school than work. So, what's on ya plate?" Truthfully, this lil' nigga had it good.

"Nothin', mane. You ain't gon' understand."

As I backed out of the garage and onto the street, I glanced at August. Frustration lined his dark-brown face.

"What don't I understand? Help me so I can help you. Somebody fuckin' witchu?"

He scrunched his face up. "Hell nah, ain't nobody fuckin' with me," he countered. "Faith is pregnant. I'ain ready for no damn baby, mane. I'm tryna talk her into not keepin' it, but she on some spiritual bullshit."

My eyebrows snapped together. I agreed that he wasn't ready for a kid, but his ass needed to man up and handle his responsibilities instead of trying to get rid of them.

"Aight, let's get something straight." He groaned at my tone, but he was going to listen to me today. "If you thought you weren't ready for a baby, you should've strapped that shit up. And tellin' a woman you've been with for six months to just up and get rid of her baby is triflin' as fuck. Spirituality or not, it's her fuckin' right to have that baby."

He exhaled, then shook his head. "I'ain ready, bruh. She probably did the shit on purpose anyway. Besides that, I'm having a hard time with two classes that I know I'm not gon' pass."

I merged onto the interstate, wondering how he could figure that if it was only the second week of school.

"I'm just sayin' you can't do no wrong in Granny's eyes. Not only am I finna be outchea with a whole ass baby, but I'm strugglin' like a muhfucka in two classes. If I fail them I know she gon' be mad as fuck."

"You can get a tutor, August. School just fuckin' started."

He tsked. "I'on need no damn tutor, bruh. It's me. Shit just be on my mind."

"More like, you make time for what you want. Hangin' 'round niggas that ain't tryna do shit but live up under their damn mamas and each other all day ain't it."

Traffic was crazy although it was barely ten. I flowed with the bustle but kept my ears on August.

"Other than Faith, wassup? Be specific."

He sighed. "How this shit with Dad don't bother you?"

August rarely talked about our mother. He was only eight when she died, but still had enough memories of her to last him a lifetime. Our father, on the other hand, August talked about him every other day. While I saw my dad once a month, August went at least twice a month, if not three times a month.

"Whoever said it didn't bother me?"

"The way you move through life like nothin' bothers you," he explained.

"Everyone handles situations differently. I can't change Dad's situation, so I'm not gon' drive myself crazy tryna figure out how I can. The best we can do is what we're already doin'."

It took some time, but I was finally healing from the sting of my father's poor choices. Forgiveness was a hard thing, especially when you loved that person. I loved my dad, cared for him like he should've cared for us, but he chose his path, and that ultimately destroyed our family.

The exit for the university approached just as August said, "You're right, bruh. I'ma get my head together and do what I gotta do. Maybe if I talk to my professors they'll help me stay focused. I'on want Granny to be disappointed."

"And Faith?"

He shrugged. "I heard you on that, too."

"Aight," I replied. "As long as you puttin' some type of effort forth, everything's gon' work out."

Entering the college's campus, I rode around until I was at the building where August's first class was and parked.

"Bet," he said, dapping me, then getting out. "My last class is out at two. I'll just hang around here until then."

I nodded. "Be careful."

"Fa sho," he responded and closed the door.

Shaking my head, I backed out of the parking space, headed off campus, and back to the crib. I prayed over my brother, asking God to protect him. No matter how much I stayed on him, August had to make his own decisions. Now I see how parents felt when their kids go astray. August wasn't even in the streets, yet he worked my nerves overtime. Here he was about to make me an uncle. Sighing, I shook my head again. I should've been the one in a relationship, settled down somewhere, and spoiling the fuck out of my woman.

As if the devil were laughing, my Bluetooth sounded through the car.

"'Sup?" I answered Vicki.

"You didn't call me back last night. Were you with someone else?"

I mugged the console screen like she could see me. "Vicki, we're not together. That means you can't question my moves. I told you last night that I had work. I can't drop everything just to call ya ass."

Her irritated exhalation came through the line. "I just wish you'd pay as much attention to me as you do your job, King. It's not fair."

"Look, I'on wanna hear that, aight?"

"You never wanna hear shit I have to say. Why're we even fuckin' with each other? If you're not gon' give me the time I deserve, then what the fuck is this even about? I'm more than a fuck, King."

Hopping back on the interstate, I replied, "You're right, Vicki. I'm sure it's a nigga outchea that's gon' give you more than some good dick. I apologize if that ain't me."

She scoffed loud as hell. Knowing Vicki, she'd start that crying shit next.

"King!" she cried as I shook my head. "One day a bitch gon' break yo' fuckin' heart so good, I hope I'm around to see it."

"Okay, bet." I hung up, aggravated by the start of my day.

Wasn't that I wasn't into Vicki. She was beautiful and had a good career. She had a fine ass body and a sexy voice that'd bring a man to his knees. I just wasn't that man. Vicki complained about me not having time for her when she wasn't even my damn woman. My career as a drug enforcement agent kept me busy but not so much so that I'd neglect the people I cared about. I guess I didn't care too much about Vicki.

My Bluetooth sounded again, causing me to grumble at the name on the screen.

"What it do?"

"Is that how you answer a business call, King?"

"When it's you, yeah," I responded. "'Cause you ain't callin' for nothin' other than—"

"East side, Seventh Ave. Get there." Lieutenant Anderson hung up in my face per usual.

The more cases I tried putting to rest, the more was heaped onto me. I knew why though. Lieutenant Anderson trusted me. He trusted my ability to get shit done. Exiting the interstate, I headed towards my destination. None of the intentions I'd had for the day were going as planned. I hated when days started like this.

Hours later, exhausted, I swooped back into the parking lot of the university with minutes to spare before August's class let out. I parked, then got out to stretch. Propping myself on the hood of my Charger, I popped a peppermint into my mouth to see if it would alleviate the headache I felt on the horizon. Coming straight from a crime scene, all I wanted to do was crawl in the shower and wipe the grime off of me so that I could dive into the paperwork needing my attention.

The double doors to the building August was in opened, and several students spilled out of them. Some looked like they were escaping prison, while others looked like they were half-dead. There was only one person who's expression caught me in a snare. I understood why my day had completely shifted. My future strutted towards me, an unbothered expression upon her gorgeous ass face. I took into account the way the distressed jeans she wore clung to her hips and thighs, and the way her simple white tee didn't hug her frame but flowed against her bronze skin like fine cotton. Her hair was pulled up into a top knot. Whisps she left out fanned her oval shaped face. I couldn't see her eyes because the shades she wore, but her cute nose and thick lips had me. The closer she came, the harder I stared.

Chapter Two

TIFFANY

CHRIS:

We have a new case in Miami. Our flight leaves Friday at 9 a.m.

Sighing, I replied to my boss's message the only way I could.

ME:

Okay.

Every day I questioned my decision to become a legal assistant. I thought taking a couple semesters off from school would be good for my mental, only to take up a position with a lawyer who had one of the best reputations in Florida.

I went to school for four years, got my undergrad degree in political science, and was on this pursuit of potentially taking up law. This year off was supposed to be my way of making a final decision on my next step. But I swear, working for Christopher Dawson was like hell. And this was only month one.

"Did I break this down correctly?"

Quickly, I shifted my attention to Dorian.

"No, you left out the first part of the expression," I explained.

Poor Dorian could play his ass off on the basketball court, but his academic skills were shit. With it being only the second week of classes, I questioned the 4.0 GPA he came into his freshman year touting. Intermediate algebra had him stuck. That wasn't my business though. At the request of his older brother, Marquis, who I'd graduated with this past spring, I was here doing my best to get him through his first semester.

"Oh, shit," he mumbled and corrected his answer.

"That's correct," I informed him. "We'll pick back up on the next section tomorrow. I have to be in Miami this Friday, so I won't be able to make our session that day. We can make it up on Thursday if you have the time."

Dorian nodded and gathered his things, placing them in his book bag.

"I really appreciate you, Tiff," he stated, dapping me like I was one of his homeboys before leaving the table we'd been occupying for the last hour.

Chuckling, I stuffed my phone inside my purse and placed my laptop in the crook of my arm as I stood to leave. The sun hit my face, causing me to squint my eyes against the rays beaming down on me. Grabbing my shades from my purse, I slid them over my eyes and trudged towards my ride. As I neared my Wrangler, a dude sitting on the hood of a black-on-black Charger caught my eye. He was fine as fuck, with his long, black, freshly twisted dreads, and his dark brown skin. His marked-up arms rested on his thighs as he observed anyone passing by.

I noticed that his lips were thick, settled in the bed of a neatly trimmed and shining beard. Under his white t-shirt, his muscles fought against the fabric. The strength of his arms reminded me of someone who spent hours in the gym. Then, he had the nerve to smile.

Oh my.

I ducked my head and continued to my car, not giving in to my body's reaction to him. Ignoring the power of his build and the smell of him that took a ride on the afternoon breeze, I hit the fob to deactivate my Wrangler. I felt his eyes on me, burning me up.

"You can't speak?"

Damn!

Shit!

I'd never heard a voice so deep, so gruff, yet so melodic, and smooth at the same time.

"Nope," I quipped.

His light chuckle stirred my middle, causing me to hurry and slide into my car. Only when I closed the door and start the engine did I release the breath I was holding. He stared at me over his shoulder with a smile still on his face. A simple *non*-interaction with him shouldn't have caused such a flood in my system. Weeks away from twenty-three, I was ashamed to say that I had no clue what being with a man was like. Sure I received attention from men all the time, but to actually have dated one was unfamiliar to me.

The first and only attempt I had at having a boyfriend ended in disaster when he met my brothers. Just thinking about it had me irritated. Forcing him from my mind, I blasted 2Chainz as I hit the interstate to head to my sister-in-law, Gianna's, boutique. Fifteen minutes later, I pulled into the parking lot next to her Tahoe. Taking my purse and laptop with me, I climbed out of my car, closed the door, and set the alarm before going inside.

"Hey, boo!" she spoke as soon as she saw me.

"Hey, boo!" I spoke back as we embraced.

I loved my sisters-in-law. Between Gianna and Jacoba, I had two big sisters that loved me, and most importantly loved my brothers. Gianna was working on a bridal gown that looked like it weighed a ton. My sister-in-law's hands were gifted, and as I beheld the dress, I couldn't wait for the day when she'd be making my wedding dress.

Over four years ago, she made Jacoba's dress, and people in the entertainment business were still singing Gianna's praises. She was already killing the game when it came to designing and making gowns, now she was on everyone's radar, with such a huge influx of business that she had to hire more staff.

"What're you getting into today?" she asked, ambling over to a chair to have a seat. Sis was big and pregnant, due in the next couple of weeks with her and Grey's little boy, Ash. I was so excited for them. Grey had been wanting more kids since Gray was born, so he and Gianna finally decided to have another one.

Sighing, I replied, "Trying to enjoy the days off I requested last week, but the boss texted me that I'll have to be in Miami with him Friday."

Gianna turned her nose up. "That's rude. Even if you're going home, it shouldn't be because you're working."

"Exactly," I seconded. That was the only thing I was happy about going to Miami for. I'd get to see my sisters, my parents, Blu, Jacoba, and their children. Otherwise, I took these few days off because it was that time of the month and my cycles always wore me clean out.

"When did you traveling with him become part of your job description anyway?"

Blinking, I responded, "Since the girl who normally travels with him decided to quit the week after I started. He pays good money for it, but at this point, I'm not even feeling this position anymore. I'm tryna stay at it because I'm learning some valuable things, and I need the recommendation for when I apply to law school. But boo, this man is tapping on my last nerve."

As if I talked him up, the distinct ringtone I had for my boss chimed. Gianna shook her head with her mouth pursed together.

"This is Tiffany," I answered, aggravated but trying to maintain my professionalism.

"Have you finished those notes for the McCarthy case? I have to be in court—"

"At ten tomorrow," I smoothly interrupted. "Yes I know, sir. They're complete. I'll email them to you now." I'd stayed up all night finishing his damn notes.

"Thanks, Tiffany," he drawled before hanging up.

"He didn't even speak first," Gianna grumbled.

Rolling my eyes, I just shook my head and stuffed the phone back in my purse. I powered my laptop on and hurriedly sent Chris the email so that he wouldn't buzz my damn phone again. Like I said, he was grating on my last nerve. I hated that he made me rethink my career path in life.

Ding!

Grey came strolling through the boutique, a scowl on his face.

"Oh, damn." Gianna sighed.

“Hey, lil’ baby.” Grey hugged me, then addressed his wife. “’Gianna Summers.”

“I’m finishing up right now, baby,” she answered. The blush in her cheeks when he looked at her brought a whimsical smile to my face. They’d been married a little over four and a half years, but their love was as new as when they first met.

He bent to her level to kiss her lips. “If I have to come back up in here, you already know what it is.”

She giggled, and her face grew even darker.

“I’m almost done, promise,” she stated, batting her lashes.

As Grey left back out the door, both of our gazes followed him.

“He’s so crazy,” Gianna and I spoke at the same time. We busted out laughing but I bet her ass hurried up and finished that damn dress.

The next afternoon, I chewed on a piece of gum as I observed Dorian breaking down some more expressions.

“You’re doing much better today,” I told him with a small smile.

He smiled back, making his dimples peek. Dorian was handsome and knew it but never came across as cocky or arrogant. Sadly, that’s what he was missing to make his handsome ‘pop’. It’s almost like he wasn’t owning what he looked like. In some way, I could dig that. Maybe if I were nineteen, I’d find him attractive. Instead, I found dudes attractive that looked like all they caused was mayhem. If he didn’t possess a little cockiness, I couldn’t take him seriously. My mind was so flawed.

“I’m actually starting to understand a lil’ more,” he responded.

“That’s good to know. Means I’m doing something right.”

He grinned and finished up the last two questions. I reminded him that we'd be meeting tomorrow instead of Friday, then he was off to catch practice. Before I even hit the exit, I donned my shades to block out the blasting sunlight. The sweater I wore while in the library came off, and I threw it over my shoulder. Head down as I fumbled through my purse for my keys, I glanced up to find *him* parked next to me. Again, he was sitting on the hood of the Charger.

Today he looked no less scrumptious and clearly didn't care that his deep brown skin was being punished by the sun. Designer shades covered his eyes, but I still felt them on me as I neared.

"You gon' speak to me today," he spoke as I passed him.

"Sure the fuck not," I mumbled with my nose turned up.

Like yesterday, he chuckled and stared until I'd left the parking lot. His smile followed me all the way to Gianna's which had me a little irritated by the time I made it inside the shop.

"You okay, sis?" she asked.

Huffing, I replied, "Would you believe some lame dude keeps trying me?"

Gianna chuckled. "At the college? Is it the guy you're tutoring?"

I shook my head and plopped down in the seat across from her desk.

"Why's he lame?" Gianna divided her attention between me and the paperwork in front of her.

"Because," I said. "He's parked next to me two days in a row now. Then, he just sits there, on his hood, like he doesn't even belong on campus."

"Maybe he's there picking someone up," Gianna guessed.

"I'on know but he's ugly and his ass needs to stay out of the sun."

She guffawed. "No you didn't! He can't be that dark, and stop calling people ugly," she chastised.

"You're right," I conceded. "He isn't ugly, he's just hard to look at. And I still stand on him staying out of the sun. His skin is so deeply brown that..."

Gianna blinked at me as I stared off into space, trying to remember everything about the man I wouldn't even speak to. While I was up here frontin' with Gianna, I wished I at least knew his name. His skin was absolutely everything to me, and the way he smelled...attracted me like fish to water.

"Girl, you sure are buggin' over a man that's 'hard to look at'," she checked.

Rolling my eyes and hiding the shame on my face, I reached out my hand for some of her paperwork. I'd help her get through inventory so that she could get her hard-headed ass out of here. I was with Grey now. Gianna needed to be at home, resting.

"It doesn't matter anyway. I'm good on these niggas."

Gianna chuckled. Seconds later, I heard her humming *Brown Skin* by India Arie. I busted out laughing and so did she.

"Don't start," I warned.

She shrugged. "Wouldn't hurt for you to have a man, Tiff. It's been too long since that last dude you attempted to bring around your brothers."

Groaning, I begged, "Don't remind me."

Gianna giggled. "He was cute though. Just scared of Grey and Blu."

"Which turned me all the way off." I grimaced. I forwent telling her about the whole date issue. "My brothers are intimidating without even opening their mouths. Ain't that some shit." I shook my head.

The dude Gianna referenced, the one who I cared not to bring up, his name was Athens. I'd met him at the mall and thought he was cute. He had the whole cockiness thing down to a T. Only thing was, he nearly shit himself when he met my brothers at a dinner party celebrating Jacoba's birthday.

Athens tried reaching out to me a few times after that incident with me blocking him. I couldn't be with a man that couldn't first match my brothers' crazy energy. Therein lied another issue I had with these niggas. What man could be in my world and be comfortable there? Grey and Blu weren't invincible, but they sure did cause these men to think twice about coming at me.

The next afternoon, I finished up with Dorian and left out of the library cranky as hell. I had to head home and pack for the trip to Miami. Chris had already texted me twice today to confirm that I'd be on time for my flight. He was so annoying I was seconds from telling him to shove this job up his ass.

"Excuse me."

Why is it mess with Tiffany day?

Not only did my cycles wear me out, but my attitude was on one thousand during this time. Everything irritated me. I kept walking like I didn't hear his ass, hoping he'd get the picture and leave me be.

"Excuse me," he said again, walking up beside me. "Can I talk—"

"I'm busy," I answered before he could even finish.

"Damn, you ain't even let me say what I gotta say." He chuckled.

“Because I don’t have time to talk,” I replied. His ass looked familiar but needed to get on somewhere.

My annoyance increased when I saw *him* parked next to me, sitting on his hood, looking like a whole day's worth of meals under the Florida sun. He glowed out here, like he'd dipped himself in coco butter. I knew he smelled good too. Whenever I walked by him, his cologne would tickle my nose. His dreads were piled on top of his head in a haphazard bun. You could tell he knew he was fine as hell by the way he licked his lips when he caught me staring behind my shades.

Smacking my teeth, I sighed because my annoyance didn't stem from him sitting there like a king on his throne. It stemmed from the leggy broad standing in his face, showing all thirty-two of her horse teeth. I shouldn't have cared. I didn't care! But damn, he was obviously into her because whatever she said had him grinning, displaying his pearly whites...and the diamond fangs.

“Hol’ up, shawty.”

Steps from my car, the dude reached for my arm which I snatched away.

“Please, don’t touch me,” I hissed, glaring at him.

Before I knew it, *he* was in front of me, smelling good as hell, all broad shoulders with his thick body blocking my view of the other dude.

“Fuck is you doin’?”

“Bruh, I was just tryna talk to her,” the dude defended.

“I’on give a damn. Getcho ass the fuck outta her face.” This dude’s voice was but a whisper but I swear it burned like fire. The other dude clicked his teeth and stalked off to the same car this dude had propped himself on the past few days.

When *he* turned to face me, my tongue got stuck in my

throat. I wasn't sure if it was the way he looked down at me, licking his thick lips like us being this close turned him on. Maybe it was the way he didn't try to back up, although my nipples damn near touched him we were standing so close to each other.

His large, tattooed hand reached up as he smoothed his long, thick fingers over his beard. I couldn't help but notice how clean his fingernails were and the tattoo covering the expanse of his hand that read KING.

"You good?" he asked.

I found my tongue and popped a hand on my hip. "I had it," I told him, avoiding his weird, brown eyes. Against his dark skin, they were odd yet heavenly.

“Ya beautiful self refuses to be nice to me,” he stated, then smiled when I rolled my eyes.

“Why should I be nice to you? You’re a stranger, and I find it weird that you’ve parked next to me three days in a row now. Do I need a restraining order?”

He grinned, causing the sun to spark off his diamonds. “That’s cute,” he quipped. “I like you.”

“So, I *do* need a restraining order? My brothers are FBI if you’re thinking of trying something funny.”

“Is that right?” he questioned, rubbing at his beard.

I nodded. He clasped his hands at his crotch and met my gaze.

“Good thing the feds don’t put no fear in me, baby. What else you got?”

Blinking, I quickly clapped back, “A nine in my purse just in case you think I’m playin’.”

When I tell you this man had the sexiest laugh ever—the sound melted the hairs off my body.

"Yeah, I like you, Princess."

"That's not my name."

"Princess sounds good though. I'on know ya name yet, so I'ma rock with that." He stuck his hand out. "Kingston. That was my baby brother, August."

Reluctantly, I placed my hand in his. His grip was strong and sure yet gentle. Snatching my hand back, I hated how he sent that weird ass vibe through me.

"King?" The chick he was talking to when I walked up called him.

His gaze never left mine when he replied, "I'm talkin'." The mug on his face turned him from beauty to beast. Damn for a second, I wondered if he had split personalities. That's how quickly his mood shifted.

"May I take you out, Princess?" he asked in the next breath.

Cocking my head, I glanced over my shoulder at the girl eyeing us.

"You're really asking me out while that chick is over there waiting on you?" *The audacity*!

"She's neither one of our concerns."

I narrowed my eyes on him.

"Don't do that," he cautioned. "It makes you irresistible."

Turning my nose up, I said, "You seem like the type that says whatever's on your mind. No matter what it is."

"I do," he confirmed. "I uncomplicate things by speakin' my mind, so you'll never have to worry."

"You say that like we're gon' have a conversation beyond this one."

"We're gon' have plenty of conversations beyond this one, Princess."

"Didn't you just watch me tryna get rid of ya brother?"

"Yeah you brush youngins off, Princess, they ain't for you. I'm a man."

"My name's Tiffany. And you being 'a man' doesn't make you special."

"It makes me somethin' since you haven't brushed me off yet," he replied. "Will you take my number, Princess Tiffany?"

I hid a smile. "Not only do I not know you, but I'm sure you're too old for me, Kingston."

He bit into his bottom lip, drawing my attention to the way he gnawed on it.

"You like gettin' a rise outta me, don't you?"

"Huh?"

Ignoring my questioning gaze, he moved on. "I know it's rude to ask a woman's age but tell me how old you are."

"Twenty-three soon."

He nodded, smiling. "Twenty-eight is too old for you?"

Honestly, I didn't know what was too old for me. Clearly, the guys my age weren't piquing my interest though.

When I didn't say anything, he said, "Take my number."

Whether it was his gentle, deep voice, or the soft gleam in his eyes, one of them shits drove me to open my phone. He rattled off his number, making sure I typed it in correctly.

"I'll be waiting to hear from you."

Turning, I squelched the butterflies running amuck in my stomach. As I neared my car, he was there opening the door.

"Thank you," I mumbled.

"Be safe," he returned, closing my door after I'd slid into the seat.

I cranked my car and checked my camera before pulling out. Kingston watched me drive off, until I was no longer in view. Damn, I wondered who the other girl Kingston was talking to happened to be. I'd forgotten about her. She was still standing there looking goofy when I got in my car and drove off. Shaking my head, I asked myself what was I thinking.

This man just flirted with one female, only to give me his number. Hell, maybe she had his number too. The thought caused me to smack my teeth. His smooth-talking ass finessed the hell outta me! Aggravated, I would delete his number the first chance I got.

Chapter Three

KINGSTON

"DEA! Freeze!"

This nigga looked dead at me and took off running, even with my Glock pointed at him. As much as I wanted to put a bullet in Smooth's ass, he was the state's witness. I needed him alive and without injury so that he could testify against his boss. His big ass sailed across a fence like he ran the hurdles in a past life, but I was right behind him, pushing garbage cans over to catch up with him. People burst out of their doors to see what all the ruckus was. Once they caught sight of my heat, they scrambled back inside their homes.

One yard Smooth dashed through had two pit bulls in it, tied to a pole. They barked, baring their teeth and tried to break their restraints. Nevertheless, I chased after him until we were on the main street, running up Cervantes. Horns blared because this nigga darted across traffic like he was made of superhero shit. Grunting, I took off through the traffic, too, damn near getting touched by a Mercedes flying up the thirty-five-mile-an-hour road. Good thing I had my dreads secured under the skull cap I wore or else the long strands would've whipped in my face.

"Freeze!" I yelled again when we made it to the clearing of a gas station. Someone came out of the store, tripping Smooth up. They both crashed to the ground. Smooth didn't have time to get up before I was on his back.

"Be still, muhfucka!" I barked, locking his hands behind his back. My knee dug into the small of his back, making sure he didn't budge.

"Get off me!" he demanded, thrashing. "I can't wait for you to come off that horse you on, nigga!" He cackled as I calmly read him his rights, ignoring the shit he said.

An undercover cruiser pulled up with two other agents, Jared and Eddie, hopping out to assist me. People stood around with their phones out recording this spectacle. Smooth wanted me to beat his ass for making me chase him this damn far. I stood to my feet and let the other two agents haul him away as another cruiser entered the parking lot.

"Mane." Jared chuckled from behind his mask. "You ran him down like he had yo' money!"

Laughing, I shrugged, still trying to catch my breath.

"Hop in, I'll give you a lift back to the scene," he said.

Back at the crime scene, I shook my head at the amount of drugs Smooth had holed up in his house. Shit was in the walls and everything. I'd seen worse, but the fact remained that Smooth was a stupid ass nigga. He was outchea beating charges because his ass decided to roll on the boss he so heavily served. Seemed like Smooth didn't give a damn that he'd just hemmed himself back up. Flipping on Beal wouldn't get him out of this shit.

The state was willing to do anything to keep Beal off the streets. Not only was he heavy in the dope game but his body count was pushing the teens. For a nigga that wasn't even thirty yet, Beal was a menace to the streets of Pensacola and the surrounding areas. Smooth was gon' have to come through, or else, the case against Beal was as good as dead.

It was approaching ten in the morning when I walked into my house. The smell of pine met me. I shook my head already knowing why. Granny was in the kitchen, wiping the counters down like the shits were really dirty.

"Granny," I stated on an exhausted sigh.

"What nie? Don't you come in here startin' nothin' with me." She huffed.

Laughing, I walked up behind her, hugged her to me, then dropped a kiss on the top of her head.

"I'll be glad when ya ass find a woman and stop bein' 'round here all in my bidness," she continued, grumbling. "Churrin' always got to clock my moves like I'ain been here longer than them," she grumbled under her breath.

Her griping brought Tiffany to mind. I just knew lil' baby was gon' call me last night. To say I was disappointed as hell was an understatement. I kicked myself for not getting her number instead. Shiidd, I'd go back up to that school and stalk her ass if she didn't call me.

"You'd be proud of me, Granny. I met this beautiful woman yesterday."

She paused wiping the counters to give me her undivided attention. I knew it would do the trick.

"Where is she?" she asked, planting her hands on her hips.

Shrugging, I explained, "I gave her my number, but she didn't call."

Granny cackled. "What? Nie that's some shit!"

Smiling, I replied, "That's how you feel about ya grandson?"

She nodded. "'Cause you bringin' her up means you must like her. I'on here about the rest of ya lil' ugly hoes."

Scoffing, I held my chest in mock shock. "'The rest', Granny? Whatchu tryna say about me?"

She tsked. "That you's a hoe! You're a handsome young man, 'round here wastin' ya sperm on floozies! August ain't no better. Done got that po' chile pregnant and think I don't know. Hm! He ain't ready for no baby, and po' Faith tryin' her best to make him grow up, but he just ain't ready."

I agreed with my granny on that one. There was no point in asking her how she knew about Faith being pregnant. She probably had some crazy ass dream.

"First, Granny, I'm not wastin' my sperm anywhere, aight. Second—"

"You are too!" she interrupted. "Any time you set those lil' demons free, whether inside somethin' or someone, you're givin' energy away that you could be givin' to someone who deserves it and matches it."

Granny said a mouthful that I stored in my head for future use.

"Nie is this woman worth ya energy?"

Without a second thought, I nodded. "She is."

"Hm. Well, save ya lil' demon seeds for her. At least be some sort of virgin by the time you get with her."

I busted out laughing so hard, it drew August's attention.

"Granny in here talkin' 'bout sperm again?" he questioned with his nose turned up.

“I sure am! You got a problem, baby daddy?”

August’s eyes bugged and flew towards me.

“Mane, why you—”

“He ain’t tell me a thang!” Granny’s small voice boomed over August’s.

He snapped to attention and refrained from clicking his teeth like he did with me. Although I went through a rebellious stage, it was never with my granny. I cut up a lot before my mother died, which her death should’ve made me worse. Instead, it catapulted me into who I am today.

“Granny—”

“Don’t ‘*Granny*’ me, August Wells. You knew better. Po’ Faith can’t do nothin’ witcha and nie she’s pregnant.” Granny shook her head.

Granny might as well had beat August’s ass from how heartbroken he looked.

“Nie you gon’ clean ya act up so you can be a daddy to that baby,” she ordered. “Faith needs to move on to better—”

“What, Granny?” August slightly fumed. I cocked my head at him.

“I’m sayin’!” Granny’s voice rose. “If yeen gon’ be good to that baby girl let her move on. Why you gon’ keep her ‘round knowin’ you ain’t ready to be settled down? That’s selfish, young man!”

I walked up to August until I stood in his face. I heard everything Granny said, but I had something else to tell him.

“Ya voice got a lil’ too loud just then.”

He jerked his head away and clicked his teeth. I chuckled.

“Apologize,” I commanded. He looked everywhere but at me until his eyes met our granny’s eyes.

"I'm sorry, Granny. It's just, how you gon' say that about me?"

She guffawed. "Was I lyin'?"

He had no comeback because Granny wasn't lying. August may not like the way Granny came at him, but it was the truth, nonetheless. One day Granny and I wouldn't be able to save him from himself. Excuses wasn't something I tolerated, and I be damned if I allowed August to slide by so easily.

"I'm out for a minute," he said, grabbing a set of keys and heading for the garage. "Don't worry, I'll bring it back in one piece," he quipped, referring to my Denali truck since his car was still in the shop.

Granny shook her head and vigorously started wiping the counters down again.

"That child's gon' be twenty-one in a few weeks, but I swear I can't tell it. I do my best not to come down on him, but it's only made him worse." I heard the frustration in her voice and hugged her to my side.

"You did a fabulous job, Granny." I kissed her cheek. "Don't let his hard-headed ass make you think otherwise. Sometimes, no matter what we do, we can't catch somebody from fallin'. They gotta land hard enough to get back up and do it right the next time. As much as we don't want him to, sadly, August may have to fall before he wakes up."

Granny sighed and resigned to the fact that I was right. That didn't mean she liked it. We wanted to save those we loved without them growing and learning through their own hardships and life's struggles, not realizing that in the absence of pain one can think they're invincible. When in reality, they've been saved so many times that they've never had to feel pain. Saving them conditioned them to think that life is perfect, even when they see others around them struggling. Because that *struggle* hadn't touched them yet, they believe it doesn't truly exist.

August was my baby, and I loved him to death. But I wasn't going to love him to nothingness. I refused to do that shit. As tired as I was, after I showered, I sought Granny out to see if she wanted to go in her garden this morning. I did all that fussing about her staying off those deck steps, and although my body was screaming for rest, I know she loved being in her garden. Like I thought, I found her standing by the sliding door, covered in tattered overalls, hand on her hip, gazing out at the backyard.

"Come on, lil' lady." I took her hand, opened the door, and led her across the deck and down the stairs. All her supplies was already waiting in an enclosed chest I kept underneath the deck stairs.

She retrieved what she needed and headed towards the row of peppers while I sat on the steps and kept a close eye on her. She'd be out here for a couple of hours, and I wouldn't dare rush her.

"Ol' mutt," she muttered to the neighbor's dog, Rattler. She couldn't stand his ass 'cause he stayed getting into our yard. I had no problems with him as long as he didn't shit on my damn lawn.

While sparking up a cigar, my mind drifted to Tiffany, wondering what she was doing that she couldn't call a nigga. Hell yeah I was pressed because shawty really had me questioning my pull game with her fine ass. I'd seen and met plenty of fine females, but Tiffany… And she had the nerve to have eyes that snatched my damn soul.

Last night, she'd met me in my dreams, doing shit to me that had me waking up with the hardest dick I'd ever had. That was saying a lot considering I had a pretty uncivilized sexual appetite. I wish I could say my mind being on her was nothing other than me wanting to knock the lining out of her but I had bitches that catered to my dick whenever I needed it.

Catering to *my mind*, however, was a different story. I took a toke of the stick, slowly exhaled the smoke and imagined Tiffany smiling. That shit broke me down for no damn reason. There was something different about her, something special. Baby girl needed to call me.

Chapter Four

TIFFANY

I scribbled notes down in my notebook, trying not to focus on the man sitting across from me. Derek Wilks was fine and one of the finest NBA players I'd ever met. He reminded me of Nelly, just taller and a tad darker. If he made one more pass at me, I was going to get up and walk out of this meeting. Chris was here to help him get out of trouble, but he was more interested in getting a rise out of me.

"Mr. Wilks, the accusations against you are serious. Do you plan on settling?"

Derek scoffed indignantly. "Hell, naw! I'ain touch neither one of them hoes."

Chris sighed. "Well, it looks like you did, Son. You need to be honest with me so that I can help you and tell you what the best strategy is. You don't want to ruin your reputation, I understand that. But lying isn't going to do anything but make us look like fools when we step into the courtroom."

One thing I hated about working for Chris is he handled cases like this—disgusting, high profile cases, dealing with millions of dollars, and most of all, straight up liars. Derek sounded innocent enough, but he rubbed me the wrong way just by looking at me.

"Aight, look," he started. He proceeded to tell his version of what took place the past weekend with him and two women he met at the club. According to the victims, Derek forced himself on them. Yet, he sat here defending his actions claiming they were the ones to accompany him back to his house.

Listening to him explain his side of the story made my nerves cringe. He really thought he was innocent too. By the sound of things, Derek was full of shit. However, it wasn't my place to say anything. I was here to record notes.

"So, what do you think?" That came from Horace, Derek's agent. From the look on his face, he knew his client was screwed.

"We'll make this go away," Chris assured.

I paused writing to glance at him. This wasn't the first time I listened to a guilty man spill his guts to Chris, only for Chris to make the same comment. I understood his job was to defend his clients, but for some reason, it irked me that he was taking this situation lightly. His reply was too nonchalant for me.

The meeting wrapped up ten minutes later with me anxious to get from around these men. We'd gotten off the plane and came straight to the hotel for the meeting. Instead of staying in the room Chris had already booked for me, I texted my mom to pick me up.

"Tiffany, why don't you join us for lunch," Chris offered.

Derek sidled up beside me, smiling from ear to ear. I just listened to this man replay his tryst with two women he picked up in the club, then allegedly *didn't* rape.

Thinking quick on my feet, I scrolled to Kingston's number and dialed him.

"Princess—"

"Sorry," I declined as Kingston picked up. "My boyfriend is on his way." I was in a whole other city claiming to have a man coming to pick me up, but I wanted to make sure Derek backed his ass up off me.

"Boyfriend?" Kingston drawled in my ear.

"Oh, if I was ya man, I'd come swoop you up, too," Derek commented.

"I didn't know you had a boyfriend," Chris added.

I ignored them, split from the men, and went to the lobby. All I had was my Brahmin bag that was large enough to fit an outfit in. I didn't bring any luggage for the two-day trip because I knew I'd be staying at my parents' house where I still had some belongings.

"Who is that?" Kingston asked.

"No one," I answered, plopping down in the nearest sofa. I watched them leave out of the entrance with Derek staring me down. I balled my face up at him and looked away. My mom needed to hurry up.

"So, who is this boyfriend you got, Princess? He know 'bout me?"

Although I didn't want to, I laughed. "What is there to know about you?"

"That I'm finna snatch his woman," he answered, not a hint of joking in his voice.

Scoffing, I replied, "You'd do that? No remorse whatsoever?"

I heard the phone click in my ear signaling that he'd hung up. The phone buzzed not a second later with a FaceTime call. Suddenly nervous, I bit into my lip and ignored the call.

KINGSTON:

Pick up, baby.

It buzzed again. Groaning I answered, flustered as hell. When Kingston's face appeared, I felt my middle contract. How the hell was anyone as fine as him? I'd never met anyone with his rich, dark brown skin and eyes the color of amber. His gaze seemed to burn right through me. It didn't help when he licked, then bit into his lip.

He smiled. "For you, in a heartbeat," he answered. "You gon' fuck my head up, I know it."

Blushing, I pursed my lips. "Whatever. First of all, you don't even know me."

"Lemme get to know you," he requested.

It was so easy to say okay.

"So, just forget all about my boyfriend, huh?"

He shot me a half-grin. "I'll make you forget about every nigga walkin' this earth."

Chuckling, I asked, "How is that even possible?" Men always said shit like that, and I never understood it.

"Oh it's possible, my baby. I'ma show you."

"That would mean I have to give you a chance. Honestly, I don't know about that."

Grinning, he questioned, "Why?"

Shrugging, I said, "'Cause I don't fuck with dope boys." Grey and Blu would kill me if I did.

Kingston chortled, the sound wreaking havoc on my senses. "I'm not a boy, number one."

"And number two, you have drug dealer written all over you," I quipped.

I saw my mother's car pulling up to the entrance of the hotel, prompting me to shoulder my bag and head for the doors.

"Damn, that's how you feel about me?"

I glanced back at his handsome face, upset at myself that I'd blessed my mind with his face and voice. Now I would be thinking about him the rest of the day.

"Yep," I responded.

He lightly chuckled. "Then you really should get to know me, baby."

Opening the car door, I took account of my mother's surprised expression at the deep voice on the other end of my phone.

"Who is that?" she asked, all in my business.

I leaned over to hug her, ignoring her question.

"You gon' introduce me, sweetheart?" Kingston asked, causing my mother's eyes to bug.

Embarrassed, I said, "Ma, Kingston."

My mother was stuck on dumb because I'd never introduced her to anyone. Kingston, however, did what he does best.

"Nice to meet you, Ma. Ya daughter is beautiful as hell."

"Thank you," my mama gushed.

"Hm, hm. She gon' marry me," Kingston continued.

Face flaming, I smacked my teeth, and said, "Bye" to Kingston before hanging up on him.

Mama guffawed. "Why'd you hang up? He's fine as hell!"

"Ma, I'on know that man," I replied, scrunching my face up.

KINGSTON:

I'll let this time slide. Next time tell ya husband to have a good day before you hang up on me.

I busted out laughing, blushing so hard my cheeks hurt.

"Okay, so who is he?"

My mama wasn't going to drop it.

"Kingston, Ma."

"You already told me his name. Who is he?"

As she started driving, I sighed. "No one for you to gush all over. I won't be talking to him again."

She scoffed. "And why not, *mija*?"

"Because," I replied, "he's not my type."

Valentina scoffed. "Sexy with a deep voice like his isn't your type? *Girl, who raised you*?"

Laughing, I shot back, "Besides you and Daddy? Grey and Blu."

Mama grumbled. "Your brothers can't dictate your life forever, sweet pea."

"Who gon' tell them that?"

She laughed. "They just love you, that's all."

"Alright, so neither one of us is telling them that."

"But... I'm serious, sweetheart. If this guy is nice, I think you should go for it. Your brothers will just have to get over it."

"You and I both know that isn't gon' happen." Especially because I suspected Kingston was a whole ass drug dealer. There's no way my brothers would accept him. While I didn't want my brothers dictating my life, I loved that they cared about me the way they did. That's why I never rebelled against them.

At some point, I'd have to bite the bullet though. Not only was I tired of being alone, but the urge to do some stupid shit like link up with a dope *man* were high on my list. Kingston made me smile, blush, and laugh all in a ten-minute conversation. Twice! Just to squelch the part of me that wanted to reach out to Kingston, I deleted his number. Now...that was... refreshing.

So, why did I feel bereft?

Blu, Jacoba, and their children welcomed me with open arms. I hadn't seen them in a couple of months but it equated to a lifetime. I loved them so deeply that I wanted to be around them every day. Sky and Royal, Blu's four-year-old twins were identical and took on their mother's features. However, they had their damn daddy's personality. I'd never been around two mean little girls who didn't give a damn who you were, they were going to assert their dominance and attitude without any reservations.

The newest addition to their family, Steel, was one going on one hundred. His sisters tried bossing him around but he didn't fool with their shenanigans. He was laid back and never cried like some of these hollering ass babies I see. Jacoba told me that Steel was such a good baby that she and Blu were heavily thinking about having another baby.

Well, she was heavily thinking about it. Blu was ready. I missed being around them and enjoying time with Jacoba whenever she had a show. She'd settled down quite a bit now and was pretty much into mommy role. I could tell that she loved her life just the way it was. For that, I was happy.

"You look tired, Tiff," Blu stated as he sat next to me. I

called myself trying to enjoy this sunset, but I knew any minute Chris would be buzzing my phone. It was past working hours, but he always found something that needed to be 'done' before the morning. I only had tomorrow to spend with my family before I had to get back on the plane Sunday to go home.

"I am a little bit," I admitted. Playing with my nieces and nephew had me wore out. Then, Violet and Emerald had the nerve to want to go to the mall tonight. He put his arm around my shoulders and pulled me to his side. I laid my head on his shoulder and stared at the sky.

"Maybe you need to stop workin' for a while. I can tell it's beatin' ya ass and it's only been a month. You just busted ya ass for four years through college. You need a break."

Rolling my eyes, I said, "Which is what I thought I was taking. It's like I'm second guessing my decision to go to law school, and it's only in direct correlation with this damn job."

Blu grunted. "Which means you need to quit that bitch."

Shrugging, I said, "I don't wanna give up. Giving this a fair chance will let me know I gave my all before walking away."

Just then my phone vibrated. I groaned, knowing it was Chris. Deciding to check the message before he called, I looked at the screen.

4235560:

I wanna hear ya voice, Princess.

Kingston! My heart rate increased.

"Everything good?" Blu asked.

Stuttering, I replied, "Yeah."

ME:

You're interrupting my sunset.

I hurried up and blocked the number he'd texted me from, not wanting to see his response. Hell, I was still trying to forget about him, and I didn't even know him. I hated how fine and irresistible he was. Like if I'd ever dreamt of my dream man, Kingston was him. Everything about him called to me. But...I had to ignore it and him.

I finished watching the sunset with Blu, then went into the house to lay down. This was the last day of my cycle so hopefully, the extra exhaustion it was causing would wear off by tomorrow. I planned to spend the day with my sisters, and they'd have me out all damn day.

The next afternoon, I was shopping with Violet and Emerald when Chris called.

"Are you joining us for dinner?" he asked, referring to him, Wilks, and Wilks' agent.

My face balled up. "No sir." If they weren't discussing business, they didn't need me.

"Very well," he replied. "Don't forget the plane leaves at eight in the morning."

"Yes sir," I responded, sounding annoyed even to myself. Hanging up, I shook my head and got back to shopping.

"This dress would be so cute on you for your birthday," Violet said, bringing me a black, shimmery number that wouldn't hit my thighs.

"Girl, bye!" I chuckled. "You know I love color."

Emerald smacked her teeth. "So, sis. This is definitely what you need to wear to usher in twenty-three."

To cap off what our sister said, Violet turned the dress around so that I could see the back. It dipped low to the small of my back. Thinking about it, a little black dress is exactly what I needed. Taking the number from Violet, I headed to the dressing room to try it on. That's all it took for me to drop five hundred dollars on something I would wear only once.

We stayed in the mall another two hours looking for a few more things and shoes to match my dress. I loved spending time with my sisters because they looked up to me. Just like Grey and Blu were loyal, protective, and loving towards me, I was the same with our little sisters. No one better not ever dare tried to come between me and my family.

Chapter Five

TIFFANY

Annoyed wasn't the word as I clocked out, grabbed my things, and tried to hurry up out of the back door before Chris could catch me leaving. Never had I spent my birthday working, let alone being at work late.

"Tiffany?" His voice stopped me as soon as I touched the exit door.

Whirling around, I fixed my face before saying, "Yes?"

Chris looked tired and worn, his suit slightly wrinkled and a dark shadow covered his brown jawline. His eyes were sharp as a tack though as they bored into me.

"I needed you to do one more thing for me," he stated, heading back towards his office as if that was the end of the discussion.

Not today!

"Chris, I actually have somewhere to be and I can't be late."

Sadly, his ass didn't even acknowledge that it was my birthday although the 'company' gave me a birthday card with a gift card inside.

He chuckled like I was playing. "Surely whoever you have waiting for you can hold off another thirty minutes," he said.

My eyebrows snapped together. I felt *Sapphire* on the horizon, and she wasn't a nice person at all.

"Actually, *my brothers*, can't wait for me. My family is here from out of town to celebrate my birthday." Why was it his business who was waiting on me in the first place? He irritated my whole being.

"Oh," he cracked. "Sorry, I wasn't aware that it was your birthday."

I smiled sarcastically.

"Enjoy your night then. First thing Monday morning, I need you to handle this document for me."

"Sure thing," I answered, turning back toward the exit and busting through it.

By the time I made it home, Blu was already in the driveway, pacing.

"I was just about to call you," he said with his face balled up. He helped me out of my car, then hugged me.

Sighing, I kissed his cheek, and explained, "Worked a little late."

His frown deepened.

"I know," I muttered, sensing his vibe. Blu was the brother who stayed on the edge of a ledge. One push and he'd be on somebody's ass.

"Well, go inside and get dressed. Everyone's waitin' for us."

Leaving my purse and phone with him, I rushed inside to find my parents sitting on the living room sofa, cuddled up.

Quickly hugging and kissing their cheeks, I ran to my room to get ready. My sisters were on the bed watching television. I quickly hugged them then darted into the bathroom.

I showered, moisturized my body, then threw on the little black dress I'd purchased in Miami. The black cocktail dress shimmered at every turn and barely hit my thighs. If that weren't enough, the back was out.

I applied light makeup, just enough so I didn't look like I worked fifty-plus hours this week. My hair, wet from the shower, curled up so bad that I had no choice but to wear it in its natural state. Combing through it to detangle it as much as I could, I applied a leave-in conditioner, oil, then used some gel to slick my edges. After donning my simple jewelry, I slid into my heels and rushed back out of the room, waving to my sisters as I went. I sailed into the living room past my parents, waving by to them on my way to the front door.

"You look beautiful, baby!" my mama called behind me. My daddy grunted his disdain for my choice of clothing.

Blu grilled me as I came hustling out of the house.

"The fuck is that?" he asked, motioning to my dress.

"A dress, boo," I answered, and met him at the passenger side door of his truck.

He grumbled as he opened the door for me.

"You're grown, Tiff. But don't have me actin' a fool tonight."

I giggled as I sat in the seat.

"It's funny now, but don't be screamin' and cryin' when I bust a nigga shit in." He closed the door with me beaming.

I wasn't scared to go anywhere with Blu because he would never let anything happen to me. If he had to bust a nigga's shit in, I'm sure the dude would've more than likely deserved it. Blu came off as mean and crazy, but he meant well. Jacoba and their kids had really made my brother *that* nigga!

"Happy Birthday!" Jacoba and Gianna shouted as I entered VIP. Grey was there to greet me with a hug and kiss on my cheek.

An elaborate cake, champagne, and several gifts littered the table holding up the center of the section.

"Look at you!" Jacoba gushed as she and Gianna wrapped me in a big hug.

"Don't hype her," Grey warned.

Smacking my teeth, I spun around so that they could see the back of the dress. Gianna's mouth dropped.

"Okay, sis! We tryna get a man tonight!" she quipped loud enough for the people in the next section. If they weren't so rowdy, they would've heard her over the loud ass music.

"The fuck is 'we'? And no the hell she ain't!" Grey barked to his wife who smiled coyly at him.

In the middle of me laughing, I felt eyes burning a hole into me. The attention was expected because there was a lot of sexiness in this section along with a whole ass celebrity in Jacoba. But these eyes, they caused every hair on my body to stand at attention. Discreetly, I eyed my surroundings as I smiled and moved towards the cake. In the rowdy section next to ours, a pair of peculiar brown eyes bore into me. Directly in front of me, he sat on a plush sofa, head slightly cocked as he licked his lips and openly stared.

Damn…there was never a sexier man. In the dim lighting, his

dark brown skin glowed and seemed almost creepy from how he stood out from everyone else in his section. The only other face I recognized was his brother's. From the looks of things, the gentlemen were celebrating someone's birthday.

I stood here in a trance, watching Kingston glide to his feet without taking his eyes off of me. He excused himself from the party. My heart ran a marathon in my chest because he was coming my way!

"You okay, sis?" Gianna asked, seeing my surprised expression.

"Uhm..." I stuttered as Kingston said something to security standing at my section, then dapped them.

Why the hell did they let him in?

Grey and Blu would flip if—wait. *What?*

My brothers, the crazy ass Summers men that didn't fuck with *nobody*, grinned and dapped Kingston like he was an old friend. Kingston talked with my brothers, but his eyes were on me.

"Who is that?" Gianna asked in a hushed whisper like she was scared Grey would hear her in this loud ass club. "Is that *him*? You liar! He's fine as hell!" she added.

Gianna only knew who Kingston was because I'd thoughtlessly brought him up one day while we were out enjoying lunch. She ragged me for it, but I assured her I was not into Kingston and that he wasn't at all fine.

Jacoba grunted and messily sang, "Giiirrllll!"

Kingston indeed was fine. His dreads were down, reaching his chest. The army green shirt he wore clung to his muscular body and did little to hide the fact that he had pierced nipples. Those only added to the level of sexuality this nigga oozed. His distressed, light washed jeans hugged him just right without being tight. Designer sneakers on his feet spoke to his taste.

Ice hung from his ears, his neck, and around his wrists. I didn't know who the hell this man was, but I was legit scared the moment he motioned in my direction. Grey and Blu, confused, glanced between me and Kingston. Kingston broke away from my brothers to step to me. My brothers looked stupefied by his boldness.

His eyes skated down my body while he licked his lips, biting into that bottom one that I wanted to suck on. I shivered under his direct gaze.

"'Sup, Princess," he spoke as his hand went around my waist. Not hearing his voice in damn near two months caused me to quake. He brought me to his chest and hugged me like I was his woman. His hands roamed the bareness of my back, then settled on the swell of my ass. I thought he was about to kiss me, but his lips fell on my forehead, then the tip of my nose, igniting me.

Like a fiend, I sniffed his shirt, basking in his scent, and felt along the planes of his corded back. I could tell that it did the same for him as it did for me. It was something about the way Kingston looked at me, with that soft ass expression on his face. I wanted to reach up and run my fingers through his neatly groomed beard.

"Aye, King," Blu interrupted. "The fuck is this?"

Gianna and Jacoba grumbled.

"Princess, you outchea not claimin' me?" Kingston smiled down at me.

My mouth fell open at the same time as I glared at him.

"How're you cool with my brothers? I thought you were a drug dealer," I fussed, looking between Kingston, Grey, and Blu.

Kingston blinded me with his smile. "You assumed I was a drug dealer, baby."

"*Baby*?" Grey mugged Kingston, which only made Kingston chuckle. "Tiff! You and this nigga—"

"No!" I quickly defended, but hesitated when Kingston ran his fingers over my face.

"Sexy as fuck," he uttered, shocking Gianna and Jacoba. His actions only fueled my brothers to step into his space. Their wives nudged them back, causing both to protest.

Unbothered, Kingston tilted my chin up until my eyes met his. "Happy Birthday, beautiful."

"Thank you," I replied, blushing.

This time, his head lowered and his lips touched mine. Everything faded as I tasted the drink on his lips. I thought this was going to be a quick peck but he surprised me. I opened my mouth to accept his tongue, which begged for entry. My arms went around his broad shoulders, holding on as this man kissed me like he loved me.

One of his hands skated up my back, and his fingers dove into my hair. He tugged my head back so that he could have a better angle. My pussy swooned, dampening the crotch of my panties as I felt his dick poking my stomach. When his teeth sank into my bottom lip, my entire body shuddered. In a daze, I didn't realize he'd broken the kiss until I felt his lips on my ear.

"I miss you. On our first date, I wanna watch the sunset," he stated.

The fact that he remembered the last thing I texted him moved me in a way that had me not denying him. The fog cleared with me finding four pairs of eyes staring at me. Two pairs were full of joy, while the other two were full of confusion.

Kingston still had me in his arms though, trapping me in his embrace.

"You miss me?" he asked, then kissed along my cheek and neck.

What was it with this nigga being all over me? Was he drunk? I noticed us being watched by more than my brothers and their wives. In the section Kingston had just left, some females curiously stared at us. Irked, I tried to break his embrace. He took my hand though, securing ours together.

"Uhm… Let's have some cake," Jacoba suggested, trying to break the ice.

Thank God for my sisters because Grey and Blu looked like they were ready to kill Kingston., who wasn't paying them any attention. His lips were stained with my gloss, only making him sexier.

This was the type of energy I was talking about when it came to me, a possible boo, and my brothers. For his energy alone, Kingston just nabbed a major win.

"Yeen tell us you had a nigga," Grey fussed.

"I didn't know—"

"And *this* nigga," Blu added, interrupting me.

"I didn't—"

"How long has this been goin' on?" they both asked at the same time.

"Guys," Gianna interjected, laughing. "Stop badgering Tiffany like she's a teenager."

"Right!" Jacoba supported.

Kingston chuckled. "Y'all gotta get used to me," he said, "'cause I'ain goin' nowhere."

Blu grumbled and stalked off to his wife who eyed him with her nose turned up. He didn't want any smoke with Jacoba. After a second, Grey let it be, too, going to Gianna's side to smooth over the frown on her face. He was a sucker for his wife just like Blu was for his. One day they'd have to understand that I didn't want to be single forever. On the same token, I didn't want my heart broken either.

As the night progressed, we danced, drank, and had a good time. After they got a few drinks in them, Grey and Blu were chill enough to loosen up. I sat atop Kingston's lap while the three conversed about a case they'd worked together.

Imagine my surprise to find out that my *dope man* was actually a damn DEA agent.

Whew!

Why that made his thugged-out ass so damn sexy… It was something about a man that oozed hood nigga but was actually the law. I mean, nothing about Kingston indicated that he was anything other than a nigga who owned the streets for a living. That shit turned me on to the point I let my back hit Kingston's chest. His hand fell on my stomach and held me in place so if I wanted to move I couldn't.

"Where you goin'?" he asked when I tried to get up.

"Restroom," I answered, standing.

He tugged at the hem of my dress, which my brothers approved.

"We'll come with you," Jacoba stated.

Now she knows damn well…

"Gianna will come with me," I said instead.

"Yeah, you stay ya ass ritchea," Blu agreed.

The crowd would rush Jacoba if she left out of this VIP. She was the reason we had security standing outside of our section.

"Girrlll!" Gianna shrieked as soon as we were in the restroom.

My cheeks burned as she hyped me up.

"The way he kissed yo' ass!"

"He's crazy," I responded, beaming because I loved it!

"Just the right amount of crazy to not give a damn about the *craziest* men I've ever known." I high-fived Gianna, then we went to handle our business.

As we came out of the restroom, my phone buzzed in my hand. It was a notification from my bank. Confused on why I was getting a notification this late at night, I clicked on the app as Gianna and I waded arm in arm through the rowdy crowd. What met my eyes stunned me.

Chapter Six

KINGSTON

I was chilling in VIP, watching my brother and his friends act a fool when I peeped Tiffany steps away, smiling from ear to ear. The black dress she wore glided over her shapely ass just right, and her back was bare. For a second, I thought I was dreaming. I thought her hair was cute swooped up in that top knot she loved to wear, but fuck, seeing that shit flowing down her back proved to me that I had to have her for myself.

I'd been playing in her hair most of the night, enjoying the textured strands running through my fingers, imaging them wrapped around my fist while I fucked the life out of her. I couldn't help it though. Lil' baby mesmerized me more than any woman I'd ever fucked with. And there were plenty. Nobody held a candle to Tiffany.

Grey and Blu were a little salty, but they knew me well. Wasn't shit about me pussy. We worked together on a couple of cases down in Miami and formed a friendship. I even knew they had three sisters. I just didn't know that Tiffany was one of them.

The object of my thoughts came back into the section, eyeing me. She tried to forgo my lap, but I wasn't going for that. Especially with all these thirsty niggas waiting for the chance to swoop in. I'd shoot this bitch up. She showed me her phone as I positioned her back in my lap and rested my hand on her stomach. She'd gotten a notification.

"What?" I asked nonchalantly.

She eyed me a second longer. "How? And that's too much."

"Don't worry 'bout allat. What I look like not blessin' my woman on her day? Lemme spoil you," I defended.

"I don't wanna be spoiled," she countered.

"Then, what you want? Tell me," I volleyed back.

Cutting her eyes at me, she ignored the question.

"Aight then." I grinned and tweaked her chin. "I'ma take good care of you, Princess."

As the night wound down, Tiffany agreed to let me drop her off at home. I made sure my brother was straight before dashing. He had explicit instructions to get his ass home in one piece. I understood him wanting to celebrate his day with his homeboys, but I'on play that drunk shit. He was twenty-one now and, no matter what I did for him, he had to grow up. It was up to him to make the right decisions. Whether he listened to me or not, I wouldn't let him make excuses for any of his behavior. I never have.

Tiffany and her family hugged it out in the parking lot. Grey and Blu grilled me and threatened my life if Tiffany didn't make it home safely. I laughed as I put her gifts and leftover cake inside my car. I stood by the passenger door, waiting for her to finish hugging her brothers and in-laws for the third time. I didn't mind though. The relationship they had was one my brother and I had. Her heels clicked across the concrete as she made her way towards me.

"I know it's late but can we find some food before we head to my house?" she asked.

"Of course, beautiful," I replied, hungry myself.

She slid inside the car and I closed the door, smiling because I had her to myself for a minute. Inside the car, I turned the air up so that it was comfortable enough for her, then set the radio to Pandora's Jodeci station. Whatever they played I vibed to 'cause wasn't nothing like slow jams.

"A taste for anything in particular?"

She nodded. "A juicy burger is fine."

I chortled.

"For real, I deserve it tonight," she defended.

Running my fingers along her delicate cheek, I said, "You deserve it whenever."

Shyly she glanced away, while my fingers ended up intwined through hers as I left the parking lot and headed to a spot I knew she'd enjoy. Three Sisters made the best burgers in the city and was only a few blocks over. At this time of night you couldn't dine in, but we could order and enjoy our food by the water.

"Ohh, you tryna give me all the feels tonight," she quipped. "This spot is my favorite."

"Good to know," I responded, parking along the street line. We'd have to walk a couple of blocks, which was expected this time of night in downtown Pensacola. I put my heat at my back just in case. Tiffany didn't even flinch, I'm sure used to her brothers being this protective.

It was cool walking those couple of blocks until I realized Tiffany had those death shoes on.

"It's okay, boo," she said, taking my hand. I set the alarm on my car and we were off.

Tiffany's dress drew attention—attention that didn't bother me in the least. I had yet to have her, and I was confident enough to know that her ass wasn't going anywhere. The line for Three Sisters moved swiftly, and we only had to wait thirty minutes for our food.

We were back in the car, with me driving a few more blocks until we ended up parking waterside. The moon was big and bright in the sky, providing the light we needed to enjoy our food and each other's company.

"So, you're in school?" I asked her.

She shook her head. "I graduated in the Spring. I'm there tutoring for now. When I'm not at the college, I'm at work or Gianna's boutique."

I could dig that. "How's work?"

She grunted. "Absolute shit."

I chuckled. "It can't be that bad."

"I'm a legal assistant that works for a man that thinks less than fifty hours a week isn't real work. Obviously, he isn't aware I'm only working with him to get a good recommendation for law school. Working as his assistant is supposed to help me learn more about law, not run me into the ground."

"Law?" I quizzed. She confirmed with a head nod. "Okay! That's wassup, shawty. As far as ya boss, he sounds like a nigga that needs his ass beat."

She laughed but I was serious. Look, she already had me thinking reckless.

"So you're really a DEA agent?" She laughed and shook her head as she bit into her burger. Off rip, I loved how she ate like I wasn't right here, staring in her damn mouth. That shit was sexy as fuck.

"Yeah," I answered. "Why does that surprise you?" I bit into my own burger, savoring the thick, superbly seasoned steak.

Her eyebrows snapped together as she shot a look my way.

"You'd catch my ass holding 'cause I would *never* peg you as the law."

I busted out laughing. This damn woman was gon' give me a run for it.

"It's the tattoos?" I questioned.

She shook her head 'no'.

"The grill?"

Again, she shook her head 'no', and sank into her burger. Once she'd chewed it, she replied, "It's *all* of you."

Why did her voice sound huskier than it had before? Maybe that was me and my tweakin' ass. Watching her eat was making my dick hard which was some bullshit.

"I guess that's what I get for assuming," she continued.

"Definitely," I agreed, which made her giggle. "You let six weeks slide by without me hearin' ya voice. I was this close to poppin' up on you, but I'ain want you to use that nine on me. You almost made me not care though."

She laughed harder. "You counted the days?"

I shrugged. "You left a nigga hangin', fallin' asleep an' shit to ya voice and face. I'ain have a choice but to count the damn days."

My confession stunned her into a brief silence.

"Stop lying," she said, then sipped her drink. I could tell she was blushing.

"I'm dead ass," I asserted. "That's why you saw me dive over that VIP section the way I did." I threw her into another fit of laughter.

"You're crazy!"

"Not yet," I stated, "but I can tell you gon' make me that way."

Grinning around her straw, she turned to the moonlit sky and sighed.

"Besides being an agent, what does Kingston like to do?"

This old school conversation was about to have Tiffany completely winning me over as if she hadn't already.

"I have a seventy-six-year-old grandmother who occupies my time. Other than her, I spend my time as quietly as I can, doing things that either feed my mind or my spirit."

She smiled. "Seventy-six? Is she a pistol?"

I nodded. "Hell yeah. You come at her sideways, she'll eat you alive. To look at her you'd think she is as frail as a lil' soda cracker. Shiiiddd, by the time she cut yo' ass up, you'd realize she's more like peanut brittle."

Tiffany died laughing.

"Knock all ya damn teeth out," I continued, making her ball over laughing.

"Aww, but you love her though," she stated.

"To death," I confirmed.

We'd finished eating and were sipping our drinks now.

"What about your parents?"

Sighing, I said, "Lost my mama when I was sixteen. My father's in prison."

"Oh," she answered, downcast. "I'm sorry to hear that."

"She was beautiful," I recalled. "Strong and determined to have the best family she could. She was raised by my grandparents who had the best relationship. My granny dealt with her husband's death better than she did her daughter's although both were untimely. That's why I love on her the way I do. She's been through a lot, and I be damned if I take her through any more shit."

Admiration shown in Tiffany's eyes. "That's very commendable. I know she adores you."

I chuckled. "Maybe."

"Hm, hm. When she hears your car pulling up in the driveway, I'm sure she's beaming with happiness knowing you've made it home safely."

I thought about that for a second. "You're right." Being an agent didn't make me safe from the shit that could happen on these streets. Truthfully, my job put a bullseye on my back.

"I am," Tiffany agreed, wringing and smile from me.

"Tell me about ya parents. Mr. and Mrs. Summers doing well?"

She snapped her head back. "Oh, so you *know*, know my people? I introduced you to my mother and you didn't say one word."

Laughing, I shrugged. "I've never seen ya mother before. If I did, I would've known you 'cause you look just like her. Grey and Blu have always been cool and sometimes mention your parents' antics."

She groaned. "My folks are doing well and my brothers aren't exaggerating. My mom and dad are like teenagers who just so happened to be inside of two middle-aged people. However, I love it 'cause they're genuinely happy. Not none of that fake shit I see a lot of couples being into."

Hell, that sounded just right.

"I bet you gave them hell."

She side-eyed me. "And? If I did?"

Holding my hands up in surrender, I replied, "Just lettin' me know what I'm gettin' myself into, baby."

She snickered. "Whatever, Kingston. You're the one that walked up and put ya lips all over me. I should be tryna figure out what *I'm* getting myself into. I know all about not judging a book, but you definitely give off an entirely different vibe than the laws. 'Round here looking like Kingston the Kingpin instead of Kingston the Agent."

I chortled.

"I bet you have women all over the city," she quipped.

"Absolutely not," I denied.

"Says the man that knows how to tell a lie and make his own brain believe it."

I damn near spit the drink out I'd just sipped.

"Aight, you got that. I'm serious though, Princess. There's nothin' about me that's deceitful. If you wanna know somethin', ask me. It's that simple."

She mulled something over in her head, then met my eyes. "Why's your dad in prison?" she asked softly, almost as if she was afraid to ask, but bold enough to. I liked that shit.

"He was Nate the Kingpin," I answered.

Chapter Seven

TIFFANY

Kingston's response rolled off his tongue so easily that it took a second to realize he was serious. I felt bad because I'd rather his father had been into drugs, than some other crazy shit, like killing Kingston's mother. Honestly, that's why I asked.

"I try and go see him at least once a month." Kingston popped a piece of gum into his mouth, then offered me a piece, which I took. He gathered our trash, opened his door, then quickly discarded it in a nearby trashcan before sliding back into his seat. He made himself comfortable like we'd be sitting here for a minute.

"Where is he?" I asked.

"Georgia. It's a six-hour drive so I usually spend the weekend there."

"Is that why you went into law enforcement?" He was probably tired of me asking questions.

"Absolutely. I've known since I was sixteen what I wanted to do with my life. I went to college, got my degree, and haven't looked back. I don't regret what I do and for the most part, my father is proud of me for not makin' the same mistakes he did. I go to work every day knowing I'm making my mama proud, and my granny too."

Slowly exhaling, I had to remember that this was my first official night with Kingston. Although he'd been heavy on mind since the last time we talked, he was still new to me. His open honesty and gentle, yet domineering vibe was really reeling me in to the point I couldn't fight it.

I felt his fingers on my chin, bringing my eyes to meet his.

"You like touching on me, huh?" I questioned, grinning.

"If you mind, let me know," he said.

At this point, I didn't mind so I didn't respond.

"We're together so get used to me touchin' on you. I can't help it."

Although my body reacted in a way that made me want to let down my window, I fought the urge and replied, "Number one, you haven't asked me to be your woman. Number two, I've known you all of one night."

Kingston leaned over the armrest, crowding my space but staring me dead in my eyes.

"My fault," he apologized.

Whatever cologne he was wearing had me trapped in his web and had all night. Between sitting on his lap, being in his arms, and tasting his tongue, I was going to have one hell of a night trying to sleep.

"I've been dreamin' about this woman. She has eyes that I hope can see to my soul. Her smile is equivalent to feeling butterflies in my stomach. I act like I'm not pressed by her presence or being this close to her. When really, she makes me wanna do shit I've never done with a female."

"Which is?"

"Make you mine," he simply answered. He leaned closer, pecking my lips.

"What happened to being friends first?" I quizzed, in between him planting kisses on me.

"You fucked that up by ghostin' me for damn near two months. That was our friend stage. I know you dreamed about a nigga—"

I smacked my teeth.

"—and I for damn sho had you on my mind like crazy. So what's good?"

Because he wouldn't stop kissing me, I just blinked at him.

"Cool," he said as if my silence was my answer. "Our first date is already planned, so you might as well say yes."

"I'm not sleeping with you tonight, Kingston."

This man chuckled against my lips. "Good, baby. I'ain plan on givin' up my innocence this early in our relationship."

I busted out laughing. One thing about it, Kingston knew how to make me laugh, and he wasn't even trying.

"I want you to be good and comfortable with me by the time we cross that line," he added.

"Okay," I conceded.

"Okay?" he parroted.

I nodded. "Yes."

"Aight." He placed a couple more kisses on my lips before going back to his side. "Lemme get you home." As soon as he said it, my phone vibrated.

GREY:

I'ain good witchu havin' a nigga just yet. Don't make me have to body that nigga.

Laughing, I typed him back.

ME:

He's completely harmless.

At least I hope so.

ME:

On my way home now. I'll call you when I get inside.

GREY:

Bet.

I remembered why Kingston won me over so easily. The way he bombarded my night and didn't flinch at the sight of my brothers gave me great hope that I could do this. I could be in a relationship with a man and him not give a damn about the way my brothers felt about it. Why did that scare me a little bit?

The next morning, I woke up feeling rested as hell. It must've stemmed from the nasty kiss Kingston placed on me last night. It had got so hot and heavy that I ended up against my front door with him begging me not to open it until he was a few feet away. Although my parents and sisters were inside, the temptation to invite him in had been strong. However, I told him I wasn't sleeping with him and I meant it. My pussy, on the other hand, was angry as hell at me. After showering and handling my morning routine, I went down the stairs to find my parents in the kitchen.

"I heard you got a lil' boyfriend," my daddy said by way of greeting.

"Daddy," I groaned.

"I'ain said nothin'," he shot back. "You're a grown woman, and I'm not pryin' 'less I need to. I had a long talk with ya brothers this mornin' about that very thing. They called me gripin' 'bout some dread head nigga. I told 'em, you grown. What they expect?" Confused, I wondered if this was really my daddy talking. He sounded and acted too damn *cool.*

"Why're you sittin' here lying through your teeth, *papi*?" My mother grilled him.

My father grumbled.

"*I* told your brothers *and* your daddy to find some business," she explained.

Laughter bubbled over just as my phone rang. Glancing at the screen, my heart stilled when I saw it was Kingston. I sprang from the kitchen then hurried up and accepted the FaceTime.

"Heyyy," I answered calmly, although my heart raced.

"Mornin', baby," Kingston crooned with a smile that played along my nipples.

I bit into my lip because how could he sound so sexy this early in the morning. It's a shame that I was glad he called first. I didn't want to come across as clingy too early on in this *relationship.*

"Good morning," I spoke back.

"I can't wait 'til I hear that shit when you wake up next to me."

Whew! I knew I turned every shade of red.

"Damn, look how fuckin' sexy ya ass is," he continued.

"Kingston," I lightly chided.

"What? I can't hype my woman? You're my woman, right?"

Playfully rolling my eyes, I nodded.

"Aight then, makin' sure we clear on that. 'Cause I'on hype females up, baby. Only you."

Smacking my teeth, I took notice of the black, collared button-down he had on.

"Working?" I asked, changing the subject.

"Yeah, handling some shit. Hopefully, I won't be here all day, but I'ain holdin' my breath."

Sighing, I hoped his Saturdays weren't always filled with work. I was already worried over if he and I would spend quality time together. And this was only day one and a half. I shook my head, ashamed that I was thinking too far ahead.

"I usually don't work on Saturdays but I have a case I'm tryna put to rest. I'ma have plenty of time for you, lil' baby."

Did this nigga just read my mind?

Kingston chuckled at my eyebrows snapping together.

"I'ma let you know now, I want all ya time. I hope that's cool 'cause in my mind, we're best friends. I understand you gon' have ya lil' female time witcha homegirls and family time or whatever, but at the end of the day, my time belongs to you, and I hope you'll let ya time belong to me."

"That's a recipe for disaster, Kingston. We'll get on each other's nerves at some point. Others would see that as controlling."

He chuckled. "You could never get on my nerves, shawty. And controlling? Tellin' you to get dressed and bring that ass to me right now is controlling. How 'bout...*damn, I wanna see that ass so fuckin' bad. Can I slide through for a kiss?* Yeah, that sounds better." His eyes took on a sensual, dark bedroom look that turned me into puddy.

Why did he just have me soaking my panties? Speechless, I gulped, feeling like I was in the middle of the desert in here.

"May I?" he asked.

"Huh?" I questioned.

"Slide through for a kiss?"

"Uhm...yeah," I stuttered.

"Bet. I'll be there shortly."

I smiled, then hung up, nervously biting into my lip. Patiently, I waited for him, not changing into decent clothes or anything. My mother made breakfast, which I left wrapped on the stove.

Twenty minutes later, I was sitting on my porch swing, watching Kingston come up the street. He was in an undercover SUV, slowly riding through. I had to laugh. This man was actually a federal agent. He parked along the curb, left the SUV running, and stepped out like Mike Lowry. His sexy, dark chocolate ass looked even better dressed in slacks and a button-down. The badge dangling from the chain around his neck only confirmed that he was *that* nigga. His shades came off, revealing his weird brown eyes. I loved the way his dreads were pulled back in a ponytail at the nape of his neck. Visually, Kingston was just...everything.

He took the couple of stairs bringing him onto the porch, then sauntered up to me with the softest expression on his face. That shit scared me. Like how could Kingston look so damn gangsta but have an expression that mirrored the gentlest soul? His cologne hit my senses, lulling me to my feet as he reached his hand out for me.

Kingston towered over me, his masculinity a turn-on in itself. When he hugged me to his body, he lifted me off my feet. Giggling, I wrapped my legs around his waist and cupped his scruffy jaw. His beard was freshly trimmed and thick as hell. Like at the club, he kissed my forehead, then my nose, then pecked my lips.

I didn't protest when his hands slid under my ass cheeks, holding me as I slipped my tongue into his minty, fresh mouth. The cotton shorts I wore didn't stand a chance as the heat of his body bled right through the material, stroking my center. Holding his head steady, I angled mine, deepening the kiss, making sure he got exactly what he came here for. My nipples pebbled hard, arousal taking over as we vied for supremacy. We moaned at the same time, nibbling and sucking on each other sensually.

A dog's bark broke our heated moment, causing me to snicker against Kingston's strong, tattooed neck. I slid down his body until my bare feet touched the porch, but I remained in his arms. His dick poked my lower abdomen, spiking my senses.

"I'ain gon' be able to concentrate for the rest of the day," he joked.

"That's kinda the point," I quipped.

"Point made." He grinned, then pecked my lips. "Now get back inside 'for somebody see ya ass out."

Cracking up, I let Kingston hug me tightly before I slipped back inside the house, locking the door behind myself.

Chapter Eight

AUGUST WELLS

"Shit," I grumbled, rolling over to catch my buzzing phone. My body felt like it was a thousand years old, and my head hurt like a bitch. Smelling something funky, I scrunched my face up. Next to the bed was a trash can filled with what looked like yesterday's dinner.

Gagging at the sight, I tried to sit up, only for my head to start swimming. My phone continued to buzz though, prompting me to force myself to sit up. Only then did the soft body lying next to me stir. Her body was bad, and her face was even sexier. Glancing around, I saw that I was in an unfamiliar room.

"Fuck," I muttered, swiping up my phone, expecting it to be Kingston. He was going to blow a gasket that I'd been out all night without giving him the slightest heads-up. Shiidd, I was grown now, so Kingston had to chill.

The name flashing across the screen sent me panicking. Dizziness and all, I rushed to get dress and out of this bitch's house as I answered Faith's call.

"Hey, baby," I answered.

"Please don't even." She chuckled. "At this point, we're done, August. I don't want anything from you, and I don't need anything from you. This baby we're having, you can choose to do what is your responsibility, or we can handle it the hard way. I hope your birthday was everything you intended it to be." *Click*!

"Fuck!" I growled, busting out of the funky ass apartment this hoe lived in. I mean, it took a minute to make it through the living room her fucking place was so dirty. Realizing I was in the hood, I checked my surroundings, and as soon as I slid into my Challenger, I checked the inside to make sure wasn't shit stolen.

I tore out of the complex on two wheels, to make it to Faith's apartment. Faith wasn't the type to bug a nigga, so I wasn't expecting her to call me again after this phone call. The last time I fucked up with her, she stopped talking to me for weeks. She didn't send not one message or anything. Her ignore game was solid.

A part of me loved Faith, I just couldn't be faithful to her. I'd tried a few times, and each time I fucked up. I was able to get myself out of the last fuck up by paying the other girl to lie and say we didn't fuck. Honestly, I wasn't sure if Faith believed it or not, but she took me back. This time though, I pulled up to her apartment smelling like straight bitch. I didn't realize it until Faith cracked her door and tooted her nose up.

"We can't talk?" I asked, knowing damn well what her answer would be.

"What you can do is get your things out of my trunk.

Otherwise, we don't have anything to talk about if it's not concerning the baby."

She closed the door in my face, locking it. Sighing, I mugged the nigga coming up the steps towards Faith's apartment.

"This why the fuck she'on wanna deal wit' me," I angrily told ol' boy.

Chuckling, he walked past me, glancing me up and down. "Don't blame shit on me, pahtna."

Faith's best-friend, Jericho, never came across as wanting my woman, but the way he smirked in my face had me thinking differently.

"If you wanted her, all you had to do was ask," I goaded him.

He cackled, sliding a key into the Faith's door to let himself in.

The fuck?

"I'ain gotta ask for shit," he replied. He stood there, waiting for me to jump.

This is what I hated about this nigga, Jericho. Just because he was from the streets, he thought every nigga owed him their respect. I didn't owe him shit, so I laughed in his face.

"Tell Faith—"

"I'ain' tellin' her shit. Get ya shit outta her trunk and stay the fuck from 'round here."

I wanted to bust this nigga upside his head, but I was already in hot water with Kingston. If I got arrested he'd have a stroke. Deciding to leave well enough alone, I retreated back down the stairs. One box sat in Faith's uncluttered trunk holding my belongings. Glancing back up towards her apartment, I found Jericho leaning on the rail, smoking a blunt, waiting for me to get gone. Laughing to myself, I put the box in my car, said fuck it to Faith, and took off.

How she let a nigga have a whole damn key to her crib and I didn't? Hell, for all I know that damn baby probably wasn't even mine.

"Granny, I'm sorry, okay," I apologized for the fifth time. She was hot as hell that I hadn't checked in last night. She angrily plucked at her flowers, while I stood here listening to her bless me out.

I'd came home, showered, and thought I was about to hit the bed for a nap, when I heard her calling my name. Ever since Kingston told her to stop going down the deck steps alone, she hadn't. She wanted to garden this morning, so I went to help her down the stairs. Now here I was getting my whole life chewed up and spit back out.

"You know darn well I was worried. But ya grown nie, can't do nothin' 'bout it. It's the respect and decency, August. You think ya mama ever pulled that with me?"

"No ma'am," I mumbled, following her as she continued to pluck from a row of beautiful roses.

"'Xactly. Just 'cause you twenty-one nie don't make you no man. In the law's eyes it does, but not in real life. A man gon' handle his responsibilities and keep his head 'bout him. You doin' that?" she questioned, stopping what she was doing to glare at me as if she knew the answer.

"Granny—"

"Aht, aht! Answer me, August. You outchea old 'nough to slang ya lil' pecker, but are you gon' take care of ya baby?"

I didn't get a chance to answer before she added, "Can't be since you was somewhere besides here or Faith's house last night. You oughta quit it!" she continued plucking and fussing. I scratched my short beard, trying not to laugh. My granny was so dramatic at times.

"Granny, my baby will be taken care of," I assured her. "I don't have to want the woman to take care of what I created with her."

Granny looked at me like if she could slice me up, she would.

"Get on, August!" she barked. "The audacity! I bet' not *ever* hear you say some foolishness like that again! Sound just like that—" She cut her rant short, growling like a mad woman. "Get on, August. I'm done witcha for the day."

Damn, Granny was good and mad. As I walked back towards the house I did chuckle to myself to keep from getting angry. Granny didn't have to finish her statement for me to know that she was talking about my dad. She had the strongest grudge against my dad for what she considered his fault for my mother being dead. As Nate's son, everything in me believed that if he'd been able to, he would've prevented my mother from being killed that day. However, my grandmother just needed someone to blame.

My dad would've done anything to save my mother. It wasn't his fault that niggas were after him. Sure he was in the dope game, but according to him, he'd never done anyone wrong for them to have come after my mom. I believed him. He took her death so hard that he closed himself off to the world. Being fucked up behind losing his wife is what got my dad caught. If he'd been on his A game, the troopers would have never caught him. But he got caught slipping and was now paying the price. I held out hope that he would see the day he was due to be released.

My phone vibrated, just as I made it back inside the house. I couldn't leave Granny in the backyard, so I sat at the kitchen table and divided my attention outside of the window to her and the message on my phone.

BAKE:

You comin' thru?

ME:

Fa sho.

I'd barely answered Bake when another message came through.

KING:

Do what you do, baby.

Groaning, I shook my head. I loved Kingston to death, but his ass needed to stay in a brother's place. He was forever trying to be my dad when I already had one.

ME:

I'm cool, bruh. Watchin' Granny in the yard.

KING:

Yeah.

Shaking my head, I chortled at his response. I should clown his ass for how he tripped over himself trying to get out of VIP last night to get to ol' girl. Shiidd, but shawty was bad as fuck, no lie. She had that Aaliyah vibe going on, and what man could resist that? His ass didn't even come back to the party after linking up with her. I hope she gave his ass some pussy so he'd stay out of my business.

Needing to make this move, I didn't even reply to King and instead went back outside to hustle Granny back inside. She wasn't too happy about it, but I'd make it up to her later.

Chapter Nine

TIFFANY

Friday night...

I was so nervous getting ready for this date with Kingston. Several outfits lay strewn out on my bed, neither of them doing justice for how I wanted to look tonight. While I wanted to be sexy, I didn't want to seem like I was throwing myself at him. Even though I wanted to.

Not physically seeing Kingston since Saturday, I couldn't wait to have him in my presence. Our daily and nightly FaceTime calls or his random text messages over the last few days wasn't cutting it for me. Our conversations were never longer than a few minutes and ended with me pouting to myself.

I hated that he worked *a lot*. Now I could understand what Gianna and Jacoba went through with my brothers and their careers. However, Grey and Blu balanced work and home life well. Maybe I was thinking too far in advance, but I hoped neither of our schedules caused us to lose interest in each other.

Kingston had to have some warlock's spell on me. That's the only reason I could explain the sheer attraction I had for him. Tingles shot through my body, already anticipating being in his arms. His energy was too strong for me to deny if I tried.

So, here I was trying on the tenth outfit, hoping this one would do because I heard his Charger pulling into my driveway. Having no choice, I zipped up the black high-waisted jeans, slid my feet into my black stilettos, and checked myself out in the floor-to-ceiling mirror hanging from the door. The white, cut-off tee I wore with an image of the ninety-six NBA draft class on it wasn't formal at all but toned down the sexiness just a little. It hung off my right shoulder adding some flair. With my hair down and flowing, I looked like a whole Vogue ad.

Smiling, I grabbed my clutch just as the doorbell rang. Jitters took over, wanting this night to be perfect. When I opened the door for Kingston, I had to catch my breath. I was talking about looking like a Vogue ad when Kingston was the whole damn Vogue issue. From his freshly twisted dreads, all the way down to his Jordan covered feet, Kingston oozed sex and a lot of other shit in all-black. He chuckled lightly; the way that made me want to melt.

"If you ready to be Mrs. Wells just say that," he stated, bringing himself closer to me.

Why did he make me blush so much? It was almost silly. But it wasn't silly at all. Kingston made me feel beautiful and not just on the outside. It's like his words stroked my soul in a way where, any other dude saying what he'd just said would've gotten him a stank eye from me. However, when Kingston said it, I felt that there was some validity to his words.

I smacked my teeth, hiding my nervousness behind a smile, just as one of his hands found my waist and the other lifted my chin. Per usual he kissed my forehead, then the tip of my nose.

"You're beautiful, Tiffany," he declared in between sweet kisses to my lips.

My eyes fluttered close, basking in the gentleness of him. He never deepened the kiss and stepped away before taking my hand.

"Let's go catch this sunset," he said.

Nodding, I preceded him out of the door, allowing him to close it behind us.

We ended up on the beach, at a restaurant I'd never been to. I for one knew how uppity this place was, but the deck did provide one of the best views of Pensacola Beach. The deck was empty of other patrons, with one table set for two, donning flowers, and several gift bags.

Kingston seated me while the cheeky hostess smiled like this was her perfect dinner. "I'll be back with your drinks," she said and hustled off.

"Kingston, what is all of this?" I asked as he took the seat across from me.

"Gifts, baby," he responded, like he hadn't given me two stacks for my birthday.

"You already gave me a birthday gift," I contested. I hated to wonder how Kingston made his money besides working for the law. His tastes were expensive, and if the gift bags told anything, he'd showered me plenty tonight.

He turned his nose up. "Money ain't a gift."

"Tuh! According to Kingston? I'm curious as to what kinda side jobs you have," I said.

He grinned. "There's no feeling in givin' money, shawty, anybody can do that. As far as my side jobs—I invest. My mother left me money, and the money that my dad had stashed away my granny put into an account for me and August."

"Oh. Well, I was good with that," I countered.

Licking his lips, he smirked at me. "You gon' argue witcha man on our first date, lil' mama?"

I giggled because he found any reason to make sure I knew we were together.

"No, I won't," I acquiesced, eyeing the five gift bags.

"Open them," he encouraged.

Sighing, I started with the biggest bag. My mouth dropped at the bag inside of it. Flicking my eyes Kingston's way, I wasn't sure whether to hop on him or simply beam with pride. Our moment was interrupted by the server bringing our drinks back.

"You like it?" he questioned, tasting his drink to make sure it was up to his standards.

I nodded. What wasn't there to like about an LV bag. Especially one that I'd been eyeing the last few times I'd searched their site. Besides the LV bag, I was gifted a pair of red bottom sneakers, Versace perfume, and two pairs of Gucci shades. It was funny how he knew my style.

Inside the last bag were three jewelry boxes, bearing the name of a very expensive jeweler.

"Kingston," I protested when I opened the first one. It was a platinum and diamond necklace bearing a charm with the initials KTW. It was stunning. There was no need in me asking what the initials stood for. Tingling sensations filled my belly at the implication. I was no less shocked at the diamond studs and bracelet in the other two boxes.

"This is too much," I fussed while he stood to come to my side of the table. He took the necklace and placed it around my neck. His hand then tilted my head back for a kiss.

"Nothing's too much for you," he stated against my lips.

He went and sat back down with me staring after him. What was it about Kingston that drew me so heavily? Shouldn't I have been afraid of falling for a dude, especially one that I hadn't crossed the line with? I was so damn out of my element with him, feeling like the amateur that I was in this courting game.

As he pointed towards the water, he said, "Our first sunset together."

Looking out over the water, I marveled at the sky's beauty as I always did. Enjoying this moment with Kingston solidified something between us that I couldn't name.

"Give me ya hand," he requested.

Placing my hand in his, he flipped it over in his larger one. Seconds later, he did something with our hands, bringing a smile to my face. It was a handshake, one that was so quickly done yet so intricate, I asked him to repeat it. He did. This was something special between two people that signified their unity.

Each time our fingers intersected he stated something different. "Loyalty. Respect. Honor."

The fourth time our fingers locked, he just stared at me.

"This one we'll get around to soon enough," he said, referring to whatever word he had for the fourth lock. He kissed my palm then grinned.

Minutes later, our food arrived. I struggled to eat, feeling his eyes on me with every movement I made. It wasn't weird or unsettling. Quite the opposite. It's like his gaze reverenced me in some way.

We made it through dinner, with me hating that the night was ending. If I expected Kingston to want to stay the night, he didn't. This man walked me to my door, kissed me senseless, then told me to go inside and lock the door. I went to bed that night both hot and bothered and upset. I craved Kingston.

Monday morning came too quickly. I rushed into work half-asleep from being on the phone all night with Kingston. He had me up laughing my head off so much that my ribs ached. I grabbed a cup of tea on the way in to see if it would sooth the sore throat I'd gained from laughing so hard.

He worked all day yesterday, preventing us from doing anything other than sharing a FaceTime with each other. After having a great night with him Saturday, I felt bereft. It was clear I wasn't used to having a man because all I wanted to do was be up under Kingston. In the throes of a passionate dream last night, I decided to not mope at the fact that Kingston was a busy man. This clingy side of me was a bitch, and she needed to get under control. Especially since Kingston and I were new to this. Power walking through the back entrance, I barely made it to my desk before Chris came around the corner.

"Everything set for Mr. Wilks?" he asked. Now this man saw me with my purse and drink still in my hand and the computer off.

It was going on my third month here, and I felt no better

about working for Chris. I was truly trying to thug it out, but day by day he irked me. Just so I wouldn't have to travel with him again, I had my doctor make up an excuse for me not to be able to fly until further notice. She didn't even put an explanation, but Chris being a lawyer knew it was illegal for him to ask me what the problem was. So, that's the only good thing that had happened to me thus far.

"Once I get the computer up and running, I'll prepare the file for you," I responded.

Wilks and Chris were getting on my last damn nerve.

"Okay, awesome!" He grinned. "I have a couple of interviews today for the vacant assistant position. I really missed you not being on those other trips. You're very efficient," he complimented.

If I was 'very efficient' why did he stay on my ass so much is what I thought to myself, but I thanked God that he'd finally taken the step to hire someone.

"Their files are in that folder." He pointed to a tan folder on top of my keyboard. "Look over them and see what you think. I'll let you sit in on the meetings."

Discreetly rolling my eyes, I did not want to spend my time in his office all damn day. He sauntered off, not even caring that I had other shit to do besides listen to him grill prospects. Thirty minutes later, I was almost done compiling the Wilks' file when a delivery guy appeared at my desk.

"Tiffany Summers?" he asked. I nodded.

He placed the two dozen roses atop my desk and with a simple head nod was gone. Surprised, I stared at the white roses, then hurriedly plucked the card from the center of it. Because it smelled like Kingston, I sniffed it before slipping the card from the envelope.

Princess,

Can't wait to touch you, kiss you, hold you...and some other shit.

King

I smiled so hard, my cheeks burned.

"Those are beautiful."

My eyes snapped left, almost rolling at the sight of Miss Aldridge. She was the only one in the office I couldn't address by her first name and it made me chuckle every time. Her lawyer's title had her head so far in the clouds, she couldn't tell what season it was, let alone what skin tone she was. Miss Aldridge was a beautiful, brown-skinned woman but wished she was the color of her palm instead.

"Thank you," I responded half-heartedly.

"New boo?" She leaned over my desk, trying to discreetly read the card I'd placed on my desk.

Swiping it up, I placed it in a different spot and asked, "Can I assist you with anything this morning?"

I really needed to FaceTime Kingston to thank him for my roses, and she was holding up my desk like we were cool or something. We'd never shared a lunch, the restroom, or the same sofa for that matter. If it wasn't something I could do for her, Miss Aldridge didn't fuck with me.

Her bundles cascaded around her shoulders as she chuckled.

"Secretive? I'm trying to see how to get my man to send me roses. Any pointers?"

Huh?

"Actually, no," I replied truthfully.

She stupidly blinked at me like I was trying to be funny when I wasn't.

"Well," she said after a few seconds had passed. "He either fucked up or misses you because that arrangement is life."

Chuckling to myself, I ignored her and repeated my earlier question. "Can I help you with anything?" Her assistant, Mina, was out this morning and wouldn't be in until this afternoon, leaving me to deal with her uppity ass.

Pursing her lips, she replied, "Yes. I have some notes I need typed up before lunch."

She handed me the notebook she cradled. Several pages were clipped together, which I assumed were the notes she needed me to type up. I only worked for Chris, but Miss Aldridge occasionally snuck herself to my desk to ask for help.

"I'll place them on your desk once I'm done," I assured her. She stood here a minute longer, needing what? I didn't even ask. When she finally sauntered off, I shook my head, and dug my phone out of my purse.

Clicking Kingston's number, I waited for the FaceTime to connect.

"Hey beautiful," he answered, grinning.

"The roses are gorgeous." I beamed.

"So are you, baby. Friday won't come soon enough. This case I'm workin' on is almost wrapped up, so I'll have plenty of time on my hands to spoil you."

I nibbled at my lip, unable to contain the amount of hope flowing through me. Here I was complaining about him not having time for me when he had serious shit to take care of. His dedication was commendable. Was it possible that my first boyfriend, *man,* could be this perfect? Hell, Kingston wasn't perfect. But he damn sure seemed like it.

"I told you I don't wanna be spoiled," I reminded him. This morning, I almost wore the necklace he'd bought me, but opted for the earrings just to feel him near.

"You never did answer what you wanted," he shot back. "Therefore, I can move accordingly. Is it that you don't know what you want?"

Irritated that he read me, I smacked my teeth.

"Ain't no other nigga spoiled you before, Princess?"

"My brothers and my father—"

"Nah, I'ain talmbout them and you know that," he interjected, but I was already laughing trying to lighten my embarrassment.

"Honestly, Kingston." I sighed, not sure if I should tell him, but urged myself to say what I had to say. I never bit my tongue for anyone, let alone a man. "You're the first man I've ever had. You've met my brothers so I'm sure you can understand why."

Kingston stared at me through the phone, gauging whether to believe me or not. As a matter of fact, it wasn't him gauging my honesty, but rather measuring what his next statement would be.

"I'ma be ya last, so yeen gotta worry about introducin' anybody else," he answered.

Like he could do, Kingston sent me laughing.

"Call me when you go to lunch," he requested.

"I will," I responded with a smile. I received one back, causing butterflies to take over my stomach.

"Later, lil' mama."

"Later, Kingston."

I hung up, blushing like Kingston was standing in front of me naked. The things that man made me feel was a shame.

Especially since we hadn't done anything except kiss. I'd never been so ready to give up my box more than I was now.

For the next hour, I breezed through typing two documents for Miss Aldridge before I had to go into these meetings with Chris. Neither of the applicants had shown yet which was strange.

Shortly after I completed the notes for Miss Aldridge, Chris sauntered to my desk with his wife alongside him. Seeing Anissa here caused me to hold back a deep sigh. Visually, I couldn't find one thing wrong with Anissa. She was that type of beautiful that had many women envying her. Her deep brown skin always popped, and her hair was always laid to perfection in the black pixie cut she wore.

"Hey, beautiful," Anissa spoke.

She went out of her way to be kind to me, and I was okay with it. Working closely with her husband, I'm sure she was more concerned about keeping me close to the chest. Being nasty to me wouldn't help her keep tabs on her man. Only, she had no reason to worry about me. I'd heard some things about him and his previous assistant, but that was just speculation and office gossip to me. Since I didn't see it firsthand, I couldn't paint anyone in a negative light. Besides, Chris was all work when it came to me.

"Hey," I replied and continued on to the next assignment I had on my list for the day. My man asked me to call him on my lunch, and I needed to pass this time quickly. I was like a fiend trying to hear his voice and see his face.

"Wow, those are gorgeous!" Anissa beamed.

Chris chuckled. "They have the lobby smelling good, too."

Actually that was the faint smell of my man's cologne permeating from the card.

"Thank you," I responded.

"I'm going to be away from the office for the rest of the day, so feel free to leave as early as you like."

Bitch, all I heard was 'leave'.

"Should I inform the applicants?"

He shook his head. "They've already been contacted."

I wasn't even going to investigate who called to inform them.

"Okay," I quickly answered so he couldn't take it back. This was a nice surprise as Chris never left the office early let alone an entire day.

"Text me if you need me," he said before they waved and headed back towards his office.

Smiling from ear to ear, I breezed right on through the rest of my morning. Chris said I could leave, so when noon hit, I'd already closed my computer down and had gathered my things to leave.

Miss Aldridge caught me collecting my keys and eyed me. Out of all the other attorneys that worked here, she was the only one steadily finding her way by my desk.

"Leaving early?" she questioned. Seeing that she had another notebook in her hand, I nodded.

"Oh, I had something else for you."

Politely grinning, I pointed to Mina's desk. "She'll be in by one."

Leaving her with her mouth partially open, I stole a glance at my beautiful roses before leaving them adorning my desk as I left the lobby. Miss Aldridge was going to have to get over it today. Something that Kingston said the other day had me calling my brother.

"'Sup, baby girl?"

"Grey, where's the DEA's office?"

"Why?"

As if I could see his face ball up, I laughed while cranking my car.

"'Cause," I jokingly snapped. "Stop being nosey and give me the address."

Reluctantly, Grey gave me the directions. Within minutes, I was pulling into the parking lot. I spotted Kingston's Charger and giddily hoped he was inside. With him driving an undercover cruiser the other day, this trip could be a blank one. I hoped not though. More importantly, I hoped he wouldn't cut up from me popping up on his ass.

Shouldering my crossbody purse, I figured I was here now, so my nerves could just calm the hell down. Plenty of eyes followed me as I walked inside the building. Stopping at the receptionist desk, I asked her if Kingston was in, and if so, could she direct me to him. The older white lady smiled and pointed towards the security check in.

"Yes he's here. Once you get through them, he's down the first hall to your right," she directed.

Thanking her, I gulped, really wanting to turn around and go back to my car. What was I thinking showing up at this man's job? If Kingston cussed me out today, I wouldn't take it to heart. Because I was straight on some crazy stalker shit right now.

Chapter Ten

KINGSTON

"Mane, I'm tellin' you I'ma make her get one of those DNA shits. Ain't no way I got another seed comin', bruh. You know damn well she got other niggas outchea besides me."

"Aye, hol' up," I said to Jared, who was in the middle of running down a story about his baby mama's attempt at trapping him again.

My eyes were on the beautiful ass creation walking down the hall towards my office. Through the glass I watched a couple niggas stop and watch her switching her fine ass up in here. She was dressed in a pair of red slacks, and a white blouse that was crisply tucked into the pants. Her hair was up in the top knot, with the whisps shit. The closer she got to my office door, the more I salivated. Nervously, she smiled when she saw my attention was on her but kept eye contact as she stood in the doorway.

I beckoned her with my fingers, shocked, but damn sure happy to see her. “Bring ya ass here, baby.”

As if my words were the key to her smile, she lit up and trekked to me, never addressing Jared’s ass who was drooling at the mouth. I couldn’t say shit because my dick bricked up at the sight of her. The minute she was close enough, I guided her into my lap. Her sweet scent had my nose flaring and my mans reacting even more. Sitting across from her at dinner the other night was still fresh in my mind. The strength it took to only kiss her goodnight caused me to lose sleep every night since. I wanted Tiffany bad as fuck but found myself holding back with her. She just shot that to hell comin’ up in here smelling all good an’ shit.

“Uh, I think I’ma give y’all some privacy,” Jared stated and got to his feet.

“I’ll catch up witchu,” I told him before he left out of the door.

“Did I interrupt? I hope you’re not upset.”

I silenced her with a kiss that did nothing but fuel the fire. Especially when my hands cupped her ass cheeks and moved her until her pussy rubbed my hardened length.

“The only thing I’m upset about is I can’t spread you open on this fuckin’ desk.” Not without every man and woman gaping at her beautiful body while I tore her the fuck up.

She prettily demurred under my appraisal. “I was headed home for the day but needed to see you.”

My pierced nipples hardened when she tugged at my beard requesting another kiss which I gave her.

“Come see me whenever you want to, baby.”

She giggled. “You don’t think I’m crazy for poppin’ up on you?”

"Be crazy about me," I encouraged, causing her to chuckle. "I'm aight with that."

"Aight," she said, "don't have an issue later down the road."

"I won't," I assured her. "Spend the weekend with me," I said in the next breath.

She chewed at her bottom lip in contemplation. If she agreed to spend the weekend with me, I'd make her time more than worth it.

"Okay," she agreed seconds later.

Happy she agreed, I tweaked her chin. "Let's go grab some lunch," I suggested.

She nodded and climbed from my lap. When she held out her hand to help me to my feet, I laughed at her thoughtfulness.

"You do realize I weigh two-forty, baby."

Her gaze shot from my feet to my face, then she promptly looked away, whatever thoughts skating through her mind caused her face to heat.

Shiidd. "Any chance you gon' tell me what you're thinkin'?"

She shook her head and hid a smile.

"I'ma have a good time makin' you blush over me," I stated, hugging her to my body.

Ushering her out of my office, I couldn't help but watch the sway of her hips in the slacks riding her curves. Tiffany was so damn sexy, I had to catch my breath every time she looked at me. I'd never been smitten by a woman, however, lil' baby absolutely had me like that.

We ended up at Tasha's, indulging ourselves in each other while we waited for our food. I enjoyed listening to her tell me about her family and the crazy shit she dealt with when it came to her brothers. Every time we talked, she had something new to tell me. Because I was overprotective of August, I couldn't fault Grey and Blu from being that way with Tiffany.

Our conversation was briefly interrupted when Faith walked into the diner. Sweetly, she waved. Faith was not only beautiful, but she had a sweet soul. August was dumb as fuck for doing shawty the way he was. She was about to sit at another table when I told her she could sit with us.

"Thank you." She smiled.

"Tiffany, this is August's lady, Faith."

Faith politely shook Tiffany's proffered hand.

"Actually, I'm just Faith. August and I are..."

Tilting my head, I questioned, "Really?" August hadn't said shit.

She chuckled and nodded. Her slightly swollen belly was barely noticeable, but there, nonetheless. Inwardly shaking my head, I wondered what the hell August was thinking. He knew how it felt to grow up without our dad present, and here he was about to make his own flesh and blood start off foul.

"No offense to you or Granny, but August has some growing up to do," Faith simply said.

"I can't argue with that," I acknowledged.

Faith shrugged.

"I've seen you around campus a few times," Tiffany stated.

Faith nodded. "That's where I've seen you! Girl, you have the prettiest skin!" she gushed.

Tiffany modestly grinned. "Thanks, but so do you. You're glowing!"

Sighing, Faith lightly chuckled. "It's the baby I'm sure. I have until March, and I'm already over pregnancy."

Tiffany's eyes widened. "Congratulations!"

Faith groaned. "Thanks, boo, but no ma'am," she replied, sending me and Tiffany laughing. She joined in.

"You know what you're having?" Tiffany questioned.

Faith produced several ultrasound pics, handing one to me. "A boy." She sighed. "I'm so nervous."

"Aww, that's so sweet," Tiffany responded. While they gushed over the baby, I made sure Faith's order was placed so her food would come out with ours.

I sat here half-listening to them become acquainted, while mulling over the fact that I needed to talk to August about his lack of responsibility for someone who hadn't asked to be here.

Before our father was arrested, he never shirked on his responsibilities of raising us although he'd been doing his dirt in the streets. I couldn't lie and say that he was a bad dad because he wasn't. Where August's ways spawned baffled me. He was nothing like me or our dad.

Talking to August would be like pulling teeth. All he'd do is accuse me of coming down on him, when really all I wanted to do was help him. My niece or nephew wasn't going to come into this world half-taken care of, even if I had to do it, like my granny had to do for me and August. Whether he liked it or not, I had to see him about this shit.

Tiffany and I parted ways after we made it back to my office. I hugged and kissed her like she wasn't going to see me again and told her to call me once she made it home. She and Faith exchanged numbers and were planning on hanging out sometimes, which I thought would be good for Faith. I only knew about her what August relayed to me, and from the sounds of it, Faith needed a solid homegirl in her corner.

Plopping in my chair, I sighed heavily, but dialed August's number anyway.

"'Sup, bruh?" he answered.

"Just ran into Faith," I said without preamble.

"So," he quipped.

My face balled up. "'So?" I lightly chuckled to calm the frustration rising in me. "You for real 'bout to let this woman be a single mother?"

He guffawed. "I'm not lettin' her be shit. If she wanna bitch about what I do instead of forgivin' me and movin' past the shit, ain't nothin' I can do about it."

"Wait," I stated, pinching the bridge of my nose. "You wanna fuck around on shawty and blamin' her for not bein' cool wit' it? That's what the fuck I'm hearin'."

August clucked his teeth. "Maannee," he drawled. "I'm young, aight. I fucked up gettin' Faith pregnant, but she should've considered not keepin' it like I told her ass."

"August," I growled. We'd already been over this.

"I know, mane," he hurried up and said. "I tried to go to her and make shit right, but she wasn't havin' it, so I dipped. I'm not beggin' no female to be in her life."

At the end of my rope I asked, "How you think Mama would feel about that, bruh?"

"Can't think about that," he casually replied. "I was only eight when she died, remember?"

Dodging his dig, I started over. "What about Dad? You think he'd be cool with what you're doin'?"

August remained quiet on the other end.

"'Cause you know he wouldn't agree," I added.

"I go see him this weekend. I'll let him know wassup. If he tells me to make shit right, I will. Otherwise, I'ma let Faith do what she's doin' and just give her money whenever she needs it."

"August you sound dumb as fuck," I barked. "A baby needs more than ya fuckin' money! Ya time, nigga! What about that shit?"

"Damn! You act like I said I'm turnin' my back on my seed. I'm just not ready to raise one right now, King. I'ma still be there the best I know how, and that's making sure it has everything it needs."

"*He*!" I growled. "You're havin' a fuckin' son!"

Seeing red, I hung up on August not wanting to hear any more of his bullshit. Frustrated, I ran my hands down my face and growled into my palms.

"Keep that same energy for where we're about to go," Jared said from the doorway.

Shaking my head, I pushed August to the back of my mind, grabbed my badge and gun, then headed for the door. Work called.

Four hours later, I left the crime scene disgusted by the amount of drugs found in one of the city's most prominent doctors' home. It was bad enough that illicit drugs ruled the streets. Doctors taking it upon themselves to abuse prescription medications was where I absolutely drew the line.

A lot of these drugs didn't have to put one in a grave. But by the time a person is addicted to them, they'd want to be dead. I hated this shit. As much as I loved my career, I often wondered sometimes if this shit was worth it anymore.

Between dealing with August and the heaviness of my career, a nigga was dead ass tired.

The week didn't pass quick enough for me. I drowned myself in work, trying to catch up on what needed to be done so that I could enjoy my weekend with Tiffany. She didn't have to say it, but I know me working a lot made her feel some type of way. Hopefully, this weekend would put her mind at ease that I was still the right man for her.

I left work early to come home and get ready to pick her up. August was in his room, packing to get ready for his trip to Georgia. He'd been dodging me since the phone call from Monday and the ultrasound picture I'd sat on his nightstand was in the same damn position. He could avoid growing the fuck up for some shit but was man enough to get his ass to Georgia to see our pops faithfully. Shit pissed me the fuck off.

Not willing to sour my mood, I simply told him, "Be safe," as I passed his door. Anything else I said would've hit a brick wall.

Chapter Eleven

TIFFANY

Three days with me… You can't even imagine lil' baby…
-King

Smiling hard as hell, I didn't see Miss Aldridge standing next to my desk until she cleared her throat.

"Wow, another bouquet?" she commented on the pink two-dozen roses resting in an elaborate glass vase where my other roses sat just days ago.

My smile faded because why did she find herself creeping up on me?

"Is there something I can do for you?" I asked, placing the card inside my purse. Go figure that Mina wasn't in today. Rumor had it that she was pregnant, and the morning sickness was kicking her ass.

"No, I don't need anything. I do have to admit that I'm curious though. Your man seems to be showering you with love." Her eyes fell to the necklace I wore. Missing Kingston, I put the necklace on today to remind me of his fine ass.

Unable to resist being a little petty, I said, "He likes to spoil me."

Her eyebrows peeked. "Oh really? Any chance he has a brother or best friend that's looking for a woman?"

I caught myself from turning up my nose. "No ma'am." It wasn't a lie. August wasn't fit to be anyone's man. After he tried to talk to me only for me to find out he has a pregnant girlfriend had me side-eyeing him since. Other than him, the only person Kingston spoke of was his coworker, Jared, who had his own baby mama issues.

"Figures." She chuckled. "Well, hold on to him, girl."

I didn't need Miss Aldridge to tell me what to do with my man. She ambled over to Mina's desk, her eyes still resting on my necklace. Her weird ass.

This last week had been rough. Chris hadn't hired a damn person and was putting more work off on me. The Wilks' case was proving to burn my hide. Every time I had to type something up with Wilks' name on it, I wanted to throw up. Sorry, but something was not right with him.

Spending the weekend with Kingston is what I needed even though I was dead tired. Kingston had to be too. He'd been working hard this week, leaving little time for us to talk. The last I'd been in his presence was Monday. Sighing, I tried not to let it get me down. If I planned on being Kingston's woman, I needed to get over him not being around me often.

My phone vibrated, grabbing my attention.

KINGSTON:

When I see you, I'ma kiss the fuck outta you.

Face burning, I quickly replied.

ME:

I'ma do the same to you.

"That's hardly working," Miss Aldridge pointed out.

Flicking my gaze over my shoulder, I schooled my features from frowning up at her.

KINGSTON:

Bet, Princess. I got something special planned for you so be ready.

ME:

Okay. Should I dress any way in particular?

KINGSTON:

Just be comfortable, my baby. We gon' have a good time.

ME:

Okay. My roses are gorgeous.

KINGSTON:

Just like my lady.

Placing my phone aside, I smiled because he'd texted me at the perfect time.

"You just spent several minutes texting back and forth. That's company money you just wasted."

This lady.

"I'm all caught up on work, so I'm actually about to make sure Chris doesn't need anything else so I can head out."

She'd wasted ten minutes standing here looking over my damn shoulder. Ew, what a way to be—educated, with a well-to-do-job, and still unhappy as hell. Some of these females killed me. On one hand, Miss Aldridge liked to assert her alpha female personality, while on the other hand all her insecurities bled through in the way she treated me.

If she wasn't downplaying my role within the company, she was giving me work to do just because she could. I wasn't stupid by a long shot. Not to mention, she knew that I was here in order to make my decision about attending law school. Maybe she saw me as competition, no matter how dumb it was.

Miss Aldridge didn't have to tell me she didn't have a man for me to know it. She flirted with every man that came through those doors, yet none of them took the bait. That wasn't my fault. She needed to come down off that high horse. Her attitude was stank and that was coming from a woman like me who possessed confidence on skyscraper. Still, I wasn't no bitch.

By the time I got off I was exhausted, but my energy picked up knowing I'd be with Kingston soon. Rushing home, I showered, and dressed in a simple jersey-knit dress and Jordans. I left my hair down because I knew Kingston liked it. I packed some clothes, my slides, and enough underwear for three days.

Oh my God! I was going to be sleeping next to this man. My face burned with joy. I heard his pipes coming up my block sending tingles throughout my body. His text message was still fresh in my mind as I stood from the sofa and hurriedly checked myself in the hall mirror to make sure I looked straight. I was already opening the door before he made it to the entryway. The smile on his face told me that he liked what he saw.

"Come here," he said, tugging me by my dress until I was in his arms.

All I could do was hold on as Kingston's lips touched mine. Immediately, his tongue was in my mouth, sliding against mine. His hands palmed my ass, sending me up in flames. I moaned and sucked his lips, causing him to growl. The unmistakable python poking my belly didn't make things better.

"Ready?" he asked between kisses. I nodded and giggled because neither of us made a move to leave.

Finally breaking the kiss, he took my bag and escorted me to the car. His hand held mine as he drove. I took in his gray sweatpants and white t-shirt loving how he looked good in anything he put on his body.

"I missed you," he confessed over the soft sounds of smooth R&B flowing through his speakers.

I was already trying to calm my pussy down from his hypnotic scent. Now he wanted to go and start it back up.

"I missed you, too," I replied just as he pulled up to a red light. He leaned over the arm rest to peck my lips, then let go of my hand just to palm my bare thigh. His touch caused me to shudder.

"You gon' have all my time, baby. I meant that. Work has been crazy, but just rock with me, and I got you."

I nodded, taking Kingston at his word. I was too caught up in him *not* to rock with him.

We arrived at a nice house, on the other side of town. This neighborhood was one I'd looked at when I was looking for a house. It boasted something I loved about any house—a porch. The driveway Kingston pulled into belonged to the most beautiful house on the block. Plants littered the front of the house which also boasted thick green grass.

"Is this your house?" I questioned.

He nodded. "Yeah. Can I cook you dinner tonight?"

Surprised, I said, "Of course you can."

He turned the car off, then came to open my door for me. Once I crossed the threshold of Kingston's house, I knew this was where I wanted to be often. His space was not only clean, neatly furnished, and well-lived in, but it was *comfortable.* It smelled like both lemon and cherries.

Smiling, I was in awe at the photos lining the foyer. There was a dining room off to right, a second room to the left that sported a seating area and fireplace, and big screen television mounted to the wall. In the living room, the photos continued. They were a mixture of Kingston, August, their parents, and grandparents. Lining the fireplace mantle were photos of his grandparents throughout their lives together. It was beautiful.

"Well, hello," a sweet voice said from behind me. Turning, I came face to face with Kingston's grandmother.

"Hello," I spoke, surprised to see her standing there. Now I could see where Kingston's eye color stemmed from. His grandmother's rich skin color was the same as his. Her long, silky, gray hair drew my attention for how neatly plaited it was.

"My, my, my," she whispered. "Aren't you gorgeous."

I smiled and extended my hand. She tsked, pushed my hand aside, and hugged me.

Kingston's granny was small and petite, even more so than I was. However, when she hugged me, every ounce of strength in her, I felt.

"Baby, this is my granny, Lily. Granny, this is my lady, Tiffany."

We were equally surprised to be meeting each other. Lily eyed me up and down, a satisfied expression on her face.

"I must say when King told me he had a surprise for me, I wasn't expectin' a woman," she stated then eyed her grandson. "You got me this time." She chuckled.

Kingston grinned. "My two favorite ladies had to meet."

I knew how Kingston felt about his granny, so for him to introduce me to her was flattering. He ushered us to one of the sofas and told us to get relaxed while he cooked. Neither of us protested and fell into quick conversation as Kingston whipped up dinner.

Granny told me about her life growing up and how she met her husband. All ears, I listened to her recount their first date, which was in a cucumber field that they both snuck into from time to time. She told me about their shared love for growing vegetables and plants and their love of family.

Her eyes took on a somber look as she spoke about her daughter. Kingston's mom was beautiful and sadly lost her life too soon. Granny's faraway smile said that, although she missed her daughter, she was happy that she had fond memories of her. She then switched the topic to Kingston and August. Her love for her grandsons was clear. Raising them had been what she needed after losing her daughter. Without them, she believed she wouldn't have made it to be her age from dealing with the grief she'd been under. I could definitely understand that.

"So, tell me about your family, suga," she requested.

Giving her the rundown on my folks sent her laughing. Especially when I mentioned Grey and Blu. She fanned herself the harder she laughed. I was glad I could make her night. Kingston finished dinner shortly after, inviting us into the kitchen and seating us like the gentleman that he was. My mouth watered when he sat a plate of creamy chicken pasta in front of me, followed by a bowl of hearty salad and fluffy breadsticks.

Outdone, I stared after Kingston while he served his granny her food. If he wanted me to fall in love with him, he was surely pressing all the right buttons. Kingston had me spoiled alright. Spoiled with his way of treating me.

Chapter Twelve

TIFFANY

I thought bathing in Kingston's bathroom would've been weird, but I stayed my ass in there well over thirty minutes enjoying his claw foot tub. I'd never seen one this spacious and thought about him being in here with me. Stopping short of feeling on myself, I hurriedly finished so that he could have the bathroom.

Now as I sat here watching him exit the bathroom, all the breath I had in me stopped short at the sight of him. Kingston's chest...goodness! I thought a man with pierced nipples would come across as suspect, but Kingston proved me wrong. His chest was sculpted in a way that had to be crafted by the man, Himself. These stories written all over his glorious, deep brown skin only added to his sex appeal.

"Stop lookin' at me like that." He had his back to me now as he rummaged through his top drawer for something. My eyes roamed the planes of his wide shoulders, strong back, down to his ass. The boxers riding his sculpted hips did nothing to deter me from wanting to know what lie beneath.

"I can look," I asserted. He had his locs wrapped up in an elaborate green scarf, causing me to wonder if anything could make this man look ugly.

He chuckled. "Aight nie, I'm tryna have a civilized evenin' witchu, baby."

"We had a great evening," I gushed, relaxing against the pillows as he neared me.

"We did," he agreed, sliding in next to me.

His scent was perfect, reaching my senses and wrapping me in his control.

"Your granny is funny as hell." I laughed, remembering some of the crazy things she'd said.

"She's my heart. That's why I wanted you to meet her."

"That's sweet of you to say."

"It's the truth," he said, bringing me to his side.

Tussling with my hair to get it out of his face, I sighed.

"Let me," he said. He perched up against the headboard, then ushered me between his open legs. We were about to settle in for a movie anyway and this was a more comfortable position. He started the movie, then focused on my unruly hair.

Kingston's strong fingers slid through my thick strands, massaging my scalp, causing me to moan. He continued massaging until I practically fell asleep against his chest. Somehow he'd managed to plait my hair into two braids.

"My granny makes me plait her hair sometimes when her fingers are hurting too bad from being in her garden all day," he explained.

"She taught you well," I said, leaning back to get comfortable. He pulled the cover over us and locked me in his strong embrace. When his lips pecked my cheeks several times, I smiled, truly content right here with him.

The next morning, I woke up to Kingston on top of me, rubbing his dick in between my parted thighs.

“It’s time to wake up,” he crooned, placing soft kisses along my neck.

Moaning, I didn’t want to move despite the sunlight spilling into the room. I wrapped my arms around Kingston’s shoulders and stretched my body. I’d cuddled up under him like a kitten all night, not moving an inch. I liked how he kept the house cool, but under the blankets he kept me warm with his body.

He chuckled against my cheek. “I’on wanna get up either, lil’ mama, but we got things to do today.”

Slipping off of me, he helped my protesting body from the bed and carried me to the bathroom. We handled our hygiene, then got dressed. As we were leaving out of the room, Kingston’s phone rang. It sounded important, so I kissed his lips and went downstairs to give him some privacy. Granny Lily was standing by the deck doors when I came downstairs. Smiling, I sidled up beside her.

"Mornin' suga," she sweetly spoke.

"Morning, Granny Lily."

She waved her hand. "Granny's alright with me. You spent the night, so you might as well call me Granny."

Cheeks flaming, I covered my mouth to hide the shocked smile I possessed.

"I'd like you to know your grandson was a complete gentleman."

She guffawed. "TMI, baby."

I doubled over laughing. "That's not what I meant, Granny!"

She chuckled heartily. "I know it, I just like to get a rise outta you," she confessed.

Sobering, I looked out over the back yard in awe. The garden taking up most of the area was stunning.

“You tend to all of that?" There was no way!

Granny huffed. "I do when Kingston or August are here. Otherwise, I'm told to stay off those steps. I'on know why those men can't let me be great. Those stairs are good and sturdy."

Tickled, I said, "You wanna go out there? I'm curious about what's all out there."

She nodded happily. "Lemme get my shoes."

Kingston hadn’t made it down the stairs yet, and regretfully, I believed it was work calling him. If so, I’d just spend the morning with Granny. I went to retrieve my shoes too and met her back at the door. Outside, I held her hand and helped her down the stairs. They indeed were sturdy but Granny was frail and slightly buckled a couple of times while we slowly descended them. Once we made it to the bottom, she was off like a kid in a candy store, and I had to keep up.

Granny introduced me to her plants she called her children. There were several different plant species, none of which I recognized. She then led me down the rows upon rows of different herbs and vegetables she grew. I was in awe. My mother had beautiful plants lining the home I grew up in, but nothing this extravagant.

"This is the spot I'm cleaning up today if I can." She pointed to a section that had some of the ground unsettled.

"That lil' mutt next door been in my tomatoes again," she fussed. That's what it looked like. Half-eaten tomatoes were strewn all over. "I keep tryna give his lil' slow self a chance but he eat my tomatoes one mo' time, and I'ma take my gun round that fence and beat his tail."

As if the old mutt heard her, he appeared on the other side of the gate looking as innocent as a child.

"Don't be lookin' over here, Rattla!" Granny scolded.

He whimpered and padded off with his tail between his legs. I cracked up.

"Let me help," I offered. "I'd love for you to teach me about the different species."

She glanced at me, pleased. "Okay, suga. Let's go get the supplies we need."

I followed her to a spot under the deck where a heavy weatherproof chest sat. She opened it revealing all kinds of gardening tools. I could only laugh. Granny was a mess.

Kingston came out of the house a few minutes later and joined us.

"You pushin' me to the side?" he jokingly questioned, hugging me from behind. I was in the middle of picking up the tomatoes and only had a few left. "This is our weekend."

Granny huffed. "Don't be stingy, King. I won't keep her long."

Smiling, I peeked over my shoulder and added, "You heard what she said."

He sexily mugged me before addressing Granny. "Twenty minutes, Granny. I'll be back from getting breakfast by then."

"No work?" I asked, but then regretted it. It wasn't any of my business.

He kissed my cheek. "The only work I'm doin' is gon' be inside you," he whispered in my ear. "I'ma take pleasure in feelin' ya thighs shake around my head while I taste you. I'ma enjoy every minute of pullin' ya hair while I deep stroke you. Ssss... Feel how hard I am, baby." He pressed his dick into my butt for good measure. My eyes widened. "I can't wait to suck and bite on ya nipples while you ride me."

I couldn't help the pulsating he caused in my core. *Great!* Now I had to go change my panties.

He chuckled. "So, you gon' lemme go to work?"

Biting the inside of my lip to keep from screaming, I simply nodded. He kissed my cheek again, then said, "I'll be back in twenty."

It took me a minute to gather myself and remember what I was doing. Granny ambled past me, laughing.

"If my first great grandbaby happens to be a girl, how about we name her Lily Marie?"

Embarrassed, I started back picking up the tomatoes, wishing Kingston hadn't put that freaky shit in my head.

Chapter Thirteen

KINGSTON

That evening…

Sunset neared, bringing a grin to my face. I had something extra special planned for Tiffany, which we were on our way to. She was dressed for dinner, in a pair of distressed denim jeans, a black blazer with a bralette underneath it, exposing all her gorgeous skin. To dress it down a bit, she had on simple Gucci slippers. Her hair was up in the bun since she had to wash it earlier.

After being outside with Granny most of the morning, she came back in to shower and wash the sweat from her hair. It was the smile on her face that did it for me though. Hearing her talk and laugh with my granny like they were two peas in a pod warmed me. I couldn't ask for anything other than for them to have a good relationship.

One thing I realized; Tiffany really liked being around my granny. She catered to my granny of her own free will. Her organic response to the woman I held closest to my heart made me want to give Tiffany anything she asked for. I planned on having Tiffany around forever, so it mattered that she got along with my people. Speaking of my people, August finally called to apologize for being an asshole. He still wasn't stuck on fixing things with Faith, but I encouraged him to for the sake of the baby. Again, he brushed it off, so I dropped it.

He said that his meeting with our dad went well, and that Nate looked better than he had in a long time. That was good news considering the last time I saw Nate he was upset due to some beef he was having with a few inmates. He assured me that he was good though. That was the week before I saw Tiffany in the club. I'd make it to see Nate in the next couple of weeks to lay eyes on him for myself.

"The water is so pretty!" She beamed brightly as we took the bridge leading to Pensacola Beach.

Within a few minutes, I was parking and helping her out of the car. I popped the trunk and retrieved the blankets and picnic basket. When she saw what we were about to do, she batted her eyelashes at me.

"You're tryna make me not wanna be without you." She sighed and held tightly to my hand as I walked her towards the white sands.

"Is that a problem?" I asked, setting us up in a spot that was somewhat empty. The sound of the water crashing along the shore was perfect for our evening together. Although it was October, the sun still beat down over us, keeping the temperature in the high seventies. Once the sun went down, a gentle breeze would flow. By then dinner would be done, and I'd have her back at my place.

When we were both seated, I opened the picnic basket, retrieved our drinks, and waited for her to answer me. The expression upon her face told me that she was deep in thought. I prayed that she'd tell me what was up, so I didn't have to guess what she was thinking. Our day had been great so far. We spent breakfast with Granny on the deck, then went shopping for whatever she wanted. She gave me hell for buying her some more shit, but hell, if I liked it, I wanted her to have it. Lunch was spent with Granny again because I hated her being home by herself.

This evening Granny wasn't having it. While Tiffany napped, I cooked, and tried to set the table for three. Granny sent me on my way though.

"Take that sweet girl out and stop tryna babysit me," she'd fussed.

I was lowkey glad she was alright because spending this time with Tiffany, enjoying another sunset was well worth it. She straddled my lap, and we fed each other grilled chicken breast, broccoli, and sweet potatoes. I couldn't resist popping her blazer open to kiss along the swells of her titties. Anytime my lips touched her skin, her breathing halted. We didn't care who walked by us, or who was looking our way.

As the sun set, I stared into Tiffany's eyes, seeing everything there that I wanted for myself. It's crazy because I hadn't had the first taste of her nectar. But instinctively I knew that after having Tiffany, I wouldn't want anyone else.

“Dinner was amazing.” Tiffany, full from all the food I fed her, melted into the passenger seat with her eyes closed and a serene smile on her face. We were headed back to my house to shower and get ready for a movie.

“I’m glad you enjoyed it, baby,” I replied, kissing her hand that I held in mine as I coasted up the highway.

“I have a question, Kingston,” she stated. I divided my attention between her and the road.

“‘Sup, lil’ mama?”

“My first name is Sapphire. Sometimes she likes to assert herself.”

Smirking, I said, “Oh yeah?”

Clearing her throat, she sighed deeply before uttering, “Yeah, like now. Would you like me for dessert?”

My ears rang from her words, and if I was a bad driver I would’ve ran off the damn road. I glanced over at Tiffany to find her eyes still closed and the serene smile still on her face.

“I mean, if—”

“Dessert, a midnight snack, and breakfast,” I interrupted.

Glancing over, I saw her smile widen. The tip of her tongue darted out to wet her lips.

“Kingston…” she purred. I tried to pay attention to the road, but I couldn’t resist peering at her again. Her lids slid open, revealing her hazel eyes, looking like a fucking scary ass seductress. “Hurry,” she softly demanded.

Thirty minutes later, I slid into the driveway hard as fuck from listening to her breathe. I had her out of the car, through the door, and up the stairs in minutes. She stood in the middle of my room, smiling at me like she thought we were about to play a board game. My dick grew in my joggers when she removed her blazer and stepped out of her slides.

Turning the light down, I also told Alexa to play *When We* by Tank. It was clearly exactly what she wanted to hear. Tiffany seductively glided towards me. As she did so, she reached up to untwist her hair, sending her strands falling around her shoulders and down her back. With breath stalling in my chest, I sat on the edge of the bed to see if lil' baby was really transforming in front of me. Sweet Tiffany, the Tiffany that blushed at everything I said or did wasn't who stood before me, raking her eyes over my body. *Sapphire* was about to get her whole life fucked up. She stared at the print my dick made, biting into her lip. She brought her body flush with mine and unashamedly rubbed herself against me.

My nose flared. I hadn't smoked a blunt since college, but I could swear I had one from how high I felt. My lids were even heavy, sitting low over my eyes. Stepping between my thighs, she demanded my attention with a simple touch. Tiffany stroked my beard and tugged me closer for a kiss. Of course, I gave in but was too afraid to touch her while she was like this. She had me under her spell.

"Kingston..." she whispered when my hands skimmed her delicate flesh. By now my dick was so hard, and the tint in my joggers had her face flushing.

"What is it, baby girl?" I gruffly asked between the sloppy kisses she placed on my lips. She could forget not having me for the night. I was on go and ready to destroy her shit.

"I've never done this before..." she confessed.

My damn heart galloped in my chest at the same time my hands palmed her ass and squeezed.

"...But," she continued breathlessly. "Fuck me like I have."

My heart thudding heavily in my chest. I snatched her closer, pushed her bralette shit down, and inhaled her titty.

"Ooohh!" Her head titled back on her shoulders. I had to steady her bowing body from collapsing. Picking her up, I stood, turned, and switched positions. She fell back on the bed as I handled her jeans. The black lace panties she wore followed, exposing her naked flesh to me.

Her scent called me so much that I knelt before her and propped her feet on my shoulders. I wanted her completely open while I...

"Ssss..." she hissed at the first pass of my tongue against her wet sex. She fisted my locs, holding on as best as she could.

"Damnn..." I dove in, eating at her and enjoying the whimpers falling from her lips. Like the freak I was, I rubbed my face in her essence, branding her all over me before licking my way to her protruding nub. I latched on, then sucked her so passionately that she fell apart on a tortured cry. Quickly, I lapped up her flavor, growling from pleasure when it kept coming. Unable to stop myself, I caught her bud again, bringing her to another release, which I slurped up.

Her thighs shook as I kissed my way up her abdomen, then ripped the bralette shit off, leaving her in just the chain bearing our initials. I attacked her erect nipples, sucking and biting at them like I told her I would.

"King..." she whimpered just as I reached her lips. Nastily, I tongued her and even licked the tears from her temples.

Her nails biting into my skin fueled me to hurry and get my damn joggers off. As the track switched to another joint, my dick angrily begged for entrance to his home. Tiffany eyed him like he was the key to her future.

"Sapphire," I mumbled against her lips as I poked at her entrance. "Once I'm inside you, I'ain pullin' out." It was fair warning. "Oh and… If this chain ain't tell you that you belong to me, allow my dick to make it known."

Her crazy ass winked at me and clutched my shoulders as I entered her, being forced to take it easy because shiiddd, my baby was for damn sure untouched. Controlling the part of me that wanted to dig into her, I slowed myself down even more and took her nipple into my mouth, toying with it. Her legs relaxed, and so did her body, allowing me to break past the barrier keeping me from inside of her.

"Ahh!" she cried out, prompting me to catch her shock with my lips and tongue.

Pulling back, I pushed forward until I was fully seated inside her tightness. It took everything I could to relax. My dick had never felt anything so pure, so tight, and so fucking wet and gushy. As soon as her hips moved, I knew she was ready. Slowly, I rocked inside of her, not wanting this to be over too quickly. Shawty had a death grip on my shit. While I wanted to feed the animalistic appetite flowing through me, I wanted to make this, and every time, good for my baby. I stroked her as gentle as I could, although she begged me to fuck her like she wasn't new to this.

Her moans and whimpers drove me to growl in her ear. It was something about hearing your woman's pussy make music with her cries. That shit was enough to make me bite back the nut rising to my tip.

"King…" she groaned as she ran her nails down my chest.

When her manicured nails grazed my pierced nipples, I shuddered.

She brought my lips back to hers and bit my bottom lip as her pussy clamped around me.

"Shiitt!" Palming her ass, I spread her open and deep stroked her, feeling her pussy quake and melt around me as I stroked her spot.

"Ahh!" she cried as her body took flight.

"Fuucck, baby!" I grunted. Every hair on my body was at attention as sweat dripped from my body to hers. If it wasn't for the sturdiness of my bed, it'd be busting the paint off the wall from how vicious I was pumping into her.

"Kiinnngg!" she gasped as another orgasm ripped through her. Her fingernails cut into the skin of my back but didn't deter me from hitting every crevice of this stupid good tunnel.

"Sss... Tiff!" I groaned feeling fire flood my existence. "Fuck!"

As our bodies clapped, I stuffed my mouth with one of her titties to squelch the moaning and grunting I was doing as my nut begged to bust. Shit felt so good, my eyes rolled. When Tiffany sexily called my name the same time as her walls clamped around me again, I let go on a deep grunt, spraying her insides with everything inside of me.

Breathless, I kissed along her wet cheeks. "I'ma forever protect you, *us*."

Chapter Fourteen

TIFFANY

Kingston's ringing cell phone aroused me from a deep slumber. Unwrapping his body from mine, he grumbled and reached for it.

"Wells," he answered. Seconds later, he said, "Yeah."

He kissed along my neck and shoulder, then shifted until he lay on top of me, with my feet clasped at the small of his back.

"I gotta make a quick run to the office," he stated as his kisses lowered to my nipples. He liked licking and sucking on my nipples, yet after last night's sweet torture, they were still sensitive.

My body overheated and wept as his kisses went lower. He spread my legs, positioning them so that I couldn't move as his tongue swiped up my already wet sex. Like the first time he did this to me, I disintegrated, whimpered, and squirmed beneath him as he moaned against my spread lips.

"You taste so good, Sapphire," he uttered causing my insides to quake.

Shit, I didn't even like my damn name, which is why I go by Tiffany. *Sapphire* got us in a whole lot of trouble last night. If it wasn't for the long soaking I had, my box would be out of commission. Kingston obviously knew what he was doing because as my body lit up in an orgasm, all I craved was him inside of me no matter what my pussy felt like.

So, I reached for Kingston, guiding him to my opening as we kissed. The taste of myself on his tongue shouldn't cause this sexual arousal in me, should it? My brain stopped short of thinking when the thick mushroom head of Kingston's dick pushed into me. I was expecting him to be well-endowed from the way he carried himself, and I wasn't disappointed. He exceeded my expectations and filled me up so much that my mouth opened on a silent scream.

Last night Kingston had taken it easy on me. That was the first comprehensive thought I could form as he draped my legs over his shoulders, stared down at me, and bared his teeth on a growl.

He touched the right spot. My tunnel tightened, and my eyes watered as I already felt my release near. Kingston grunted with every stroke he sent to my chest. He said he had to run to the office, instead he was buried deep inside of me, working his dick so good that I erupted around him, gasping for air as I did so.

"Ooohh, shiittt!" he gruffly groaned and picked up his pace. "Let daddy feel that again, baby!" he demanded.

So, I did, enjoying the sound of our bodies, and him chanting my name as he came. I fell back asleep and only faintly remembered him kissing my lips before he left.

“Mornin’, suga,” Granny spoke. She was standing by the patio doors again, and because I enjoyed our time yesterday, I told her to grab her shoes. If Granny could skip, she would have as she went to retrieve them.

Today as we descended the stairs, I got a good understanding for why she shouldn’t have been going down them. Yesterday she struggled a little, but today was worse. I didn’t mind though, because I understood her need to be free and do the things she wanted to do without waiting for someone to help her. Still, once we made it to the area of the garden she intended to work on today, I put on my best motherly voice.

“Granny,” I started. “I don’t care what time of day it is, if you ever want to come out to your garden, please call me. Kingston and August may be off doing their thing, but don’t let that keep you from thinking you have to wait for them. I’m gonna leave my number with you just in case you need it.”

The smile she gave me was brighter than the sun.

“Just promise me you won’t come out here by yourself.”

She tsked. “You sound like that old man of yours.”

I cackled. “Still, promise me,” I said.

Sighing, her wise amber eyes met mine. “I promise,” she replied with a genuine smile.

Satisfied, I grabbed the gloves she’d given me yesterday and went about helping her tend to her vegetables.

Kingston arrived home a little while later, breakfast in hand, and frustration etched across his face. He placed the food on the deck table, then met us in the garden. He went to his granny's side and kissed her cheek before coming to squat at my side.

"Are you okay?" I asked between him pecking my lips.

"Everything's cool, baby."

"Liar." I slightly chuckled.

He grinned. "Nothin' that bein' in ya presence won't fix. Is that better?"

Nodding, I said, "Much better."

"Come get cleaned up so we can eat," he said.

Granny and I both did what he said without putting up an argument. After breakfast, he told Granny to get dressed. Instead of the Charger, Kingston ushered us into Denali.

An hour later, we were miles away from Pensacola at a plant farm that spanned as far as my eye could see. Lowkey I wondered if Granny would be able to walk for the amount of time it would take her to find what she wanted. Kingston, however, was a step ahead of me, producing a wheelchair.

Granny was so happy to be here that she didn't even protest at the sight of the wheelchair. She sat down, perked her feet up, and enjoyed the ride with a content smile upon her face. If she only knew how beautiful it was to see her grandson catering to her. Their relationship was something I'd fallen in love with over the time I was around them.

If I didn't know the type of man Kingston was, I'd think he was doing this all for show. But the minute one of the farm attendants referenced Granny as Miss Lily, I knew this man right here loved bringing his grandmother here.

Patiently, Kingston let Granny take her time to find what she wanted. No matter how far we walked, no matter how hot it was under the October sun, no matter how many times Granny picked up one plant to examine it for ten minutes before putting it back, Kingston never complained.

As we left the farm, I had only one question for myself. Who was going to protect my heart from this man?

Sure enough as night fell, a torrential rain beat down over the city, highlighting my current mood. I wasn't ready to leave Kingston. Sleeping next to him the last two nights had me so used to him that I wondered how I would sleep tonight. The fact that I had to get up and go to work in the morning didn't make my night ahead any better.

This was the problem with losing my virginity to a man like Kingston. He was addictive *before* we made love. Now I was just like a fiend, who's drug wouldn't be in reach at the drop of a hat. Shit, I legit wanted to be a big ass crybaby. Kingston's hand squeezed my thigh rousing me out of my depressing thoughts.

"You know you can stay with me, right?" he stated. "Allat poutin' ain't necessary, love. I'll drop you at work in the morning."

Smacking my teeth, I mushed him in his head. "I'm not pouting for one thing," I defended.

He chuckled. "Next time you mush me, you gon' be screamin'," he warned.

I busted out laughing but kept my hands to myself. When he pulled into my driveway, I waited for him to let me out, then darted into the house to grab some more clothes while he stood on the porch to smoke. I'd left some of my clothes he purchased me at his place, so I only packed what I needed. As I headed back out of the door, my phone rang. It was Blu.

"Hey," I answered as Kingston took my bag. My gangsta DEA agent was such a gentleman.

"I'on get a phone call or nothin' since you got a nigga nie. What's good?"

Snickering, I replied, "I text you every night, Blu."

"That's lazy as hell, lil' baby. Call me like you did before that predator lookin' ass nigga popped up."

Cackling, I joked, "Aww, boo, you miss me?"

"Yes, he does!" Jacoba hollered from the background. "Please tell him you're okay so he can quit sulking," she added.

"For the record, I *am* okay," I informed Blu, causing Kingston to chuckle. He placed my bag in the back seat, then opened the door for me to get in the car. As he went to his side, I beamed knowing I was going back home with him.

"Aight, shawty, if you say so. Don't think I'm too far to come body a muhfucka if I have to."

My eyes bucked. "Blu!"

"Tiffany," he said back in the same tone. "Ain't nothin' to it. And you know it, so warn his palm tree head ass."

Hollering with laughter, I ignored Blu, and replied, "I love you. Tell my sis-in-law I love her and kiss my nieces and nephew for me."

"Will do, baby. Do what the fuck I said," he added before hanging up.

I shook my head and laughed. I knew better than to think Blu was playing. Unlike Grey, Blu was certified. Once lit, there wasn't any calming Blu down. So, as Kingston drove back towards his house, I prayed he didn't mess this up. Blu couldn't kill the first man I gave my box to.

Three weeks later...

KINGSTON:

I enjoyed breakfast.

My face flamed at the message on my phone screen, causing me to almost swallow my coffee down the wrong pipe. Hell, I didn't even drink coffee but dealing with Kingston's ass, I wasn't good for shit this morning. I hadn't been good for shit the last three weeks.

After I went back to his house, I hadn't been home yet, except to check my damn mail and take the trash out. Like Blu, Grey was on my case heavy, complaining that I hadn't been to chill with him, Gianna, and the kids in a while. Tomorrow was Theo's birthday, so I planned to spend the day with them since Kingston was going to Georgia to visit his dad.

Kingston and I were stuck to the hip when we weren't working. I picked my car up because I wasn't about to have Kingston hauling me all over town. I still met with Dorian twice a week, and the campus was clear across town.

KINGSTON:

Licked the whole plate clean.

My dick on hard.

Ya panties wet?

Go to the car and FaceTime me.

The last text sent me into a giggling fit.

ME:

I did too. You did. How hard? Yes. And hell no!

I touched the charm hanging from the chain around my neck, remembering how Kingston had me spread open this morning. The heat stemmed from him coming home last night with a necklace that matched mine, although his was much larger to match his masculinity. We were an official couple. The type that did simple things that meant a big deal, like watching the sunset together and wearing matching jewelry.

Placing my phone back down, I tried to get back to work. Chris was already on edge because one of his clients no-showed his court date and hadn't answered any of Chris' calls. What was bad is that his client was out on bail and a state's witness. Either Rashad was in the wind or someone killed him.

Rashad Townsend was another client I hated typing up notes for. He was a drug dealer that turned on his own people to save himself. Now, I wasn't for anyone dealing in illegal matters, however, a bond is a bond. Once he flipped on his crew, Rashad lost all of his clout. Or so one would think. Someone had the balls to bail him out of jail. Nobody just had five-hundred grand laying around to drop on an informant.

"Girl, that phone is on fire." Mina chuckled.

KINGSTON:

Concrete. Brick. Steel. Long and fuckin' hard too.

Whew!

KINGSTON:

I need lunch. You gon' come feed me?

Poised to respond, I was interrupted by Chris who came rushing down the hall.

"He's running," he stated. "Just got word that he's clearing out one of his houses."

Confused, I wondered why Chris would air Rashad's business out like that. Of course, Mina and I were the only ones in here, but Rashad wasn't supposed to have any 'houses', especially not with drugs in them.

"I need you to come with me," he said.

"For what?" I asked before I could stop myself.

"We need to beat the police there. He's going to put up a fight, and I can't let them kill him. I need you there to record anything you hear and see."

"Chris," I started. This is why he needed to hire a fucking assistant who traveled with his ass! No way in hell was I about to—

"Let's go!" he ordered.

Pissed, I snatched my phone off my desk, the recorder, and hustled behind him. Absently, I didn't understand why Chris was so bent on saving this nigga. Obviously, Rashad had a complex and loved putting his life in danger. If the streets weren't after him, then the state was.

Chapter Fifteen

KINGSTON

"Move! Move! Move!" I ordered my team.

Rifle pointed ahead of me, I rushed through Smooth's spot, ready to put a hot one in his ass. Three weeks ago he was bailed out of jail, only for his ass to skip his first court appearance, which was a red flag, one that wasn't taken lightly. Within minutes of getting word from an informant that Smooth planned to run, we had his spot surrounded. This lowkey fucked up my day as I was in the middle of talking shit to my woman when we got the call.

According to the informant, Smooth had bricks stashed in this house that he'd been able to keep off the radar because the property wasn't in his name. After further digging, it was found that this house was under a business that didn't even exist—at least not on paper.

Several guns were strewn about the living room. Duffle bags

sat on the couch and bricks of what I knew was cocaine spilled from them. Stacks of money littered the coffee table. What got my attention were the gaping holes in the different parts of the wall. A sledgehammer laid propped up in the hallway, however, there was no sign of Smooth.

"*Clear!*"

The crackling in my ear came from Jared who was down the hall, clearing the rooms.

Pop! Pop! Pop!

Shots came from above me, sending Jared and Eddie, who was behind me, ducking for cover. A round grazed my left shoulder, piercing my flesh but only fueling me to let off a succession of rounds into the ceiling.

"Fuck!" Smooth belted.

"Attic!" Eddie shouted.

Jared took position before I put a few holes through the door.

"Bring yo' ass out!" I called to Smooth.

"Fuck you!"

Bullets rang out again, prompting the three of us to light up the ceiling. Seconds later, silence echoed off the walls. Jared pulled the latch for the attic stairs, pointing his gun in the opening just in case Smooth was playing us. Jared went up first, with Eddie behind him.

"Medics!" Eddie called through his walkie talkie.

Shaking my head, by the sounds of it, Smooth wanted gunplay and ended up picking the wrong muhfuckas to play with.

"We got this." That came from Kobi, another agent I was cool with. He then pointed to my arm. "Go handle that. You drippin' all over the scene, bruh."

Grunting, I bypassed a couple more agents and the medics as I went outside.

Shit. Granny was gon' beat my ass. Halfway across the lawn, my attention darted to the woman I woke up next to this morning. Mugging her, I swiftly stalked to her.

"Tiffany! The fuck you doin' here?" Injury forgotten, I regarded her startled expression with my own angry one.

Her eyes were wide and flicking from my face to my shoulder.

"Is my client dead?" This came from the nigga standing a couple of feet away. Giving him a second look, I realized it was Smooth's lawyer, Chris. Putting two and two together, I grilled him.

"You got her outchea at a crime scene?" Angry, I got into his face. His bitch ass cowered. "You know how fuckin' dangerous this shit is?"

"Kingston!" Tiffany grabbed me by my good arm, fruitlessly trying to pull me back.

Officers witnessing the exchange came over to investigate.

"I'm just here to check on my client," this nigga said in his defense.

"Fuck ya client!" I barked. "You got my fuckin' woman somewhere she shouldn't be. Tiffany, get ya shit and let's go 'for I beat this nigga's ass!" Bullet injury and all, I was gon' break my foot off in this nigga!

Tiffany hustled off to a car parked at the end of the block.

"She's my assistant. She's required to go where I tell her."

I had it in mind to walk away, but he opened his damn mouth.

"King!" Jared was in front of me, pushing me back. "Nah,

mane, not here. Take ya girl and go getcho shit fixed. We got it from here."

Glaring at Chris as I walked away, I silently warned that nigga not to cross me. Flustered, he gulped. If a muhfucka wanted to see me get out of character, fuck with my family or my woman. Silent warning or not, Chris had better take heed to what the fuck he knew my stare meant.

"So, we just gon' be mad at each other the whole night?" I glanced at Tiffany in the dim interior of the Charger, smirking at the mug on her face.

We'd just left the hospital from me getting stitched up and were on our way home. After she cried on my good shoulder, she proceeded to ignore me the rest of the time we were in the ER. She drove, as my arm wasn't good for shit until the pain subsided. I refused pain meds and opted for some Ibuprofen, which I'd already popped. Hopefully, by the time we made it home, they'd kick in.

"You're ignorin' me?"

Tiffany cut her eyes at me in response.

"I was careful, baby," I stated.

"No you weren't. Careful is *not* getting shot," she rebutted. "I'm not built for this shit," she mumbled, shaking her head.

Although she was doing sixty up the highway, face balled up I leaned over the armrest, into her space.

"Whatchu say?" I questioned.

Rolling her eyes, she repeated her statement.

"You'on have a choice but to be built for this, lil' baby. I'ain goin' nowhere. You plan on goin' somewhere?"

She smacked her teeth.

"I'ain think so," I responded and placed a kiss on her cheek. "And since we came to that agreement, I'ma need you to find another job."

We'd talked about her wanting to go to law school and how this job was beneficial for her. I thought it was the typical secretarial shit. But after today, I didn't like her being at Chris' beck and call. Especially not behind some dangerous shit. Just like a bullet caught my ass, one could've easily found her.

"I can't." She scoffed. "I have until May and then I can call it quits. Besides the fact that I want to make sure law is what I wanna do, if so, then I'll need Chris' recommendation if I wanna make it in."

"You'on need shit from him to make it in, shawty. You're intelligent as fuck and graduated summa cum laude. Any school would be proud to have you." She beamed at my compliment, but it was the truth.

She sighed. "I wish it were that simple, boo. I've been waiting for him to hire another assistant, the one that's actually supposed to do the shit he has me doing. Until then, I have to stay at it."

Grunting, I neither agreed nor disagreed. "What you think Grey and Blu would say about what happened today?"

Her neck snapped back. "I know you fuckin' lyin'! You gon' tell my brothers on me?"

Chuckling, I replied, "Nah, shawty. The way you just answered is enough though. One more incident with Chris and you outta there. I'on give a damn who I gotta threaten to get you into law school."

She groaned. "I always said that a man would have to be like my brothers in order to be in my life." She shot me a look. "Wasn't really expecting you to be just like them."

Grinning, I hunched my good shoulder.

"How are you supposed to drive to Georgia with your shoulder messed up?" she queried.

"August will drive," I answered.

Shifting my thoughts to August, his ass hadn't even checked on me today. My message to him went unanswered. He'd been salty since I checked him about Faith. By now he would usually be over our spats. For whatever reason, he was holding on to our last argument like I told him I hated him or something.

Hopefully, this ride to Georgia tomorrow would help us come to some happy medium. I never imagined my brother and I not being close. He wasn't the little boy that looked up to his big brother anymore. Admittedly, that broke my heart. But like any other time I felt heart break, I bottled it up and stored it in a place where I'd never revisit it again.

That night as I held a sleeping Tiffany, I reflected on the look on my granny's face when I came through the door. Her seeing me injured had her crying and upset. Over my career I'd been in a few scrapes, but nothing this serious. Once I was able to calm her down, she ended up cussing me out.

August came down the stairs and wasn't too happy to see that I'd been shot either.

"I hope you ghosted that nigga!" he'd said.

We did send Smooth to his maker, but I didn't tell August that. News wouldn't break until morning, but the streets already knew Smooth was gone. Sighing, I brought Tiffany's soft body closer and reflected on times when my mother was still alive.

Maria had the most beautiful smile and a laugh that attracted anyone's attention. Just like Granny, Mama was a handful. One time she beat this lady's ass for coming to our house to confront her about some shit that had to do with my daddy. I was eleven then, however, the memory stayed with me.

"I'm tired of this shit, Nate! How many more bitches am I gon' have to deal with?"

Mama and Daddy were quietly arguing, thinking August and I were sleep. I couldn't sleep though because I was worried about my mama.

"Marie you know damn well she was lyin'!" my dad harshly whispered back. "You've been so insecure lately and for no damn reason."

My mom cackled sarcastically. "'For no damn reason'? Nate, this woman claims to be pregnant with your baby. When the cops come arrest me for putting my hands on a pregnant woman, how do you think that'll look to our boys?"

"You're worried about the wrong thing. She isn't pregnant, first of all. And second, I'd never let anything happen to you."

I heard my mom smack her teeth. "You're not invincible, Nate. You promised me you were gon' get ya shit together. I've been holding you down for twelve years and never once complained. But I'm tired. I deserve better. So do your sons."

It seemed like minutes passed before my dad responded. "You're right, baby. Everything I do is for y'all. I'ma make things better."

I remember sneaking back to my room with tears in my eyes. My mother was hurting and begging her husband to get his shit together. They seemed so happy up until I witnessed that fight. Several days afterwards, I had the courage to ask my dad if the lady Mama had fought was truly pregnant. He vehemently denied it and told me he'd never hurt Mama in that way. I believed him. The issue itself never came up again. No more women ever showed up at our house again, and things seemed to go back to normal.

In just five more years, we'd lose my mother to senselessness. Sadly, my daddy never changed his ways to appease her. If anything, my mother just dealt with it to hold her family together.

"You okay, baby?"

Tiffany stirred in my arms, then turned to face me. Instead of answering, I kissed her lips.

"Talk to me," she coerced. "I can tell something's wrong. What is it?" Her hand smoothed up my chest, until she cupped my jaw.

"Just thinkin' about my mama. I wish y'all could've met each other. You remind me of her in a way. She was fiercely independent, yet gentle and protective at the same time. Can you believe she has two brothers that I haven't seen in years? They don't even check on their own mother."

She ran her fingers through my beard and tsked. "I wish we could've met also. As far as your uncles, I see their pictures around the house. Granny never talks about them, but I see her staring at their pictures often. They're missing out on a great lady. Granny is what I imagine my mother will be like in her seventies. All I can say is, God gave Granny you. You take such good care of her and it shows. I know your mother is looking down on you, proud of her son." She kissed me and let our lips linger together for a minute.

Tiffany had my heart in her clutches. I couldn't wait to get off of work just to rush home to her. Anytime she tried going back to her place, I casually reminded her that my place *was* her place. It'd been over three months since I first laid eyes on her, and just like then, I saw my future in her.

We'd been making love unprotected, and I damn sure waited for the day when she'd tell me she was carrying my seed. I'd never do the shit my dad did to his family. Protecting the woman I loved, and the children we create would be my highest honor. I wanted it all, and I wanted it with Tiffany.

The next morning, August and I hit the road before the sun came up. Because I was tired, I reclined my seat and rested even though Drake blasted through the speakers. August's intentions at keeping me from engaging him was clear.

An hour into our ride, I was jarred awake by the music abruptly stopping.

"Mane, it doesn't bother you that we gotta see Dad like this?"

Blinking the sleepiness from my eyes, I regarded my brother. The unit resting on his face was one of concern and frustration. It's like he was the eight-year-old kid that never got to fully enjoy his parents before they were both ripped from him.

It's different when your parent is deceased, and you can no longer lay eyes on them. But our dad was alive and healthy yet had to be accessed through the system. Shit was fucked up.

"It does bother me," I answered. "I already told you that."

"So why won't you help him get out?"

My eyebrows snapped together. "How am I supposed to do that, August?"

"You the opps, mane. Don't tell me you'on have no pull, 'cause I know you do. You lead an entire team by yaself, which means you got some pull."

Tilting my head to the side, I questioned where August's way of thinking stemmed from. Yes, I did head my own team. Sure, I did have pull. But not for no bullshit like helping a man that refused to help his damn self.

"Pops got himself in that shit, bruh. I'm not sayin' I don't love him, or would love to see him free, but I can't help him."

Mama was upset again. I came home from school to find her in the bathroom, crying. She quickly tried to wipe her tears, but she wasn't quick enough.

"What's wrong, Ma?" I stepped into the bathroom with her and shut the door. Bleach scent dominated the tiny bathroom as she was in the middle of cleaning.

"Nothing, baby," she lied. A small smile touched her face when I gave her a skeptical look.

I was sixteen now, and nothing could slide by me like she thought it could. Keeping quiet about things I witnessed around our house was draining as hell. Today, I needed my mama to tell me what was wrong, so I could try and fix it.

"Is it Dad?" I questioned.

Her head slightly dropped as tears dripped from her eyes.

"Mama." I sighed. Going to her side, I hugged her to my chest. My mother was little, and although I was sixteen, I towered over her.

"Please, Kingston, when you get older and find you a good woman, don't hurt her. Okay?"

My mom's tearful plea made it straight to my heart. She didn't have to say anything else. I knew my dad had fucked up again. Yet, instead of leaving him, my mother was in the bathroom cleaning as if it was just another day in her life. Because she wanted what was best for me and August, she'd never leave Nate. Even if that meant she had to suffer in silence.

Before I was old enough to understand, I thought my dad loved the ground my mother walked on. He couldn't though. Not when he had her down like this. I rubbed her back and told her everything would be okay.

Little did I know, a week later my mother would be dead. Musing over the years when I became old enough to understand what love did and didn't look like, I realized that my mother wasn't being loved properly. While my dad wasn't physically or verbally abusive towards us, his lack of emotional support was akin to abuse.

There I was thinking I had the best father in the world only to become older and realize Nate had been feeding us half-assed parenting. Love for my dad overshadowed so many things that I wish it hadn't. Love caused you to love people that didn't deserve it and to care about people that couldn't give a fuck about you.

Because he created me, I loved my dad and would never turn my back on him, but I didn't care for the man he was. Nothing I felt is how August felt. August only knew what our dad showed him now, and that's love from behind a glass partition.

"You're right, bruh. I hate admitting it to myself, but Dad's situation ain't ya battle to fight."

Smirking, I chucked my lil' brother on the arm. "Damn, where this nigga been at?"

August cackled. "Shut up, mane."

"Nah, for real. That was some real shit you just spoke."

He glanced away from the traffic to mug me, then he grinned. "I've just been thinkin' a lot. Every time I make this trip it gets heavier. I just wish he would've made better decisions. It's like he puts his weight on our shoulders without him actually doin' it."

I agreed. A person didn't have to physically put weight on another person. Being in situations that caused a loved one to grieve, stress, or worry was putting weight on them. Emotional weight carried hefty prices.

"That's why I'm on you so heavy about Faith, baby. You don't want your youngin' outchea not knowin' you. Money can give a lot, but it can't give time or love. I'ma stand in front of you when you right, and I'ma stand in front of you when you wrong. Either way, I'ma always have you. I'on give a damn how mad I make you, and how you try and shut me out, I'm ya brotha, and I'ma always correct you, but I'll never let anything happen to you."

He nodded, accepting my words. The rest of the ride was filled with Drake, which was cool. At least I got something through my brother's head.

"Anything I can help you with, King?"

I shook my head and handed my license to Tressa.

"You sure?" she quizzed.

"My lady wouldn't like me lettin' another woman touch me," I informed her.

Her eyebrows peeked. "Oh, really? Your woman?" Her chuckle was full of doubt. "Yeah, okay," she stated and handed me back my license.

Tressa's thick body had drawn me to her months ago. She and I had an arrangement, one that catered to me mostly. Outside of this prison, Tressa was a whole other beast. A pricey one at that. Her body was stupid thick and, at the time, I couldn't resist.

I was married…I mean, taken now, so a nigga was off the market. Fuck it if Tressa was salty about it. Putting her out of my mind, I allowed the guards to usher me to the room where the visits took place. My dad was already seated behind the glass partition when I approached and sat.

He had a wide smile on his face as I picked up the raggedy black phone.

"Havin' a woman looks good on you," he quipped.

"'Sup," I spoke.

He cackled. "Boy if you'on lighten up! I swear—it's like *you* the one locked up." He laughed.

"It's funny how you think this is a game. You think we like seein' you like this?"

His laugh faded and was replaced with a sheepish grin. "I know, son. There's nothin' funny about bein' 'round a bunch of crusty ass muhfuckas for the rest of ya natural life."

"Pops—"

"Might as well be. If the good Man allows me to see the day, what I'm gon' do when I get outta here?"

"Plenty," I replied.

He scoffed. "Not so. I like that you think positively, King, but we both know different."

We regarded each other quietly before he laughed again.

"Nie tell me what's been up witchu and this lil' lady you got," he said.

For the rest of the visit we talked about everything from Tiffany to my job. Whenever I tried to broach anything concerning him, he'd deflect the topic back on me. Once our time was up, I went back to the car so that August could have his time.

As I waited in the car, I texted my woman. Tiffany was good at making me laugh. I really needed uplifting right now.

ME:

You miss me?

Chapter Sixteen

TIFFANY

ME:

Like crazy.

Although I was still mad at Kingston for getting his ass shot yesterday, my man's message sent my heart racing. He was miles away with me on his mind, and I couldn't help but feel some type of way about that. I'd never been with a man, so trust wasn't an issue that I had to deal with. I was literally learning everything with Kingston, which was both exciting and scary.

Sighing, as excited as I was to be with my family today, I still missed my boo. My parents, sisters, Blu, Jacoba, and their kids surprised us by coming to town for Theo's birthday party. He was in heaven surrounded by his cousins. Theo was such a sweet young man and catered to his younger cousins the same way I catered to him.

I spent way too much money on his presents, but he deserved them. I'd been spoiled by my brothers and my parents, and now I was doing the same for my nephews and nieces.

KINGSTON:

I'on wanna go to bed without you.

ME:

Me either, baby. I wanna rub my booty on you.

"You want some cake, Granny?"

My attention was grabbed by Gianna who was busy fussing over Granny. I'd brought Granny with me to get her out of the house. I was glad I did because she was enjoying herself. Everyone immediately fell in love with her and vice versa.

The moment my mother learned Granny had a garden, she'd been ready to sit down with her and discuss all things plants. Valentina hadn't left Granny's side, and for that I was grateful. Granny's eyes lit up the second she laid eyes on my mom. I'm sure seeing my mother made Granny think of her own daughter in some way. They sat here talking like mother and daughter, laughing, and telling tales that each had gone through with their husbands.

This was also good for my mother. Both sets of my grandparents had long since passed, and my mother was young when her mom died. So, she stayed glued to Granny's side the entire afternoon.

I enjoyed the blissful expression Granny wore. It hadn't faded since we got here. If she wasn't talking to my mother, she was fussing over the kids, or playfully joking with Grey and Blu. Blu was a little salty that Kingston was out of town, as he had a bone to pick with him about hogging my time. Granny came to

Kingston's defense, telling Blu she'd take him over her knee. My brother, the one that barely cracked a smile, blushed and laughed so hard that Grey and my sisters were still ragging him about it.

I loved my family. The beauty of my sisters and how mature they'd grown to be made me smile. I missed the days when we used to play in each other's hair and talk about boy shit. Now they were both young women that were like two peas in a pod. Our daily calls weren't anything compared to having them within reach.

They chilled next to me, as we did what we do best. I divided my attention between them and Kingston, who was heavy on my mind. He hadn't been gone a full day, but I was missing him making me laugh to the point where my side ached.

KINGSTON:

Image

Stop fuckin' playin' wit' me, cuz what I'ma do wit' dis?

Out of nowhere a coughing fit came over me as I hid the screen.

"You okay, suga?" Concerned, Granny chucked me on my back.

I nodded and cleared my throat past the clog that was in it. Kingston's dick did too much to me for him to have sent this picture. Violet and Emerald busted out laughing, having seen the look on my face. They knew Kingston and I were texting back and forth and could only imagine what was on my screen.

ME:

I can't wait for you to get home.

What I had in mind to do to him wouldn't happen soon enough. Next time he took his ass to Georgia, I was going to be riding shotgun.

It was bittersweet leaving Grey's house to go back to Kingston's place, but evening neared, and I knew Granny was tired. We both needed to get home so that we could settle. I hugged everyone, fighting back tears because I hated being so far away from them. Sure I could move back to Miami, but then I'd be missing Grey, Gianna, and the kids just as much.

Granny got several hugs, and Blu even escorted her to the car. Granny threatening to beat his ass got Blu together really quick! She had to be as strong as she was to raise two men without any support.

We made it to Kingston's safely. I helped Granny inside, and although she tried to shoo me away, I ran her bathwater. Her tub was equipped so that she'd be safe getting in and out, but I still told her to let me know when she was done, so I wouldn't worry.

Leaving her to it, I went to the room I shared with Kingston, basking in his scent as soon as I hit the door. Needing to feel him near, I'd wear one of his t-shirts tonight. Our FaceTime call wouldn't be enough for me tonight. I wanted him next to me.

The next evening...

KINGSTON:

Be there in ten min, baby.

Excitedly, I dimmed the bedroom lights, turned on Maxwell, and went into the bathroom to start a hot bath. I'd been waiting all day for this.

Granny and I spent a time out in the garden, with me laughing at the neighbor's dog watching us, watch him. His eyes followed me whenever I went near the tomatoes as if he was daring me to touch them. The gate separating him from Kingston's yard was sturdy, but somehow his big ass found his way over, under, or around it.

Once we came in from the garden we prepared dinner together, ate, and spent some time deciding what kind of Thanksgiving dinner she wanted to prepare. The holiday was swiftly approaching, bringing all the wonderful feels with it. My holidays were always spent with my family, but this year, I hoped Granny, Kingston...and even August, would be a part of our festivities.

My day had gone well until I became bored out of my mind waiting for Kingston. I didn't want to bother him while he and August were on the road, so I tended to my own business by running to the nail shop for a fresh set and a pedicure. I made it home just in time to get things prepared for my man.

I turned the bathroom lights out and let the candles I'd lit illuminate the space. Lavender oil scent that I'd added to the bath water filled the air, cocooning me in sweet scents. I swooped my hair up into a ponytail, looked at myself in the mirror, then decided against it, letting my bundles flow. Tub full, I cut the water off, then went back in the room to retrieve our glasses of wine.

Kingston jiggled the doorknob to the room, prompting me to quickly perch myself atop the bathroom counter and crossed my legs.

"Baby," he called.

Purposely, I ignored him, knowing he'd find his way to me. Sure enough, seconds later he appeared in the bathroom doorway, his eyes taking in my naked body. My hair cascaded over my shoulders, and down my body, almost reaching my waist. The thick strands hid my nipples which stood at attention from Kingston admiring me. Our chain rested around my neck, just like it did his, reminding us of who we belonged to.

"Hey, baby," I spoke, then tilted my head to the side. "You just gon' stand there? I thought you missed—"

The words weren't out of my mouth good before Kingston was in front of me, spreading my thighs, and sending his tongue down my throat.

"Mmm..." I moaned into his mouth as I gripped his dreads and sexily nipped at his lips.

He brought my pussy to feel the length of him and groaned when I boldly slid my hand down to his joggers and slipped it inside to fist him. His large hands came up to squeeze my titties and pluck at my nipples before he inhaled them one at a time. I swear how rough he was with me wasn't a turn-off at all. How could he be rough, yet so gentle? Or maybe I was just interpreting his roughness for gentleness due to how turned on I was. Either way, he had me melting.

"Let's bathe so I can handle this," I purred against his lips.

Kingston stumbled back with a devilish look upon his face as he ripped his clothes off and slipped out of his shoes. Leaving the counter, I glided past him and to the tub where I stood and waited for him. He gripped his dick while staring at my center. When he licked his lips, I had to look away.

"After you," I said, motioning to the steamy, bubbly water.

He didn't protest and made himself comfortable. I handed him the flute of champagne, then eased in the tub behind him.

Kingston was a big man, but as he positioned himself better, he reclined against my titties. The sight of his bullet wound almost had sadness seeping in, but I squelched it by running my hands over his shoulders and firmly massaging his taught muscles.

"If you tryna be Mrs. Wells just say that." His husky voice sent my core fluttering. Smiling, I recalled that he'd said this to me before yet continued massaging him without responding.

"Damn," he groaned as my hands moved from his shoulder blades and up his neck, weeding out any knots I felt.

Kingston didn't have to tell me for me to know that he was stressed from his visit with his dad. I heard it in his voice and saw it in his face as we talked last night. Me catering to him tonight was to help him relax and to let him know that I had his back. However, I made a note to do this for him as often as I could.

After I felt he was relaxed enough, I bathed him, then myself, before getting out and grabbing our towels. I handed him one, trying to keep my eyes off the monster hanging between his strong thighs, only for my eyes to collide with his piercings. That shit was so fucking sexy on him.

Pivoting on my feet, I switched out of the bathroom, feeling his eyes on my ass. The tips of my hair clung to my skin from where it'd been wet. Throwing my towel aside, I didn't even dry off and climbed in the bed. It dipped behind me as Kingston kissed his way up the backs of my thighs. While I wanted to feed him my box, tonight was about him and how much I missed him while he was gone.

"Bring ya ass here," he demanded, clutching my thigh when I dodged his lips.

Giggling, I turned around, then coaxed him to lay on the bed. His dick stood tall and thick but curved beautifully. He took himself into his hand, biting into his bottom lip as I crawled up his body, stopping at the thick mushroom head of his dick. Pushing his hand aside, I took over, wetting his tip before taking him into my mouth.

Maxwell's voice did little to cover up the sounds Kingston made as I bobbed on him. He loved pulling my hair, which I let him do. It turned me on more than I thought it would, and I had fallen in love with him pulling my strands. My hand worked in time with my mouth, bringing him to the brink before I pulled back. I'd barely sank down on him when his hands landed on my hips.

Shit! The whole house definitely heard that. Too turnt, I didn't even register the pain. My head fell back on my shoulders as I sank to his base, moaning from how full he made me. I planted my hands on his chest and scraped my nails against his studded nipples, causing him to growl. Slowly, I rode him, taking my time so that he felt every flutter my tunnel inflicted upon him. For a minute, I was doing good. That was until his fingers dove into my scalp. He gently jerked my head to the side and sank his teeth into the flesh of my throat.

"I'm not goin' anywhere, baby," he uttered in my ear. "Don't ever leave me," he begged.

My walls collapsed around him, surging heat through my body that had me silently screaming. Viciously cursing, Kingston flipped us over, spread my legs, and feverishly pumped into me. His lips attacked mine as he fought to drown the grunting and moaning falling from his lips. It was no use. As my tunnel tugged at him, his release peaked, sending him over the edge as he growled uncontrollably and shook above me.

He collapsed upon my breast, leaving our bodies entangled. Contentedly, I stroked his dreads as tears clouded my vision. Being in love shouldn't have been so scary. Yet, I was terrified. I wouldn't be able to handle it if Kingston broke my heart.

The next day...

My morning was going great. Kingston woke me up with sweet kisses, together we prepared for work, and he hugged me for several minutes before we went our separate ways. Things went even better when another bouquet of flowers was sent to me shortly after I arrived at work.

Princess,

You own me, sug.

-King

With a note like that, nothing could spoil my day.

Or so I thought.

This email staring back at me soured my entire soul. Not only was Chris making it mandatory that I attend a company party, but it was for Miss Aldridge. The queen had finally made partner, and the celebration was to take place the Friday after Thanksgiving. Not only did I plan on being with my family for Thanksgiving, but I didn't even fool with Miss Aldridge to the point I wanted to celebrate anything with her.

"How dare them hold her party at a time when we should be enjoying our family?" Mina echoed my sentiment.

Bothered, I rushed through the rest of my morning. Dorian had a test coming up, so I agreed to get off early to meet him at the school library. Nowadays, I only tutored him once a week since his practices began earlier due to the season beginning soon, and his grades were improving.

When it was time for me to go, I didn't even waste time saying bye to anyone but Mina. As soon as I got in my car, I facetimed Kingston and placed the phone on the mount so that I could free my hands to drive.

"Baby girl," Kingston answered.

Normally, I would take the time to appreciate how good my man looked, but right now I was too upset.

"Chris is making it mandatory for me to go to a dinner party for one of his colleagues that just made partner. I wouldn't be so upset if it wasn't on the day after Thanksgiving." I flew out of the parking lot and headed towards the campus, wishing I could just go home. My period had to be near because my emotions were all over the damn place.

"You already know how I feel about that nigga and that damn job, shawty," Kingston replied. "In the time since you've been workin' there have you even considered law is what you wanna do? That *is* why you're there, love."

"You think I shouldn't?" Doubt creeped in.

"No, baby," he mumbled. "What I'm sayin' is I barely hear

you talk about being a lawyer. Is it *still* what *you* want to pursue?"

Mulling Kingston's question over, I sighed. "It's a love I have for law enforcement. Grey, Blu, and you give me hope that people that look like us can thrive in environments where some think we don't belong or hate us for being in. If I don't pursue law, there's nothing else I can see myself doing career-wise."

Kingston nodded. "Which is why I'ma support you if you gon' stick it out. I'll even go to the lil' bitch ass party witchu. Hell, I'on need no invitation. If my woman is gon' be in the buildin', then so am I."

I busted out laughing. "See, that's why I love you, Kingston. You—"

"Hol' up, hol' up," he interrupted.

I glanced at the screen to see him staring so close to the phone that all I saw was his eyes.

"What'd you just say to me?" he questioned.

Replaying in my mind what I said, my heart stopped. As I pulled into the campus parking lot, I was stuck on mute not knowing what to say.

"Play it back for me, Tiffany," he coerced.

"Uh... I just pulled up to the library, and Dorian's outside waiting for me. I'll see you when I leave." I quickly hung up, mortified that I'd told this man that I loved him! I mean, it wasn't a lie, but still. *Oh my God*! My brain shouted in shock.

Gathering myself, I grabbed my phone and purse, then got out of the car. Dorian was, in fact, pacing in front of the library doors. His tall frame never ceased to amaze me. Kingston was tall, but Dorian had him beat.

"Hey," I spoke.

"'Sup, Tiff?" He opened the door for me then escorted me to

the table we always used which was back in a little cut. It kept people from interrupting us, or else they'd be trying to get Dorian's attention while he was studying.

Half-way through his notes, a familiar scent crept into my nose, causing me to glance up from the papers he and I were perusing. I died when my eyes collided with Kingston's as he was steps away from me.

"'Sup, D," he spoke to Dorian who dapped him. "You ready to kill it?" he asked Dorian.

Dorian nodded. "Fa sho, big dawg. Tiffany's makin' sure I keep my grades up so I can stay on the court, too. Playin' ball is cool, but I gotta get a degree outta this shit just in case."

"Absolutely," Kingston agreed. "You got the whole city behind you, so keep ya head up," he encouraged.

Dorian grinned.

Kingston turned his attention to me. My mouth was partially ajar, surprised to see him here. He got right in my face until our noses practically touched. I smelled the mint and cigar on his breath, and still, he turned me on.

"What'd you say to me?" he questioned softly, staring dead into my wide eyes.

"Ba—"

"Say it," he softly demanded.

"I love you," I whispered. The words barely left my lips before his were on mine. Deeply, he kissed me like we weren't in this public ass place. He broke our connection but pecked his way up my cheek.

"I love you, Princess Sapphire Tiffany...Wells." Between each of my names, he kissed me. Him tacking on his last name sent me laughing. This is what I wanted to tell him. I loved him because he consistently made my day. His ability to make me laugh, the way he made me feel whenever he looked at me, and the way he touched me… The fact that this man just told me he loved me, I could scream in this library!

"I'll see you when you get home," he stated as our hands locked so quick and smoothly that it was second nature now. He pecked my lips once more, then retreated.

"Damn, Tiff." Dorian chuckled. "You got a sister or somethin'? Big dawg just ruined all my lil' chances witchu."

We both laughed.

"I'm kiddin'," he said. "Not about the lil' sister part, though."

Smacking my teeth, I grinned and told Dorian to get back to work. His ass wasn't about to be out here breaking either of my sisters' hearts. Hell, I needed to protect my own at this point. Kingston trampled all in and through my shit.

Chapter Seventeen

KINGSTON

"You flew outta here like some shit was wrong." Jared chuckled when I eased back into my office.

I had a meeting to hold but had to get to Tiffany to look her dead in her eyes so she could repeat what the fuck she'd said to me. My dick was hard and my heart soft as fuck from her confession.

"Get everybody together," I told Jared, who left my office to do what I said.

Until everyone arrived, I scrolled on my phone for Grey's number. I knew by way of Tiffany that Gianna was the shit when it came to designing dresses.

"What'd you do to my sister?" he snarled.

Feeling chipper, I replied, "Got her pregnant, Uncle G." Of course, I was bullshitting, but the way Grey spazzed out on the other end, I chortled. "I'm fuckin' witchu, nigga. At least, I may be," I added.

"King!" he barked.

"Aye, on some real shit, I need a favor." I chuckled.

"I'm listenin'," he said after calming down.

"My lady needs a dress—a bad ass one. I need to surprise her. You think wifey can help me out?"

Grey grumbled on the other end. "Don't go up in my wife's shit causin' problems, nigga. I'll swang through that bitch an' kick yo' ass."

"I'll be on my best behavior," I promised.

"Like you got a choice. I'll drop you the address and tell her you gon' slide through."

"Bet," I responded. "Good lookin' out."

"Fuck you, nigga," he mumbled then disconnected the call.

Just as I placed my phone down, my team trickled into my office. Without preamble, I got down to business. I uncovered some interesting information earlier while digging further into Smooth's case. The state was pissed because their witness was dead, and I was pissed 'cause that muhfucka had the audacity to shoot me. If Smooth hadn't died, I would've beat his ass into a coma.

"The house we shot up traced back to a business owned by none other than Christopher Dawson." Murmuring commenced around the office.

"The lawyer?" Jared asked just to make sure.

I nodded.

"Mane, that's a lil' too coincidental," Flannigan added.

"And the fact that his ass was bold enough to show up to the scene," Kobi chimed in.

I was still heated that Chris had the balls to bring my woman to a fucking crime scene.

"He has to be tied to the money and drugs," Jared said.

Shrugging, I stated, "Tying him to the money and drugs will be a lil' more complicated. He owns several rentals, so we can't just assume he's caught up in Smooth's shit. Is it likely, hell yeah. But we gotta chill and see where his muhfuckin' ass is gon' lead us. He's a lawyer, so he ain't dumb enough to let himself be easily caught. What I'm more concerned about is the fact that I've never heard his name mentioned on the streets, unless it involved a case. So, either we got a legit lawyer or a lawyer that's untouchable like a muhfucka."

Everyone grumbled. Anyone in law enforcement knew that 'ghosts' were hard to catch. They moved so damn smooth that even the people working for them didn't have a face to the name or had no name at all. Shit was draining as fuck.

"We'll keep our ears to the streets," Flannigan spoke.

"Do that," I drawled and dismissed them.

Not only was I frustrated over the whole situation with Smooth, but bodying a nigga was something that was never easy —necessary at times, but not easy. I'd rather stick a person in prison so that they could have some chance of reform rather than ending their life. Wasn't a soul blessed behind someone else dying. Shit made no sense to me.

Sighing, I finished up my report on the shooting and shifted my mind to better thoughts. My lady told me she loved me. I'd slide through Gianna's boutique for Tiffany's dress, then hit up my tailor for a suit to match.

After the way she handled me last night and catered to me like her king, locking Tiffany down was my number one priority. There was no way in hell I was gon' let her do that same shit for another man. Hell, not while I was still breathing at least. Fuck it, I'd haunt her in my afterlife, too. Any man who tried to get within ten feet of her, I'd set his feet and head on fire, then let the flames meet in the middle. The fuck.

Gianna's boutique had a few customers in it when I walked in. All eyes fell on me as I sought her out.

"May I help you?" the beauty standing before me asked.

"I got him, Trice," Gianna came up and said. Trice looked between us with her eyebrows arched above her eyes.

"This is Tiffany's man, Kingston," Gianna explained.

"Oh!" Trice laughed. "Tell me somethin' boo, 'cause Lawd… I was gon' have to clock out before Grey shows up." She laughed. She waved and sauntered away, still tickled.

"Tell me what you're looking for." Gianna walked me through her showroom, showing me different dresses she'd made. Tiffany wasn't lying when she said her sister-in-law was dope.

"I'm lookin' for something that says, 'fuck me' but 'respectfully'. I'on wanna have to shoot up the company party."

She scoffed, then busted out laughing. "Oh my goodness! Sadly, I know exactly the look you're going for." She led me to a sparkling, body conforming, sapphire blue dress, that from the front was modest enough. But when she turned it around, my mouth dropped.

"Oh, hell yeah," I praised. "This gon' look good on her." I

snapped a picture of the dress and texted it to my tailor, letting him know to get me right.

"How soon do you need it?"

"Thanksgiving," I replied.

She nodded with a gentle smile. I rattled off Tiffany's measurements, causing Gianna to eye me up and down.

The door chime sounded with us both glancing at the door.

"The fuck you doin' standin' so close to my wife, bruh?"

Trice's laugh could be heard clear across the showroom.

"Grey." Gianna prettily chuckled. "Now why're you comin' up in here being messy? I have customers, boo."

Grey shouldered me out of the way, then kissed his wife. Nigga bumped me so hard, I damn near knocked over the mannequin holding Tiffany's dress.

"Sis-in-law, you betta getcha nigga," I warned. In an instant, Grey was in my face, snarling. His wife yanked him back while I laughed. "What I say?" I sarcastically asked.

"Nigga—"

"Baby, stop it," Gianna fussed. "You're acting like Tiffany's a little girl. If y'all get to fightin' in here and he kicks your ass— Ahh!"

Gianna yelped loud as hell when Grey lifted her off her feet and hemmed her up like *she* was a little ass girl. She laughed hard as hell and wrapped her legs around his waist. Her customers were all in our business, being nosey as fuck.

"Just kidding!" she relented. "I know he can't kick your ass, bae," she stated while kissing all over his face.

I grunted my disagreement, but since Grey and his wife were having a moment, I didn't want to embarrass him.

"Now gon' on so I can sell this man his woman's dress," Gianna chided.

Grey's face balled up at the dress, but he held his tongue.

Smirking, I said, "It's fye, ain't it."

Grey placed his wife back on her feet and kissed her lips. "Lemme bounce 'fore I break my foot off in this nigga."

"Don't leave on my account," I taunted as Grey passed me.

He stopped with us standing shoulder to shoulder. "Just in case yeen figured it out, my pull up game is strong as fuck."

Grinning, I replied, "Mine, too, bruh-in-law."

He bared his teeth at me then stormed off. I could've sworn I heard him call me a bitch ass nigga on his way out of the door.

"Lord," Gianna mumbled and shook her head. "How you wanna pay *bruh-in-law*? I should charge you extra for messin' with my man."

Handing her my card, I said, "We're practically family, lil' mama. Grey will be aight."

She pushed her lips to the side, rolled her eyes, and motioned for me to follow her to the register.

Tiffany didn't want to attend the party because, like anyone else, she wanted to spend the holidays with her family. Lowkey, although Granny planned on cooking, I was already trying to find a way for us to spend the holidays with Tiffany. The last thing I wanted to do was make my lady feel like she had to choose between me and her folks.

I understood her relationship with her family. A part of me wished my uncles were closer to me, August, and Granny, but sulking over the situation didn't do anything for either of us. I had cousins outchea that I didn't fuck with, and it was because of the lack of relationship I had with their fathers. Families weren't the same anymore, so I dare not come between Tiffany and her family. If anything, I wanted to be a part of them.

After I left Gianna's, I went by the store to grab something special to cook for Tiffany. I swear her telling me she loved me had me moving some type of way—a good way. Like I was light on my feet or some shit.

Falling in love with Tiffany was easy. Truth be told, I fell for shawty from day one. No one or nothing could take my eyes off of her. She had me wide open, feeling shit I never thought I'd feel for a woman, which was dangerous. Love caused people to do stupid shit like lose their mind if the other person decided to walk away. As crazy as I was about Tiffany, I already knew losing her would be something I couldn't handle. I had to do anything possible to keep my shawty.

"You cookin' for her again, bruh?" August commented when he came into the kitchen. He was supposed to be on the deck, looking after Granny. Instead, he was in my business.

"Why is that a problem?" Tiffany appeared in the kitchen and asked.

August grumbled. "A relationship is supposed to be fifty/fifty. Why y'all can't cook *together*? King looks like a whole househusband standin' at the stove with that apron on," he clowned.

Tiffany cackled while I grinned. "You feelin' salty? All you have to do is get you a girl you can cook for. My man looks sexy." Capping off what she said, Tiffany sidled up behind me, wrapped her arms around me, and laid her head on my back. She already knew what touching on my chest did to me, yet she stood here feeling on me like I wouldn't fuck her up in the middle of this kitchen.

"I'm just sayin', I'on wanna know allat," August quipped. "Or *see* allat."

"Well, take ya ass back outside." I chuckled and so did Tiffany.

August grumbled again and made his exit. Tiffany chose that time to tweak my nipples. Sitting the spatula aside, I turned to face her. She naughtily bit into her.

"Nie why you doin' that while I'm tryna cook?" I backed her into the counter and trapped her there.

"'Cause I want you," she purred, bringing my body closer to hers.

Damn, it was something about the way she touched me. I never knew what affection was nor how to give it until I met Tiffany. It took being with her to understand the necessity of affection. Without it, there was no true vibe between two people. The connection wouldn't be as strong, and it would be easy for anyone to slide in and destroy what was being built.

That's why every time she touched me, I felt it in my soul. Whenever she looked at me, she branded herself on my brain. I'd cataloged every part of her in my DNA. I wanted to make sure she felt the same shit when I looked at or touched her.

Swooping down, I seized her lips, twirling my tongue inside her mouth so good that she moaned. She rubbed against my stiff dick, making him angrily hard.

"See this is that bullshit." August's voice did nothing to deter me from feasting on my woman's tongue and lips. Our smacking was the only thing I heard.

She cupped my jaw and kissed me just as nastily as I kissed her. Unable to resist not being inside of her, I went back to the stove to turn the food off. Thankfully, everything was done because when Tiffany beckoned me to follow her, I took the apron off and did just that.

As soon as we were in the room, she had me up against the door, kneeling before me as her fingernails dragged against my nipples, puckering them. I attacked my bottom lip and watched behind heavy lids as she stuck her tongue out and licked all over my thick head. Her silky member touched a spot only she knew about, sending my body shuddering. This was another reason I loved this damn woman. She took the time to learn my body, just as I took the time to learn hers. Tiffany knew how to please me, and each time, I went up in smoke as if it was the first time.

Gripping handfuls of her hair, I held on as she gagged on my tip.

"Shiittt!" I grunted, feeling my nut rush through me. "Tiff..." She stared me in my eyes, that shit making my brain spin. Baby knew what her eyes did to me and used them to bewitch me into groaning her name.

She moaned on my head, scraped my thighs with her fingernails, and deep throated me, sending me over the edge. My body shook as I held her head still, growled, and pumped furiously between her jaws as she fisted and sucked my nut out. Once done, she cleaned me up, kissed her way up my abdomen, stopped to bless my piercings, then kissed along the tattoos on my neck.

"I love you, King," she whispered. Spent, I lazily echoed her feelings. When she pecked my lips, I opened my mouth to accept her tongue.

Tiffany officially had me 'til death do us part.

Chapter Eighteen

TIFFANY

Chris was salty that I requested today off for a mental day. To get under his skin even more, I requested the week of Thanksgiving off since he wanted to interrupt my holiday with some nonsense.

Kingston was at work, so I figured I'd enjoy a day of relaxation. I thought it would be nice to invite Faith, who was excited to join me. We hit it off well the first time we met and had kept in contact since then. Faith was innocent and sweet, however, intuition told me that underneath her gentle brown eyes laid heavy burdens.

Once, I asked her about her family, hoping we could trade funny stories about our relatives. When she told me that she was raised in foster care, my heart took her in at that moment. I didn't care that I'd just met her. Faith became my little, big sister that day.

Every morning and night I sent her a text message, just as I did my own sisters and brothers. She revealed little pieces of herself to me, like the fact that she was nervous about being a mom, and that her best friend was doing everything he could to help her through the process of pregnancy.

Not once did she mention August and I never brought him up. It's like sis had resigned to the fact that August wouldn't be in his baby's life. Kingston was so bothered by August's lack of taking responsibility for the being he'd created, that he and I vowed to each other to be there for Faith whenever she needed anything.

Still, she remained guarded. It was in the way she talked. Almost as if she was questioning whether to trust me or not. I found no fault in her being guarded because I, for one, understood how mean, jealous, conniving, and envious women could be. Which is why I never had friends. It'd always just been me and my siblings. Associates I had throughout my school years never lasted because they'd be jealous of me for one reason or another. If it wasn't for the way I looked, it was because of the smarts I possessed.

With Faith, I felt that the more she got to know me, she'd see within me the genuineness to truly know her. I wasn't one of these females that looked for connections out of tainted motives. For some reason, Faith's spirit connected with mine. So, I took heed and welcomed her in. Just as I was hoping she'd do with me.

I saw her walking through the doors of Three Sisters and waved her over. Faith was a walking pregnant bombshell. Her caramel brown skin glowed, right along with the bright smile on her timeless face. Anyone could see why August went after her. Only he was looking on the outside and failed to know what laid inside of Faith.

"Heeyyy!" she cheerily greeted.

"Hey, boo!" I hugged Faith, happy to see some light in her eyes.

"Goodness!" I exclaimed. "You look amazing!"

She blushed. "Thank you, chile," she replied as we sat down.

"Baby doing good?" I asked. I'd been knowing for a few days that she had a doctor's appointment today. I offered to accompany her, only to find out that her best friend, Jericho, was taking her. Lowkey, I'd never met Jericho, but Faith made him sound like such a nice guy.

"Baby boy is doing awesome," she replied, full of joy. "I went from being scared as hell to wanting March to hurry up and get here so that I can see my baby's face."

I smiled with her. "Aww, boo. I know he's gonna be so handsome."

She grinned, knowing it was the truth. Not only was she drop dead gorgeous, but August was fine as hell, too, with his immature ass. We were interrupted by the waitress who took our drink orders. Since we knew what we wanted, we ordered our food, too.

Faith's phone went off, prompting her to sigh.

"Excuse me a sec," she said before answering it. "Hello? I'm eating. I don't have an attitude." Her eyes rolled as she smirked at me. "I just saw you an hour ago. Nope. Sure. I guess. I'm not moving to Atlanta, Jericho. I won't think about it. Okay. Talk to you later."

She hung up chuckling, so I joined in.

"He thinks he's my man or something," she quipped. "And that's too far from the truth."

"How long have y'all been friends?"

"Five years," she stated.

I gave her a look which made her laugh.

"Seriously, nothing's between us like that. He's just a really bomb ass friend to me."

I shot her another look, making her laugh harder.

"What?" she bashfully asked.

"Don't what me, Faith," I ragged.

Our attention was averted to some dude walking past the window. Through the glass he couldn't see us, but we saw his fine, chocolate ass. It was the expression on Faith's face that had me watching the dude until he walked inside of the restaurant. His gaze searched someone out.

"Lord," Faith mumbled as his eyes landed on her. She turned back around in her seat and covered her face.

"Who is that?" I asked. If he was about to start some trouble, I had my gun on me. Wasn't anyone about to mess with my girl. I didn't give a damn how fine he was. There wasn't a man finer than mine, and I even threatened Kingston once.

He slid into the booth next to Faith with a broad, white smile on his face.

"Good afternoon," he spoke to me and extended his hand. "Jericho."

Surprised, I shook his hand and simply said, "Oh. I'm Tiffany."

"I'ain tryna interrupt, just stopped by before I hop on the road," he said.

Faith cocked her head at him. "You are interrupting though, and I just saw you at the doctor's office."

Jericho chuckled, then glanced at me. "She's actin' hard 'cause she's in front of you. Normally, she'd say *'aww boo, you gon' miss me'*," he mimicked, causing me and Faith to bust out laughing. The color staining her cheeks told me that he wasn't lying.

"*But* I just saw you an hour ago," she reiterated. The waitress came back with our drinks and couldn't walk away for being in Jericho's mouth. Faith peeped it, too, but said nothing.

He shrugged. "When has that ever mattered?" The way he eyed her made *me* squirm in my seat! That's the look Kingston gave me before he proceeded to attack me. Jericho seemed like that's exactly what he wanted to do to Faith.

Faith blinked at Jericho, a million questions dancing in her eyes.

Jericho put his arm around her shoulders and pulled her in for a hug. "I'll be back the weekend unless you need me before then," he told her. I felt some type of way when he placed his large, inked up hand on her belly and dropped a kiss on her forehead.

"It was nice to finally meet you, Tiffany. Faith talks about you a lot. I'm happy to see her happy. So, please feel free to get on her nerves as often as you can."

Again, Faith and I laughed. Jericho kissed Faith's forehead one last time before leaving the table. She stared after him as he stopped at the bar area. He motioned over to us, pulled out his wallet, and handed his card to the bartender.

Faith smacked her teeth. As if Jericho heard her over the rattle of other patrons and the music playing over the speakers, he glanced her way and winked.

"I'ma beatcho ass," she stated. Only I heard her issued threat. But he had to have read her lips because he laughed. After the bartender handed him his card back, he blew Faith a kiss, waved to me, then was out of the door.

Clearing my throat, I waited to get Faith's attention before saying, "That man *is not* yo' damn friend, sis!"

She giggled. "He's my best friend," she corrected.

"Shiiiddd!" I answered, sending her cackling. Our food came then, smelling good and steaming. She prayed over our meal like the sweetheart she was, then we started devouring our burgers like some grown men.

"For five years you've been *best friends* with a man *that* fine? Baby you the goat!"

Faith was so tickled, she turned red in the face.

"Yes," she confirmed. "He's a couple of years older than me. Back then he wasn't looking at me as anything other than someone he looked out for."

"So, you're saying you would be with him?"

She scrunched her nose up. "Girl, do you see me? I'm pregnant with another man's baby. A man that couldn't care less that I'm even carrying his seed." Her mood dimmed. "What's crazy is that I know what a good man looks like. I've seen it in Jericho. I beat myself up for getting caught up with someone like August when he's nothing like the man I could see myself with. August could see from a mile away that I was green when it came to men. That's what being naïve got me. I fell for his bullshit and sadly, I regret it."

We both ate, while I pondered on her feelings. This was the first time she'd ever opened up to me, and I didn't want to spoil it or fuck it up. Whenever I needed advice, I went to my mother, Gianna, and Jacoba. Between the three of them, I had a whole camp of counselors around me.

"You carrying a baby doesn't make you exempt from having a good man, Faith—whether he's the father or not. Having a child is a blessing. The person in whom you conceived him with may not have been your ideal choice, but everything happens for a reason. Sometimes, we must wade through the bullshit to get to the treasure. In other words, maybe we need our heart broken once to really understand how to treasure the man who's going to protect the same heart with his life. Sounds crazy, I know."

My heart hadn't been broken yet, and I prayed Kingston never did break it. If he showed me all the signs of a good man, just to destroy my perception, I wouldn't know how to bounce back from the hurt.

"I understand exactly what you're saying," Faith responded. "Forgiving myself for being with him is the hardest part I'm facing. It's crazy how we can think we're so smart and end up feeling so dumb behind a man." Her eyes teared up then.

"Don't cry, Faith." Hell, she was about to make me cry.

She chuckled. "It's these damn hormones. I don't even love August, I'm just angry that I let myself get involved with him. I should've known better."

"What you're not gon' do is allow the situation to emotionally break you. Allow yourself to heal from *you* and how you feel about yourself. You're a beautiful woman with an equally beautiful heart. I'd like to think that God has great things waiting for you."

She blinked away her tears and continued to eat. Seconds later she said, "I'll accept that."

Smiling, I replied, "I'ma stand on it with you, sis."

Light revisited her eyes just as her phone vibrated. When she read the message, a soft expression graced her face.

"Jericho says thank you for putting a smile on my face." Her eyes seemed to tear again, and I knew why.

"That man *is not* yo' best friend," I muttered.

Faith died laughing, lightening the mood.

"Enough about me and *my best friend*, how're things with Kingston?"

Sighing, I fanned jokingly fanned myself. "Would you believe he's the first man I've ever dated?"

She looked surprised.

"Exactly, boo." I chuckled. "If we don't work out, who's gonna come behind *him*?"

Faith tsked. "Don't even speak that. Kingston is a good guy. He's never been disrespectful towards me, and he treats his granny like a rare diamond."

I smiled at that.

After we left eating, Faith and I went to the mall. We agreed that neither of us needed anything but didn't deter us from going crazy inside of several stores. The time I spent with Faith proved that we could be good friends. Hopefully, she saw the same thing.

Now that I had a man in my life, and I saw that it wasn't so bad, maybe having a homegirl wasn't so bad either. I was further pleased when Faith and I planned our next outing.

Sheltered Tiffany was outgrowing the cocoon of family. So far, all was well.

I could sigh in relief. Dragging out of the house to the car, all I wanted to do was crawl back in bed. Seeing that Kingston had the passenger seat set up for me to go right back to sleep made my morning. Plus, it was nippy out here, and he made sure to have the car warmed up before bringing my ass out here.

Early birds and bugs made all kinds of noise in the predawn morning air. In a few more hours, the sun would wake up. Admittedly, I was tired as hell from work. Tutoring was still going well and caused no issues for me. It was working with Chris that had me stressed to the max.

Because Chris knew I'd be off this week, he'd worked me like a slave all last week, even invading my tutoring time with Dorian. Rashad's case had been closed, but loomed over Chris' head now that Rashad was deceased. Chris took all his cases seriously, but besides the case with Wilks, this situation with Rashad had him bothered.

Kingston hadn't brought up the shooting anymore. He'd healed nicely and simply considered it as a part of his job. Being shot at sounded scary as fuck, but the way Kingston handled being shot was even scarier. He brushed it off like it was nothing.

"You comfortable?" he asked, chuckling. I'd kicked my slides off and balled up under the covers, then laid my head against the pillow. He had the seat reclined and everything.

"I'm perfect," I replied. He shut the door and got in himself.

"Rest ya eyes, baby. We'll be there soon," he said and cranked up Erykah Badu.

As loud as it was, I enjoyed the music just as much as I enjoyed Kingston touching me every now and then. It's like he was reminding himself that I was right here next to him. He had nothing to worry about. I'd always be by Kingston's side.

Chapter Nineteen

KINGSTON

Tiffany's sleepy ass had the nerve to stretch like a cat as soon as I cut the car off. Damn she looked so sexy with her hair all tousled. Whenever I questioned whether or not she was the one for me, I imagined this is how I'd see her every morning—no matter how old we grew to be.

The grocery delivery service wasn't too far behind us and showed up at the perfect time. I got Tiffany settled in on the living room sofa while I made us some breakfast. August ragged on how I catered to Tiffany, but in my mind, she deserved it.

I never took her affection for granted. I'd been with plenty of females who wanted to love on me the way that Tiffany did, however, she'd been the only one to make me want that shit. I realized how important it was to cater to and be catered to.

Tiffany often catered to me. Whether she was popping up at my job to give me a mid-day kiss or her text messages throughout the day, reminding me how good of a man I was. It was definitely the way she massaged a nigga damn near nightly, without so much as a complaint. Hell, and I couldn't forget about the way that every night I made it home, Tiffany would already have my bath or shower ready, coupled with candles and a drink of my choice. By now, lil' baby knew that my favorite drink was D'usse. Either dinner was prepared, we went out, ordered in, or Granny cooked.

She did all that for me while still holding down her day. Tiffany didn't have to tell me for me to know that she was stressed out. She'd nod off if we sat in one position for too long, and even when asked, she barely liked to talk about her job. Because of my run-in with Chris, I guess she figured telling me anything that had to do with him would have me showing up at her job.

Chuckling, I thought, I sure the fuck would. I'd show up to her job and choke that nigga to death if he ever did some sideways shit like he did by bringing Tiffany to that damn crime scene. So far, she hadn't complained of anything extreme happening, so I was chillin' until then.

Anyway, yeah my woman deserved her damn breakfast, lunch, and dinner cooked if she wanted it. The bond we were building would be impenetrable as long as we continued to hold each other down.

After breakfast, I quickly showered and dressed. I scheduled visitation with my dad early so that I could enjoy the rest of the day with Tiffany. We'd be here for two days, and I wanted her to enjoy every minute of it.

She was on the phone with Faith when I came back into the living room. She'd partially undressed, revealing her beautiful derriere in nothing but a pair of black panties. As she paced the hardwood floor, my eyes followed her sexy stride.

"Just relax yourself, Faith. You have to bake that baby for a few more months. My nephew can't come too early."

Hearing her refer to *my* nephew as hers had me grinning harder than I should've been. Tiffany caught me staring and traced her footsteps to me.

"Hold on, boo," she said to Faith. "Leaving?" she asked me.

Nodding, I kissed her lips and simultaneously slid my hand into hers. Without thought, her dainty fingers played effortlessly with mine.

"Be careful," she stated, then kissed my lips once more.

"I'll be back soon," I assured her.

I made it to the prison an hour later. As usual, I was ushered to the back without incident. Again, there my dad waited, grinning from ear to ear.

"You didn't bring ya girl to see me?" he asked as soon as I picked the phone up.

"Why the fuck would I bring my lady up in here?" At some point I wanted Tiffany to meet my dad, but it wasn't gon' be behind these walls. He'd have to settle for an over the phone meeting because I refused to bring her here.

My dad looked at me incredulously. "Embarrassed much," he grumbled.

"If I was embarrassed she wouldn't even know about ya ass, let alone ride with me all the way here. She includes you in her nightly prayers, so trust me, no one's embarrassed." The first time Tiffany prayed for my dad, I swear I fell in love with her ass even more. I don't give a fuck what anyone says. A praying woman is the strongest person in a man's circle. Whether it's his grandma, mama, sister, or his woman—those prayers are the ones that keep niggas strong.

Whenever Tiffany prayed for me, I bowed my head and trusted God for whatever she said. She was so unselfish and made sure to call out everyone's name. I mean, I couldn't, *wouldn't* find better than her. Her heart was so pure that she even prayed for Chris and his family on occasion.

Nate cackled. "Folks taught her right, huh?"

"Yep. They're good people," I answered.

"Oh." His eyebrows arched. "Either you cappin' to keep the nookie, or you're serious."

Cocking my head at him, I asked, "First, don't ever refer to my woman's private parts, and when have I ever lied to you? Why wouldn't I be serious? Her family *is* good people." He was starting this visit off on some bullshit and I'ain like that. He was disrupting my spirit.

"Whoa." He chuckled. "You're defendin' them like they're blood or somethin'."

Sighing, I said, "I'ain come here to argue witchu, Pops. Thanksgiving is Thursday, and I wanted to make sure I got to see you before then."

"Mrs. Lily cookin'?"

I nodded. "But we're spendin' the day with Tiffany's family."

The big grin that normally graced his hard face, dimmed a little.

"Listen, Son," he started, further disrupting my spirit. "I'm all for companionship, but you're actin' like you and this girl are married. You shouldn't be tyin' yaself down so soon. You're not even thirty yet."

Smirking, I questioned, "Is that what you told August? He hasn't made the first move to fix shit with his baby's mother."

Nate chuckled. "I told him not to allow a baby to keep him from living his life.

I shook my head in disdain. "The fuck kinda parent tells their child that? He was man enough to lay down and make a baby, yet you're tellin' him what he's created ain't his concern. That's bullshit, mane."

"It's not bullshit. It's the truth," he countered. "What good will August do being around a kid he doesn't even want? Torture the kid? Do something to it out of frustration or anger?"

Disgusted, I stared at this nigga.

"It's better for him to leave that girl and her baby alone. He told me himself that she's fuckin' that friend of hers anyway."

Rubbing the bridge of my brow, I shook my head again. "Faith ain't fuckin' that nigga, Pops, and neither you nor August is gon' speak down on her name. If he'on wanna fuck with her, I'ma let him feel that pain when his ass wakes up one day. Seein' as how he'd rather take ya advice than mine, I'm done tellin' him shit. When his ass hits a brick wall, ain't a muhfucka that's gon' be there to save him."

"Whatchu tryna say? You speakin' bad on my son?"

"*You* speakin' bad on ya son," I growled. "You tellin' him to run away from his fuckin' problems rather than tellin' him to man the fuck up and handle that shit."

Nate chuckled. "Whatchu know about bein' a man, King? That badge made you soft as fuck. If I missed anything about actually bein' in ya life, it's that I missed teachin' yo' ass how to be a man."

Shocked, coolly, I assessed my father. He looked no different than he had any other time I'd been here. However, something laid beneath his cocky smirk.

"Look, I'on know what ya issue is—"

"My *issue* is that I'm in fuckin' prison, and my first-born son, who claims to be a man, doesn't have the balls to get me outta here. That's my muthafuckin' issue."

Nate put the black phone back on its hook and got one of the COs' attention. He didn't take a second look at me before being taken out of the room. How did my good intentions of seeing him for the holidays turn into me not being shit?

On the drive back to my house, I worked overtime trying to right my energy. Regardless of how any man felt, hearing my dad degrade me the way he did bothered the fuck out of me. I didn't allow anything to ever rattle my cage but Nate successfully did.

His perception of me was of course flawed, however, the son in me felt some type of way that the man who helped create me thought less of me. With everything I'd accomplished in life, my father should've been more than proud of me. Instead, he took what I worked so hard for and used it against me.

As the day progressed, I tried shaking myself loose of the negativity the visit with my dad cast over me. I took Tiffany shopping and let her have her way. She claimed to not want to be spoiled, but I spoiled her regardless. Lunch was spent at a barbecue spot I frequented when in town. We ended up at a plant farm where Tiffany bought Granny some plants she knew she'd love. By sunset, Nate's shadow still loomed over me.

Here I was, standing on the deck holding Tiffany in my arms as we watched the sunset, yet my mind was elsewhere. This was our time, something special for both of us, and Nate's ass couldn't get out of my head.

"Baby?" Tiffany turned in my arms and linked her arms around my neck. "Tell ya boo what's wrong, so I can make it better."

I tightened the comforter shielding us from the cold and said, "You are my boo," then asked, "Whatchu mean?" I had to deflect. Talking about my issues with Nate wasn't what I wanted to do with Tiffany.

She caressed my beard and tugged at it until our lips were close. "I feel it," she whispered, then pecked my lips. "Something's wrong with you."

Smirking, I questioned, "You feel it, huh?"

Shyly nodding, she wrapped her arms around my waist, then laid her head on my chest.

"Your heart is hurting, King. I feel it," she insisted. The only time Tiffany referred to me as King is when I was deep in her guts, on some freaky ass, soul-mating, spiritual shit.

Biting into my bottom lip, I contemplated what to say as I lifted her chin so that our eyes locked.

"This is why I'm in love witcho ass," I stated. Her face softened into an expression of complete love and joy as her eyes watered. "It's the simple shit, Princess. From the first time you walked past me like I wasn't shit, I've been in love with you."

Although she teared up, she laughed at my confession.

"Dead ass." I chuckled. "I was like, how this woman gon' just walk by me and not speak? You saw me starin' atcho ass. Lowkey you made a nigga shy as fuck."

She smacked her teeth. "Kingston? Shy? Nah, that doesn't even go in the same sentence."

"You make me feel a lot of shit, Tiffany." Gazing into her eyes, I prayed that she could tell that my feelings were genuine.

"You got me watchin' sunsets and rushin' home after work just to share bubble baths and massages. The way you love on my granny... There's not a place in my soul where you don't exist."

Tiffany blinked back tears and sniffled but held my gaze. Sighing, I knew she wanted me to let her inside my head. The trust and loyalty spilling from her eyes wouldn't let me deny her.

"Shit went sideways with my pops. Basically, he thinks I'm allowing him to suffer in prison when I have the means to get him out."

Her eyebrows snapped together. "How is that even possible?"

"It isn't," I answered. "Not if I want to maintain the person that I am and the character I possess."

Mulling over what I said, she sighed. "Your father wants you to engage in something illegal, just to get him out of prison?"

Glancing towards the now darkened sky, I couldn't take the pity filling her beautiful eyes. That's the last thing I wanted her to feel for me.

"My mother taught me to stand on loyalty, and by no means should I ever turn my back on the people I love. To hear someone I love call me less of a man because he feels like I turned my back on him... I would do anything for my pops. But..." I shook my head and let my words trail off.

Tiffany's fingers smoothed over the taut set of my lips, relaxing them. As I looked to the heavens for answers, she stroked my scruffy jaw.

"You're amazing," she whispered.

Swallowing the clog in my throat, I struggled to get a hold of my emotions.

"Kingston Wells is strong as fuck from the inside out. You're an amazing grandson to a seventy-six-year-old woman that loves the hell outta you. Although your brother is hard-headed, the love you have for August refuses to let you give up on him. You travel miles to come see a man that you will forever call Dad even when he breaks your heart." She palmed my jaw and turned me to face her. "You're amazing, King."

"If you're tryna be Mrs. Wells—"

"Shut up!" She chortled and smacked me on my chest. "I'm tryna be serious," she chided.

"Me too, lil' baby," I responded.

A pretty smile graced her face as she sobered. "Like I said—you're amazing, Kingston."

Technically it was still early. However, as the kiss Tiffany and I shared intensified, my dick rose to the occasion. I swooped Tiffany off her feet and carried her out of the brisk nighttime air back into the warm interior of the house.

Inside the bedroom, I placed her on her feet. Seconds later, she was naked and crawling into the bed as I palmed my hardened dick. The marks I'd put on her ass and thighs a few nights ago still marred her skin. Shit, I needed to be gentler with my baby.

Tiffany laid on her back and let her knees fall open. "Come eat, baby," she beckoned.

Swiftly discarding my joggers and beater, I joined her on the bed. Her nectar called to me, sending my mouth straight to her wet sex. I barely had my first lick of her juices when her thighs started to shake.

"Oooohh!"

Her moans reached my ears, just as her delicious flavor registered in my brain. Eating Tiffany's pussy caused her just as much pleasure as it did me. The more I ate, the more I was ready to bust. I stuck my tongue in her tunnel, enjoying how she cried out in pleasure as her walls sucked at me. Growling, I propped her legs up until her feet rested on my shoulders, then locked her thighs in place with arms.

"Shiiitt!" she wailed when I rapidly flicked my tongue over her hardened nub. Beautifully, it peeked at me, begging me to wring her dry.

Clamping onto her soul, I moaned and sucked, making love to her stiff clit as she disintegrated underneath me. Her body shook uncontrollably as juice spilled from her. Hurriedly, I gave chase, lapping up every drop as if it was the key to my next breath. Flipping her over, I pulled her to her knees and blessed her sexy ass.

Reaching back, she fisted my dreads, sobbing into the pillows as I stuck two fingers into her tight pussy and sucked on her untouched hole.

"I want this, baby," I crooned. I'd never went this far with Tiffany. She asked about my piercings, why I had them. I explained to her that I liked freaky shit. I loved when she bit on my nipples and how she'd play with them while giving me head.

"You trust me, Princess?"

"I trust you," she half-cried, half-moaned as she came around my fingers.

As I sucked her juices off, I leaned over to the nightstand for the lube I used whenever I needed to get one off. Popping the cap back, I squeezed enough on her puckered hole, then added a little on my mans.

Tiffany, still high off her last nut, pushed her ass back, begging for me. Chucking the tube to the side, I eased up behind her and had to still myself from the look on her face as she glanced over her shoulder.

Her lips were swollen from my kisses, and tears tracked her cheeks. All that glorious hair lay strewn all over her face and head. She nibbled at her bottom lip, with a slight smirk on her face. This damn woman…

As I slowly worked my way into her tight hole, sweat dripped from my skin. Tiffany reached back to palm her ass cheeks, separating them as she begged me to take her.

I pushed past the tightness keeping me out and gripped her hips to steady myself.

"Ahhh!" the slight yelp mixed with moan slipped from her lips as her eyes rolled.

Lowering us to the bed, I held her under her hips with one arm. Reaching up, I grabbed a fist full of her hair and pulled her head back, giving me access to her neck as I sunk deeper. This was her first time, so I had to go easy.

I groaned into her ear. "I'ma fuck you good and slow, baby."

"Whatever part of me you want, you can have," she sexily moaned.

See. Simple shit.

The minute I felt her body relax, I supported my weight with one hand planted on the mattress, while the other sought out her tunnel, dipping back into it.

"King!"

I fingered her and thrummed on the hardness of her clit to the time of my strokes. Slowly, I pushed in and out of her, grunting from the sheer pleasure I felt.

"Kinngg! I'm cummin'!"

I moved my fingers quickly as her walls clamped around my

digits. Using my thumb as if it were my tongue, a fondled her nub until she was squirting around me.

"Tiff! Fuck, baby!" Snatching my fingers out, I stuck them back into my mouth as my hips quickly dipped, swiveled, and moved. I'ain just fuck my shawty while I was in it. I was nasty enough to fuck her crazy, but sweet enough to make love to every inch of her.

Fuck! My nut was right there. "Daddy wanted to be gentle on this ass, baby," I insisted, but my dick had a mind of his own as my hips sped up.

"Uhnnn! Uhnnn!"

Tiffany's moaning had every vein in my dick and neck standing to attention. On a silent scream she clawed at the sheets as her body shook, signaling she'd had another orgasm.

"Argghh!" Two strokes later, I nutted so good inside of Tiffany that I collapsed on her back and didn't move until my heart slowed and my breathing regulated.

The next evening, I took Tiffany to Stone Mountain Park, talked her through the Summit Skyride which took us to the top of the mountain, then enjoyed the look on her face as she watched the sun cast beautiful colors over Atlanta as it set. Tears streamed down her cheeks, which I kissed away.

"You're amazing, Kingston Wells," she uttered against my lips.

"I love you," I told her, meaning every letter that made up the three words.

Chapter Twenty

TIFFANY

"Don't bring that cocky shit up in my house," Grey warned Kingston as soon as he opened the door for us.

"Grey, don't start," I grumbled, pushing past him to go inside. Like I knew it would, the house smelled divine.

“I’on get a damn hug or anything,” Grey complained while my attention was on my mom, dad, and sisters as I hurried to hug them.

"You must be Kingston? Greyson, and this is my better half, Valentina," my dad said, offering his hand to Kingston.

"Yes sir. It's good to finally meet you," Kingston spoke and shook my dad's hand.

"As long as you're treating my baby girl right, I have nothin’ bad to say," my dad commented, surprising me.

"Just like I told ya sons, she's safe with me."

"Aww," my mama chimed in and hugged Kingston before moving to embrace Granny, who looked on amused.

"The hell?" Blu came out of the kitchen, Steel in his arms as he addressed our dad.

"You're actin' too cool, Pops," Blu said.

"I agree," Grey added.

"Do y'all think we can make it through dinner without the three of you fighting?" I questioned Kingston, Grey, and Blu. How was it my dad could be okay with Kingston, yet his sons were acting like complete idiots?

"I'm good, baby," Kingston responded. The cocky smirk he wore told me that he enjoyed this little back and forth.

"They'll behave," Jacoba came into the living room and declared. She glared at her husband first, then coolly glanced at Grey.

"Isn't that right, fellas?" Gianna sounded from the kitchen.

Grey and Blu grumbled while the rest of us chuckled.

Aside from that little hiccup, Thanksgiving went off without a hitch. As Granny prayed over dinner, we all held hands and listened to every word she prayed. There wasn't a dry eye by the time she was done. During dinner, I sat between her and Kingston, enjoying them laughing and vibing so freely. Mama was back to clinging to Granny who soaked it all up.

The smile on Kingston's face made my year. August not being here could've spoiled his day, but Kingston didn't allow it to. Just as parents sometimes have a hard time severing the umbilical cord from their children, such was the situation with Kingston and August. The minute August said he was staying home instead of coming to dinner, the look on Kingston's face had been full of disappointment. Yet, Kingston said nothing and swallowed whatever feelings he felt.

Then, there was Kingston's dad. Atlanta had been a joyous affair after he shook off the sadness surrounding their visit. Remembering how heartbroken he was, I reached over and smoothed my hand over his handsome face, thankful to see him having a good time. He grinned, clutched my hand, and brought it to his lips. Our love for each other showed in our locked gazes.

Once again, Grey and Blu loosened up when they realized Kingston wasn't going anywhere. My man made that very clear when he referred to me as Mrs. Wells, shocking everyone at the dinner table.

That's how our night capped off, with Kingston dodging verbal jabs from my brothers, while the women in my circle gushed over how sweet and unbothered my boo behaved despite being jeered. Kingston was for sure embedded in my heart—deeply embedded. That night we were awaken out of our sleep by Kingston's ringing phone. His heart thumped against my cheek when he saw the number on the screen.

Frantic, he answered.

"King, this is Sergeant Nichols."

"Your father was involved in an altercation and has been transported to the hospital for treatment," he answered.

"Shit!" Kingston swore, scaring me.

"I can't give you the details yet, but he was stable at the time of transport. He'll be under police supervision while in the hospital, but I've notified the staff that you're able to visit him." The warden dropped which hospital Kingston's dad was at, then offered his prayers for Nate.

Kingston hung up the phone, swearing repeatedly as I rubbed his chest.

Harshly sighing, he relaxed enough to say, "When we get home from the party, I'm gonna head to see my dad."

"Baby, you don't need to go to the party with me," I said, assuring him that it was okay for him to go handle his business.

"Nah, I said I was gon' be by ya side and I meant that. I'll call the hospital and make sure he's good until I get there." Nodding, I listened to him make the phone call and confirm that his dad was stable and resting.

Kingston laid back down; the weight of the world was on his shoulders. I knew he was reflecting on the conversation he and Nate had the other day. Guilt could try and eat at my man. As he fitfully but slowly drifted back to sleep, I laid my hand on his chest and prayed for him, Nate, and most definitely August. He wouldn't take the news well.

This funky ass party for Miss Aldridge wasn't something I looked forward to until my eyes fell on the dress Kingston surprised me with. The dress fit me like a glove and made me stand out amongst the rest of the partygoers. Well, Kingston and I stood out as we not only matched, but his gangsta, rough-neck vibes ruffled a few feathers. Many in attendance knew him and spoke in passing.

He and Chris steered clear of each other the entire night, which was smart on Chris' part. Every time he walked by our table, Kingston eyed him until he was no longer in our viewpoint. I was thoroughly happy when Miss Aldridge finally made her appearance and stood at the podium to offer her thanks and gratitude for everyone's support. She was a true diva, showing up to her own party an hour and a half late. As her eyes swept the dining hall, they zeroed in on me and Kingston. Briefly, she faltered over her words.

An uneasy feeling settled into the pit of my stomach as her gaze bounced back and forth between us. Clearing her throat, she continued with her speech as if I imagined what just happened.

"'Sup?" Kingston spoke into his earpiece. "Has he made any changes? Cool. Aight, be ready to head out when I get there."

"Everything good?"

Kingston kissed my lips and nodded. "I'll feel better when I see him."

I completely understood.

The party was almost over and although Kingston and I shared a drink and a dance, we were both waiting for Miss Aldridge to finish her speech so that they could wrap up this shindig. I did my due diligence by showing up, and it was admittedly a good time with Kingston.

Ten minutes later, he and I were having one last drink before leaving, when the guest of the evening slinked to our table and sat her ass across from us. Miss Aldridge looked beautiful this evening just as she always did. Her red designer gown left nothing to the imagination yet was still classy. The look on her face, however, told me that this night wasn't about to end too well.

"It's funny seeing you here, all cozied up." Her eyes smoothly swept over me, then to Kingston, and the way he had me nestled to his side.

He lightly chuckled and ignored her as he pecked my ear. I side-eyed him though. Pensacola wasn't an overly large city so I was bound to run into one of his conquests. That wasn't my issue. My issue was that Miss Aldridge was too comfortable being in our face.

"Just a little while ago you were in my bed, and here you are." She snickered. "If the help is what you're attracted to, why didn't you just say that? I wouldn't have lowered my standards for you."

My eyebrows snapped together. *The help?*

At work, I did my best to control my temper with this bird. But we were off the clock, and she was definitely asking for these hands to teach her uppity ass a lesson.

“Miss Aldridge,” I warned, “we’re not in the office.”

Kingston shushed me, causing my eyes to snap in his direction.

"Why you ‘bout to sit here and argue wit' a female that wishes she was sittin' where you are right now? Don't ever come off ya throne to address any female that can’t even shine the shoes I put on ya sexy ass feet. You know how much I love ya feet, right?"

Nodding, my face flamed from both shame and arousal.

He dropped a lingering kiss on my lips. "That petty shit is beneath you, Princess.”

Victoria chuckled. "Filling her head with bullshit."

"I fill her head with a lot of things and they definitely ain't bullshit." Kingston smirked at me, his meaning registering. He turned to Miss Aldridge. "You remember how these inches feel, right?"

Her eyes became saucers and her nose flared.

He lightly chuckled. "Yeah, I thought so.”

"Fuck you!" she hissed, drawing the attention of the couple sitting next to us.

I laughed out of anger, wanting to tag this heifer.

"Ask my lady for permission," Kingston continued.

"And that's heavy on the *hell no*," I added, glaring at her disgusted expression.

She fumed. "You're sitting there all smug now, but this nigga will do you just how he's done every other bitch. You think I was the only one he was fucking before you? You're sadly mistaken. I'd advise you to make him wear protection if I were you. There's no telling what he's paid for."

Anger sliced through me like a steak knife.

"Night, Vicki," Kingston calmly barked.

She slinked away just as she came, this time laughing.

I eyed Kingston again. "What is she talking about?"

"Nothin', baby," he answered, running his fingers down my face. I'd never questioned Kingston until now. I didn't like what 'Vicki' implied.

"Should I be worried?" I asked, taking my fingers from his because he wasn't about to have me looking stupid.

He mugged me. "Really?"

"Yes, really!" I snapped.

He bit into his lip, clearly angry but I didn't care.

Sighing, I broke away from his side. "I'm ready to go." I was over the night and him. No matter if it came from Vicki's lips, there was something to what she said, and the implication made my stomach turn.

Kingston reached for my hand, which I reluctantly let him have. I waved goodbye to everyone and smiled like everything was cool. I ignored Vicki's victorious and haughty smile as we exited the dining hall.

As soon as we were in the valet area, I snatched my hand away.

"Lil' baby—"

"Don't say shit to me," I interjected. "You just made me look like a complete fool."

"That bitch is gettin' exactly what she wants and that's you bein' mad as fuck for no reason."

“She’s a bitch for callin’ you out?” I countered, glaring at him. Although, I didn’t care one bit for *Vicki*, niggas always tried to dog females that called them on their shit. I wasn’t about to let Kingston do that in order to deflect from the truth. Thankfully, valet pulled the car up.

"Just take me home. I'm done for the night."

"Done with who?" he asked, bringing his body close to mine.

Ignoring him, I went to open the door only for him to gently snatch me back so that he could do it. Aggravated, I plopped into the seat. He closed the door and stalked to the driver's side, rubbing his beard as he glared at me through the front windshield. Rolling my eyes away from him, I ignored him when he slid into the driver's seat and slammed the door.

"You trippin'," he stated while driving off from the curve.

"Yep," I confirmed. "Now take me home like I asked. To my house,” I clarified.

The rest of the drive was quiet. No music or anything played as I sat here mulling over what the hell Vicki said. Kingston and I hadn't used protection at all since we’d been intimate. If he was out here fucking other bitches, paying for it, what the hell was he doing with me? Angry tears blurred my vision but I hurriedly blinked them back.

Why cry? I'd freely given myself to him. He’d done things to my body and mind that I could never take back. There wasn't any going back.

Kingston pulled into my driveway with me getting out before the car stopped good.

"Tiffany!" he barked, coming up behind me as I rushed to the front door. I had to get inside before I could no longer hold the tears at bay.

"Please go home, Kingston." I fumbled with the key, trying to unlock the door then finally got it open. Whirling on him, I asked him point blank, "Was she lying?"

He glanced away, a hollow chuckle dripping from his lips. That's all I needed to slam the door in his face. It felt like forever that I stood by the door crying until his car's pipes faded in the distance.

My phone sounded, prompting me to quickly suck up this crybaby shit. It was Gianna.

"Hey, boo!" Gianna sounded innocent enough, but I knew Grey put her up to calling me. Whenever there was motion at my front and back doors, or the windows, he'd get a notification. I wondered if he watched me and Kingston's little spat.

"Hey, sis!" I tried to sound as cheery as she did, however, my voice hitched.

"Tiff." She sighed, causing me to break down. "I'm on my way."

Gianna and Jacoba showed up about thirty minutes later. Gianna cradled Ash in her arms, who was fast asleep.

"How much finessing did it take to make Grey and Blu chill?"

"A lot." Jacoba laughed and took me into her arms.

"Tell us what's up," Gianna said as we got comfortable on the sofa.

Shaking my head, I swiped at the stubborn tear clinging to my lower lashes. "I'on even know what happened. One minute we were happy, and the next... Is it naïve to hope for a man that's loyal?"

Gianna pushed my hair back behind my ear, and replied, "Let's start with why you think Kingston isn't loyal?"

Hunching my shoulders, I gave them the details about what happened at the party. Both were upset but not at Kingston.

"Her entire goal was to knock you off the seat of happiness. She's seen you glowing and being showered with gifts which I'm sure made her feel some type of way. You, yourself, profess to not want female friends because of the cattiness and jealousy."

"Take it from someone who knows," Jacoba added. "Dealing with females is hard, especially when they're after your man. So what he *used to* fuck her. Same goes with whatever bullshit she's talking about him paying for it. Men do that shit all the time, Tiff."

Balling my face up, I winced. "I'm sure they do, but I'm not dealing with a man that's paying for pussy."

"*Paid*, boo, past tense," Gianna corrected.

"Right," Jacoba seconded.

"Why are y'all taking his side? I'm the one that's a mess right now."

"We're taking logic's side," Jacoba said. "Logic says that this man has been all over you since the day he snatched you out of the club."

"Exactly," Gianna chimed in. "Logic says that this man *has* to feel some type of way about you to come see me about this bomb ass dress you have on. And you already know he paid me well for my time. Speaking of time, when in the hell does he have time to cheat on you when y'all are damn near glued at the hip?"

Shocked, I took extra pride in the garment I wore. Kingston really did show out with this one. I hated that Gianna and Jacoba made sense. Still, I wasn't completely sold.

"They're sneaky as fuck, so there's no telling. Especially

when he's in Georgia. He goes up there to see his dad every month."

Shit! Instant sadness overshadowed my hurt when I remembered Kingston's father was in the hospital. Instead of me being by his side to walk him through his hurt, I was over here wallowing in mine. Gianna and Jacoba stayed with me until they were sure I was good. I got my tears out and prepared myself for bed before they left.

As I slid under the covers, I recalled everything that Kingston and I did together and how close we were. I imagined him wrapping his arms around me and rocking me to sleep. Something pulled at my heartstrings for me to call him just to see if he'd gotten on the road yet, but I refrained.

Why did this shit hurt like Kingston and I had been together for years instead of two months? Well, since he considered our first time meeting as us becoming friends, he and I had known each other for a little longer. Sighing, I thought if Kingston truly loved me, then the truth would present itself. Until then, I cried myself to sleep while whispering prayers for Kingston, August, and Granny.

When I woke up the next morning, I called my gynecologist's office. She was available on Saturdays for emergency appointments only. Feigning vaginal pain, I requested and received an appointment. Really, I couldn't sleep because I had dreams about shit that scared me to my soul. Gianna and Jacoba made everything seem fine with Kingston's sexual lifestyle, but Vicki's words played heavily on my mind. I had to get myself checked in order to ease the fear within me.

I left out of the doctor's office feeling sicker than I did when I went in. What felt like ten tubes of blood, and one confirmed pregnancy later, I was having the worst weekend ever.

Chapter Twenty-One

KINGSTON

My pops was stabbed twice in his abdomen. Per the doctor's report, other than blood loss, Nate came away without losing any of his organs or his life. The shank nicked his colon, requiring emergency surgery and two blood transfusions to get him stable. Thank God the warden and I were cool, or else, I wouldn't have been able to see my dad. Reflecting on our last conversation, I contemplated toeing the line of everything I believed in just to free Nate.

Being in law enforcement made me see the good and bad side of the law. There was just as much corruption as there was good. Those who wore a badge and used it for negative gain disgusted me. It was a bit critical, but I held those who literally had the power in their hands to a higher level of accountability. I wore my badge with pride because at the end of the day, I stood on it.

However, I didn't take into account the way I'd feel when standing by my pops' bedside, watching him rest while his wrists were cuffed to the gurney's rails. Shit tugged at my heart. August low-key glared at me from across the gurney, most likely blaming me for this shit. Hell, I just felt like the world was on my shoulders. Not being able to call my woman or to have her here with me fucked me up even more.

Last night, I wanted to kick Tiffany's door off the fucking hinges. She slammed that shit in my face like I wasn't shit to her. What hurt more was her judging me without hearing my side. Tressa, the CO bitch from the prison, was who Vicki referred to me fucking. I never fucked either of them raw and made sure I had yearly checks just in case some shit fell through. I was responsible at all costs because I didn't put anything past these females outchea.

Tiffany was different though. Her innocence captured me and held me captive in a way I couldn't explain. All I knew is that I wanted to be with her and give her everything I could offer a woman.

ME:

I tried calling you twice, baby. You gon' pick up?

It fucked me up that she hadn't responded to my message that I sent over an hour ago. Coupled with the fact that she was ignoring my phone calls, I was increasingly aggravated as the day passed. August and I didn't leave the hospital until visitation was over. Pops was in and out, not really able to talk to us. At least he knew that we were there for him.

ME:

I need you to call me, shawty.

Exhausted and pissed off, I placed my phone on the nightstand next to my nine and wallet. I hadn't slept since Thursday night. My body was sore from the ride and my eyes burned from frustration. Tiffany knew damn well my pops was in the hospital. A nagging voice told me *fuck her* for not caring about the situation I was in, but my heart wouldn't let me curse her for shit. Not even as I called her several more times and messaged her like I hadn't already.

Stretching over the bed, I rubbed my eyes and fought sleep. My stomach grumbled in protest as I shouldn't have been lying down but eating.

"I'm goin' to grab dinner," August came to my door and said, reading my mind.

"Aight," I answered.

He lingered in the doorway, obviously wanting something.

"'Sup?" I asked.

"You and ol' girl fell out?"

"Tiffany, August," I corrected.

"You and *Tiffany* fell out?" he questioned.

"We're straight," I lied. Hell, at this point I wasn't sure about shit with her.

"Well, you walkin' 'round this bitch like you heartbroken or some shit." He snickered.

My eyebrows dipped. "Bruh, this shit ain't funny, aight."

August hunched his shoulders. "You always got advice for me when I fuck shit up. Everything is always perfect in King's world. I guess seein' you down an' out is strange."

Grumbling, I replied, "You act like you got some shit on ya chest. What's good?"

He'd been acting funny all day. If he had something to say he needed to be man enough and say it.

August clucked his teeth. "Ain't nothin' I say gon' change shit, so I'll chill."

He went to walk off when I called his name. "Look, bruh—"

"Nah, you look, King. Ya fuckin' pops is in the hospital battlin' some real-life shit, while you sittin' in here mopin' over *Tiffany*. I'on get you, dawg."

August couldn't possibly understand what falling in love was like. He had a good woman in Faith yet chose to not give a fuck about her or his child.

"I wouldn't expect for you to know how I feel about either situation, August."

He chortled. "See," he pointed out, "this is why I don't say shit. You still gon' do King and not give a fuck."

This time when he walked away, I let him. His perception of me not giving a fuck about our pops only fueled me to want to make things right. A few phone calls, and I could be the man my pops wanted me to be. Yawning, I closed my eyes and envisioned Tiffany lying next to me. I must have drifted off because her touch felt too real. The heat of her pussy grinding against my deck had me moaning and reaching for her hips. Said hips were thicker than I remembered but only made me smile.

Ring!

Damn, that shit would have to wait. I missed my baby so much that I needed to feel the inside of her before I did anything else.

"Damn, baby," I groaned when her nails bit into the flesh of my bare chest.

"Mmm..." The moan sounded nothing like Tiffany's, prompting my eyes to pop open.

"Ahh!" Tressa screamed as I pushed her off of me and reached for my heat.

"The fuck!" I bellowed, angry that she was in my shit.

"King!" she shouted frantically. Her half-naked ass jiggled as she cowered in the corner of my room with her hands over her head.

"The fuck you doin' in here?" I demanded to know. Tressa and I had an understanding, and my house wasn't a part of that shit. Snatching my phone up, I saw no missed calls, so I clicked on my recent calls. When Tiffany's name shown on the screen as having called me a couple of minutes ago, I growled.

Stalking over to Tressa, I held the gun to her head as I dialed Tiffany. "Answer me!" I ordered, causing her to scream louder.

"August let me in!" she shrieked in fear.

"And you thought it was okay to bring ya ass to where I rest my muhfuckin' head?" Tiffany's phone went to voicemail. I dialed her again as I dug the barrel of the gun into Tressa's temple. Irate as Tiffany's phone quickly went to voicemail without ringing, I snatched Tressa up by her hair. "You answered my fuckin' phone! Bitch, I should cave ya shit back!"

"King!" August snatched me back, shock written all over his face. "The hell is goin' on? Fuck is you doin'?"

"Why you let her ass in here?" I barked, angry at him for causing this shit.

"How the fuck was I supposed to know she ain't welcome here, nigga? I thought you'd be cool with it." August's attempt at defending himself only further pissed me off.

"Get the fuck outta here!" I barked to a wide-eyed Tressa who beat a hasty retreat. She left behind the smell of her perfume that didn't smell near as good as Tiffany's natural scent.

"Mane, King, that was reckless as hell," August lamented. "You *that* fuckin' gone over ol' girl that you're 'bout to body a bitch? The fuck has gotten into you?"

Elbowing past August, I rushed to the front door to make sure Tressa's ass was gone.

"King!" August called behind me.

"Shut the fuck up! When you gon' grow the fuck up, nigga? Huh? You knew damn well not to let that bitch in here!" I was so angry I couldn't think straight. Stalking back to my room, I snatched my phone up to try Tiffany again.

"Fuck!" I snarled when it went straight to voicemail again.

"Kingston." Granny's soft voice broke through the haze of anger I was under. She'd made the trip with us because I refused to leave her home by herself the entire weekend.

"Calm down, Son," she said, her voice straining with concern as she beheld the gun in my hand. Damn, I forgot to put it up. I had yet to tell Granny what took place with Tiffany, but I'm sure she knew something was up. Tiffany not being by my side gave it away.

"I'm sorry, Granny," I apologized, hugged her, then ushered her back to her room. She barely came to Atlanta but this house was just as much hers as it was mine.

"You want me to pray witchu?" she asked.

Chuckling, I said, "I'm good, Granny. Just had a lil' issue I had to handle."

"Sounded like a big issue to me," she replied.

Sighing, I kissed her forehead, and told her everything was fine. "Go back to bed."

Once she was settled, I closed the door and backtracked to my room where I placed the gun back on the nightstand. The light blinking on my cellphone sent my heart racing, hoping it was a call or message from Tiffany.

JARED:

Hope all is well with Pops. Hmu if you need me.

Deflated, I sent him a message back.

ME:

He's stable. I'ma be here until they discharge him.

Just as I sent the message, another one came through. A smile broke my face.

MRS. WELLS:

I pray your dad makes a full recovery.

That's it? I appreciated her prayers but no 'I love you' behind the period had me feeling some type of way. Foregoing a text message, I rang her phone just to hear her recorded voice telling me to leave a message.

"Princess, don't fuckin' do me like this, aight? A nigga dead ass need you right now. I need you… I need to hear ya voice and not this recorded shit, lil' mama." Frustration seeped from my words. "Call me, mane."

I hung up, then palmed my head in resignation. The part of me that felt dead as fuck—that was Tiffany's absence. Between my pops and my woman, I felt my life caving in on me. I'd been able to bear some tough times and face them without folding. Pressure was never an issue for me. Yet, I sat here lost, wondering if all my good was for naught. Because apparently, everybody wanted to see the dark side of Kingston.

When my pops finally woke up, his normal boisterous personality was nowhere in sight. He took one glance at me and August yet didn't address either of us. The silence August and I sat through for the days we spent by our pops' beside was deafening. Whenever we tried to engage him in conversation, he'd feign exhaustion and pretend to be sleep. The only people he seemed to have conversation for were the nurses and detectives who came to question him about the incident.

Listening to him recount what happened to him burned my soul. August got up and left the room halfway through Nate's statement, while I tried to digest the fact that my pops was living in an everyday hell. I wasn't shocked to know that Nate had a name for himself behind those walls. Nichols kept me abreast of my pop's moves whenever he could, and for the most part, my pops had been laying low. His abrasiveness rubbed off on the wrong jit who'd felt some type of way about it and decided that he and his homeboys would jump my pops since they couldn't take him head-up, one-on-one.

With any hope, the jits would be moved to a different area so that this shit wouldn't happen again. Sadly for them, they'd added more charges and years to their sentences over some bullshit. Four days passed before my pops was discharged from the hospital. He'd continue recovering in the prison's infirmary. This was the first time in twelve years that we'd been able to hug him—the feeling was foreign as hell and brought tears to August's eyes.

Ever since the shit went down with Tressa, August and I had

been casually trying to communicate again. He never apologized, but honestly, I didn't expect him to because he never did unless I made him. I was serious about him growing up and apologizing to someone of your own free will was a part of growth. I just hated that no matter how much I loved my brother, he was stubborn as fuck—just like the man we hugged for the first time in over a decade.

On the ride back to the house, I cut the radio off and said to August, "Regardless of how you feel, I love you and I love Pops. You'on get it now, but I swear I have ya best interest at heart, bruh. I want nothing but the best out of life for you. I'on wanna see you where Pops is or feel like I hear Mama cryin' 'cause her baby boy went astray. I'm doing all I can to help you make it in life, August. All I'm askin' you to do is help yaself, too."

For a minute, he said nothing, just gazed out of the window. Thinking he wasn't going to respond, I went to turn the volume back up when he stopped me.

"I hear you, aight? I've *been* hearin' you, King. Just 'cause I don't do shit ya way doesn't mean I'm not gettin' shit done. Have you noticed that I'ain been out in a minute? No homeboys or nothin', just tryna chill and get my fuckin' grades up."

"I have noticed," I confirmed. "I'm proud of you for that."

"So why you still on my fuckin' case then?" he asked.

Glancing his way, I caught the sadness in his eyes.

"You're right, mane," I conceded, although something I couldn't put a finger on weighed on me heavily. He was staying out of the streets and doing everything to bring his grades up, but not once did he mention Faith or the baby. Small victories mattered, so I shouldn't complain. Leaving things where they were for now, I turned the music back up.

My mind drifted to Tiffany, who's voice I hadn't heard in

days. I missed shawty so much that I stood on my balcony every evening, wondering if she was watching the sunset with me on her mind. Anger still simmered inside of me from her shutting me out. I sent her flowers today, hoping she'd send me a sweet thank you text like she always did. When no text came, I felt myself snapping. Tomorrow I'd be back home. Her ass was gon' talk to me one way or the other.

Chapter Twenty-Two

TIFFANY

The next evening...

Work had been hell today. Partly because I was nauseous as hell, and the other part because I was stuck looking at Vicki's ass who found it in her weird life to keep coming in my presence every five minutes. I no longer donned the chain Kingston bought me, and although I had a fresh vase of roses delivered to me today, I threw them in the trash. Kingston could do whatever he wanted but I wasn't taking his ass back. He shattered my heart in the worst way. Everything he'd said to me was bullshit and the weight of that was almost too heavy to bear.

While I held out hope that Vicki was somehow lying, the moment I heard that woman's voice moaning...it shattered everything within me. Instead of running to Gianna and Jacoba for a shoulder to cry on, I sucked it up and fought my way through the night and last few days. It was rough, but I'd finally made it a full day without breaking down.

Besides, I had to get it together. Now that I was growing a life inside of me, I had to think about the things I needed to get in order. Financially, I was set. As far as my future in law, I was definitely on the *never mind* side of the fence since finding out I was pregnant. Hell, I hated being a paralegal... Well, I hated it because of the man I worked for. Still, there wasn't a day that I found my work joyous, but otherwise tedious and overwhelming —and I wasn't even a damn lawyer yet!

Sighing, I realized most of my frustrations stemmed from having to tell Kingston that I was pregnant. Thankfully, my nerves had settled since all of my test results came back negative. In that sense, I thanked God that the first man I decided to sleep with didn't hurt me in that way.

The other night I'd been lonely and wanted to talk to him, which prompted me to call him. After leaving the doctor's office, I'd felt some type of way about him that entire afternoon and into the night. I missed him like crazy and needed him to tell me that us having this baby was going to be alright.

Knowing Kingston, he'd take pride in being a father; *that* I wasn't concerned about. What concerned me is us not being on good terms. People always say that babies can't change broken relationships. Then, you have those that believe the opposite. In my case, I didn't want to be with a man just because I was having his baby. Also in my case, Kingston...cheated on me. I'd never be able to forget it even if I did forgive him.

FAITH:

Hey, boo! Thank you for the dinner! It's really sweet of you *heart emoji*! I'm about to smash it!

Smiling at the message, I replied back.

ME:

You're welcome, boo! I know today was long and didn't want you to have to worry about cooking when you made it home. Relax and enjoy your night.

FAITH:

heart emoji Will do, and I appreciate you from the bottom of my heart.

Tears welled up in my eyes as I texted her back. Faith and I talked earlier, and I could hear the stress in her voice. She was becoming increasingly emotional as her pregnancy progressed. When she wasn't working, she was home alone unless Jericho visited, and she admitted to feeling lonely and afraid.

For over an hour, I talked her through her feelings, allowing her to vent how she needed to. She didn't reveal much, but enough for me to know that baby girl carried some heavy loads. I promised her that we'd spend more time together, which made her happy. Deciding that I could make her day a bit better, I had dinner delivered to her. This was something I know Kingston would've done for her.

The doorbell rang, breaking my thoughts. Pulling up my camera system, my heart lurched from seeing Kingston standing on the other side of the door. Laying eyes on him after not seeing him for the last few days caused my body to heat. I missed him so much but couldn't bring myself to cave to him. He'd finessed me right into a broken heart, and for that, I hated him. I felt so stupid. My eyes blurred because the one time I decided to fall in love, it was with a man that could break my entire soul.

The doorbell sounded again, followed by, "Princess, open the door."

Kingston's calm voice irritated me. He'd left several voicemails and text messages, all of which I ignored before blocking him. Since he had another woman I didn't understand why he felt the need to show up on my doorstep. If me ignoring him wasn't enough, I didn't know what was.

Seconds later, I heard the loudest bang, causing me to scream and cover my ears. My heart jumped in my throat when Kingston calmly strolled in my house like he hadn't just broken my damn door down! My house alarm shrieked, which didn't bother him. Hurriedly, I jumped from the couch to disable it, all the while glaring at him. Once I stopped the noise, Kingston was right behind me. His eyes were dark with anger. But I was angry, too. Just then my phone rang. It was Grey or Blu. They wouldn't stop calling until I answered.

"Get outta my house," I demanded, going for my phone that was on the end table.

Kingston snatched it out of my hand. "The fuck is wrong witchu?" he asked, cocking his head. He'd never looked at me like this before. The menacing stare, lip curl, and lines dotting his forehead told me that he fought to control his temper. He chucked my phone across the room.

"I said—"

"What the fuck is wrong witchu?" he interrupted.

"Kingston, you have only a small window before my brother shows up. I suggest you do what the fuck I said."

Kingston snatched me up, causing me to buck against his embrace.

"Getcho hands off me!" I punched him in his face, making him growl. He stalked to the kitchen where he deposited me on the kitchen island and held me in place as I tried to squirm from his grip. He grabbed both of my wrists and pinned them to the countertop. Angry tears slid down my face, pissing me off.

"I'ma ask you again," he said. "The fuck is wrong witchu?"

"You think I'm stupid, Kingston? I heard you..." The thought made me gag. "I heard you with that bitch. You're a liar and a piece of shit."

"Take that shit back," he snarled.

"I'ain takin' shit back!" I snapped back. "Get the fuck off of me." I started squirming again, only for him to tighten his grip.

"You ignored me. Blocked me. All for some shit you thought you heard."

"Don't try to stand here and play me, Kingston." Now he was making me angrier by thinking I was really that naive. "Is she who keeps you company while you're in Georgia? If I would've known about her, I never would've crossed the line with you. You made me believe all this bullshit." My voice broke as I choked back tears.

"I used to fuck her when I'd go to Georgia," he stated, infuriating me. "I haven't touched another woman since we've been together."

I laughed in his face. "You're a liar, and I don't believe you. I *heard* y'all."

Clasping my wrists in one of his hands he used the other to produce his phone. He scrolled through his contacts before pressing a number. He clicked the speaker just as a woman's sultry voice split the line. She was the same chick. My stomach rolled as I fought against his grip.

"Aye, I need some services," Kingston stated, causing me to recoil. Yet another thing that was indeed true. He *paid* this woman to sleep with her!

She chuckled. "Oh really, King? I tried to give you some services the other night. I thought you were kidding when you said you had a woman. I apologize for that, however, don't tell me it ended that quickly."

Blinking at the phone, I registered what she'd said.

"You gon' meet me or nah?"

"At the room? I'm never showing up to your house again. Putting a gun to a lady's head is very disrespectful, King. You better be glad I love you."

Hearing her tell my man she loved him, pricked my nerves.

"Yeah the room," Kingston confirmed.

"Be there shortly," she replied and hung up.

"And you have her number stored in your phone which means you intend to use it."

He blocked then deleted her number.

"Kingston, none of that is gon' make me take you back."

"Oh, we ain't together anymore?" He was back to pinning my hands to the counter.

"No we aren't. I'm done with you, and I want you to leave."

This nigga chuckled crazily. His head dipped to my neck, as he inhaled my scent. I then felt his lips.

"Don't!" I warned even as my body begged for it.

He kissed his way up my neck, then my cheek, and temple. I hated how my body melted, but I still fought.

"When I told you that you could trust me, I meant that shit. When it comes to me and you it ain't no games. The first time I ate ya pussy, and you gave me ya innocence, I promised to protect what was mine. That means protecting what's yours. I'm yours, Princess Sapphire Tiffany Summers."

By the time his lips touched mine, I was a puddle of tears. He unlocked my hands, and by second nature they smoothed up his chest as I draped my arms over his shoulders. Unable to let this kiss last, I nudged him back. He wasn't about to finesse me again.

Swiping my tears, I said, "Please leave."

Back in my face, he countered, "I'm not."

"Kingston, leave!" I demanded.

"I'm not!" he replied calmly yet firmly, locking his hands on either side of me.

"Take back what you said about me," he said.

"You just kicked my door in," I rebutted. "And refusing to leave is making shit worse."

"You wouldn't answer me, so what was I supposed to do? Take it back."

Screeching tires had me groaning. "Grey just pulled up."

He mugged me. "I'on give a fuck. Take that shit back!"

The words fell from his lips just as Grey barked my name. He came barreling into the kitchen with his gun drawn, but then quickly sat it on the table and charged at Kingston. They collided and hit the refrigerator so hard that it bucked and almost toppled over.

"Guys!" I fussed, jumping from the counter.

"Bitch ass nigga!" Grey growled as he punched Kingston in his face.

"Grey, stop!" I cried. He and Kingston swung on each other, each connecting as they struggled through the kitchen and into the dining room. As if things couldn't get any worse my phone rang again. I knew it was Blu. He was on his way here, too.

Shit!

Rushing to get my phone as glass shattered, and what sounded like the walls being busted open, I quickly answered Blu's call.

"Blu—"

"The fuck is goin' on?" he interjected.

"They're fighting," I stated, panicked because neither of them were slowing up.

"I'ma kill that nigga!" Blu growled. I heard his engine sound, which meant he was already enroute.

"No!" I begged Blu, but it was no use. He hung up on me.

"Grey! King!" I implored. "Please stop!" I screamed.

Kingston pushed Grey off of him, giving me enough space to get between them. I stood with my back to Grey, doing what I could to hold my brother back.

Kingston's expression was one of hurt as he peered at me with his head cocked.

"So, you turnin' ya back on me, Princess? Over some bullshit?" he questioned. The cut above his eye did nothing to take away from how handsome he was. This Kingston standing before me was anything but the loving man I knew. Quite frankly, he looked insane with his dreads all over his head, and his teeth bared like he was ready to attack.

"We're over, Kingston. I meant that." It broke my heart to say it, but there was no going back. "Please leave."

He stared at me for a minute as his beautiful eyes seemed to tear up. But then, he glared at Grey who wanted another piece. Kingston chuckled, turned on his feet, and headed for the doorway. My heart broke even more with every step he took.

I turned into Grey's arms and cried. All this time he'd been trying to protect me from this very feeling—heartbreak. Minutes after Kinston sped out of my yard, Blu's truck pulled in on two wheels. He saw me crying and made a U-turn.

"Blu," I called to his back. "Don't." I rushed to his side, allowing him to embrace me as I cried some more.

No matter how heartbroken I was, Kingston had better be glad that I still loved him. Or else my brothers would be out for blood and wouldn't stop until they ended him.

Two weeks later...

Sunsets weren't the same without Kingston. Every evening I watched them alone, reflecting on the day he took me on top of the mountain just to enjoy what I loved most about my days.

Things in my life seemed to go back to times before he and I met. It was all work, per usual, and tutoring. Dorian was finally at the end of the first semester, and with hope, he'd pass his exams with flying colors.

I was back to being in Gianna's shop when I had the time. Being the good sister-in-law she was, she didn't throw anything in my face when it came to Kingston and Grey. The two of them fighting was something I never wanted to witness again. I'd never seen either of them so angry.

Over the last week, morning sickness had started to kick in full throttle. I kept ginger ale and crackers by my side like my nine and prayed no one noticed. Until I told Kingston, no one could know. Not even my family. I hated keeping it from them, but I had to. This was something I needed to handle on my own without them getting involved.

As promised, I spent more time with Faith. She didn't understand how being around her brought so much uplifting energy to me. Faith was naturally a beautifully spirited person, and I swear it was contagious.

"You good over there?"

I glanced up at Granny's question, smiled, and nodded. I'd been coming by for a week now. Just like I missed Kingston, I missed Granny after not being around her. I couldn't make her pay for Kingston's mistakes. I was glad I listened and did what my heart told me to do. Granny had accepted me with tears and open arms.

What I loved about this sweet, old woman—she never once tried prying information out of me. I'd just sit in the garden with her and tend to the plants. Occasionally, she'd check on me to make sure I was okay. If you asked me, a part of me wondered if she knew I was pregnant. If so, she didn't give anything away.

I peered at the sky and sighed. I hated that my time with her was relegated to an hour.

"Alright, Granny, let's get you back inside."

Kingston would be getting off soon, and I had to be gone before then. Being in the house, smelling his scent, being in familiar territory was a chore—one that chipped at my already broken heart. Granny didn't fuss. I helped her to her feet, dusted her pants off, causing her to giggle, then escorted her into the house and to her room.

"I'll be here until you're out of the bathroom," I assured her. She tsked, waved her hand, and shooed me off. Laughing, I went to sit in the living room until she was done.

About ten minutes later, I heard the sound of unmistakable pipes. Heart stuttering I rushed to the bay window in the dining room to make sure it wasn't Kingston.

"Shit!" I swore, then hurried to grab my purse so that I could leave. He wasn't due home for another hour. I had his and

August's schedules down pat. Much to Chris' dismay, I'd began leaving work earlier just so that I could come spend time with Granny.

Kingston was coming up the walkway when I left out of the front door with my head down. He'd already seen my car, so he knew I was here. Still, I tried to ignore him and go straight to my car.

"Princess."

His deep voice slowed my hasty departure. Then, I felt his hand reach out and land on my stomach.

I gasped. *Did he know?*

"Please, talk to me," he implored.

Tears stung my eyes as he tugged me to his body. While I rejected his embrace, he held and rocked me until my body complied. Turning my face into his chest, I inhaled his familiar scent. Seeing our chain still around his neck made me weak. His lips touched my neck as he squeezed me tighter and lifted me until my feet dangled.

"I miss you," he gruffly mumbled between kisses that he placed all over my neck, face, and lips.

Fighting tears, I pushed him off of me.

"Tiff," he called, holding onto my hand as I tried to walk away. "You know me, baby girl. Regardless of anything... You know me. In ya heart you know I'ain fuck up, my baby. You're fightin' because you're scared, and you need a reason to walk away from me."

Tears finally escaped, sailing down my face. He moved to bring me back in his arms, but I pulled away. Not looking back, I power walked to my car, got in, and within seconds was out of the driveway. Wishing I could run back to Kingston, I broke down.

Chapter Twenty-Three

KINGSTON

My heart sank when she pulled away from me, causing me to feel helpless as hell. I sat on the porch steps watching her drive away, wanting to chase after her. I swear she felt how bad I was hurting and didn't give a damn. She didn't want to hear me out, further frustrating me. With Tiffany, it's like the blow to my soul was deathly. The screen door creaked open, and Granny stuck her head out. When she saw me sitting here, she shuffled to my side. Chuckling, I helped her sit beside me.

"Finally caught her, huh?" she quipped. Actually, I knew since the first day Tiffany came by that she was here. A nigga could barely function at work while spending my time buried in my phone watching her work in Granny's garden. A little weird, but if that's how I was able to see her beautiful face and see her gorgeous smile, then so be it.

"How am I supposed to get her back?" I asked Granny.

"Depends on what you did, sweetheart."

"What if I didn't do anything?" Reluctantly, I explained what happened with Tressa and how everything was just a huge misunderstanding. "From Tiffany's standpoint, I understand why it could seem like I'm lyin', but I've never lied to her. I would never lie to her."

Granny sighed and took my hands into hers. "Lord," she started, bringing a smile to my face, "bring Tiffany back to the man that loves her. Also, Lord, help Kingston not to mess it up this time. Amen."

"Amen," I agreed around a chuckle.

"That's the only way to fix it—a lot of prayer. Tiffany is a sweet woman, but very much independent and head strong. She's loyal but not a pushover." Granny grinned. "People can look at her and think she's soft as cotton candy, but like me, she's fiercely strong and doesn't take any crap. She's fiercely strong, King, and you can do nothing but respect that. Even if it's hinderin' you from gettin' her back."

I conceded with a nod. Those were wonderful and accurate assessments of Tiffany and characteristics that I loved about her.

"Now be patient. She's the sweetest, pure soul I've ever met next to Marie. I swear Tiffany reminds me of my baby girl so much. Breaks my heart that Marie comes to me in so many ways. It's like she doesn't want me to forget about her. As if I could."

I blinked back the moisture in my eyes and studied Granny. The accuracy of her statement chilled me to the bone. The dreams I'd been having about my mother made sense now. Every time we talked, she gave me a piece of her. It's like she never allowed me to lose sight of who she was and how much she loved me.

"I never want you to feel like you see Nate in me," I confessed to Granny. "Yeah I look like him, but I never wanted to take on any of his mannerisms, nor his characteristics. Mama makes sure I don't."

Granny palmed my cheek.

"You've done amazing for yaself, King. I love the man that you are and can only hope that you get every blessin' comin' to you." She smiled, but it didn't reach her eyes. In fact, her eyes dimmed a bit.

"August..." She simply said and shook her head. "I'm afraid that Nate has gotten into his mind."

My eyebrows dipped.

"I never wanted to keep you and August from the man that fathered the two of you. Nate was very much a manipulator and could finesse anyone out of anything. Marie didn't find that out until August was born. By then Maire was too loyal to walk away from her marriage. She never once complained about the things she was going through, but as her mother, I knew. Nate hid his ways so well, but I could always see right through 'em."

This was the first time Granny said more than one sentence about my pops. From the way she spoke, I knew there was deep-rooted pain there. If my granny could hate Nate, she would. But she was too good to hate. It occurred to me that, although I looked just like Nate, Granny never treated me with anything other than love no matter how much she disliked the man that made me.

"Not that you need a reminder, King, but I'm askin' you to please look out for August."

Grinning, I pulled her to my side.

"Quit actin' like you're goin' somewhere, love. I got August, and I got you."

She tsked, then sobered as she propped her head against my

chest. Her fly away, silky, gray strands whipped all in my face as a gentle breeze surrounded us.

"I love you, Granny," I told her.

“I love you, too, Kingston.”

For the rest of the evening I was in my head and conflicting thoughts bombarding me.

As I dragged from a cigar, I observed the sky as God masterfully painted over the horizon. I never took the time to appreciate His or the sky's magnificence until Tiffany came along. In my world full of harshness, she was the sweet aroma that chased away any darkness within me. How could she expect me not to fight for her? She'd made me fall in love and had me thinking long-term shit. No other woman could come after her —at least she'd never be able to have my heart. It belonged to Tiffany, and I wished she'd see that. I didn't regret kicking her door in or scrapping with Grey. The only regret I had was walking away when I should've shot Grey and snatched my woman up.

Chuckling, I shook my head. Nah, I wasn't gon' be that muhfuckin' crazy. I'd scare lil' baby, and I couldn't do that. I didn't want her fearing me. I wanted her ass to love me. Licking my lips, I could still taste her flavor. It'd never go away. How the fuck was I supposed to let go? I didn't have to be taught how to love Tiffany. The shit just came naturally. Too bad letting go didn't come naturally. Because the way I felt for her, I'd hold on to her forever.

The buzzing on my phone drew my attention.

JARED:

You comin' through?

Shit! Somewhere in the middle of Jared talking about getting together this evening, my mind drifted off the other places... mainly Tiffany.

ME:

Fa sho. Be there in thirty.

I didn't feel like going to the club, watching no ass-shaking, or listening to niggas finesse some females. But the atmosphere would be good to clear my head for a while. At least I hoped it was. I'd stay for a little while, then bring my ass back home.

Exhaustion dogged me like hell as I hadn't recovered from going to see my pops. He was recovering well, however, his melancholy remained. Granny said that Nate was a manipulator, something I'd been mulling over as well. There was truth to her statement or else Granny wouldn't have said it. The question was, how good of a manipulator was Nathaniel Wells? Because if he thought manipulating me into believing I wasn't shit for not coming to his rescue, then he had another thing coming.

As I quickly showered, I remembered the concern in Granny's voice when she spoke of August. No matter how much I tried and needed to, I couldn't cut the cord. Because if I wasn't there to protect my brother, who else would?

A few days later

"King."

I glanced up from the blocks I stacked to see my mother standing in my room's doorway. "Yes, Ma?"

"I have a surprise for you," she said. She walked farther into my room with a smile on her face. She joined me on the floor and begin building on top of the structure I'd already erected.

"What is it?" I asked expectantly.

"You're getting a baby brother," she replied.

Excited, I jumped to my feet and hugged my mother. Being around this big house by myself for the last seven years had been tough!

Mama giggled. "I'm glad you're excited! There's a ton of responsibility as a big brother, you know that, right?"

I nodded emphatically. "I won't let anything happen to him," I vowed.

Mama laughed. "It's more to it than that, baby boy."

"Tell me!" I prompted excitedly.

"It's more than physical protection. Sometimes you gotta help protect his mind."

"How do I do that?"

Grinning, my mother tweaked my cheeks. "All you have to do is encourage him, pray for him, and most of all, always let him know that you love him."

"I will, Mama! I promise!"

"King!"

"Huh?"

"You'on hear me, mane?" August chuckled. "You puttin' all the bulbs in one spot."

"If y'all hadn't waited 'til the last minute my tree wouldn't look so raggedy," Granny fussed.

I busted out laughing. "That's my fault, Granny. I'll do better next year."

"Hmm hm," she griped. "Christmas is in three days and I'm just nie gettin' my tree," she continued.

August snickered. "Granny it's decorations all around the house and you're fussin' 'bout this tree."

"And I can!" She pouted, causing us to laugh.

While Granny read August the fifth degree, I was just glad to be spending this time with him. When I proposed he help me put the Christmas tree up, he jumped at it. We'd been at it for an hour now, trying to make sure it turned out perfectly. This had been something my mom used to do with us, and I remembered how exciting it had been. Honestly, it brought that feeling back as I decorated the tree. I couldn't help but imagine Tiffany being here to enjoy this moment with me.

The thought of not spending the holidays with her soured my mood, but I shrugged it off and pushed through. I'd purchased her several gifts that I planned on leaving on her doorstep Christmas morning. I wanted her to know that I still loved her and missed her deeply.

"You're off in space again," August stated.

I glanced at him confused.

"I asked if you'd go with me to get some things for Faith and the baby."

Surprised, I said, "Of course, mane."

He nodded and continued hanging garland.

Peeking Granny's way, I caught the satisfied smile on her face. Unable to help myself, I smiled, too.

Chapter Twenty-Four

TIFFANY

"No thank you," I said for the fourth time when Anissa tried to offer me something to drink. My stomach was already rolling, and she kept trying to offer me liquor after I told her I was good.

I was only here at her and Chris' house to attend this so-called business dinner. If you asked me there was more dinner than business. I touched nothing though because I was queasy just from the smell of the food.

"You've barely eaten," Chris mentioned.

Glancing across the table, I hunched my shoulder. "Not hungry. I'd really like to get home if we're done."

He'd talked meaninglessly about nothing, never really going into what I was actually here for.

"This has to do with the recommendation that you need," he started, perking me up. "You have a few months left with me, and honestly, I think you've done a great job."

Smiling, I said, "Thank you."

"Law school is a big task to undertake, however, we're here to tell you that we'd be more than happy to help you not only get in school, but excel," Anissa added.

"Wow," I gushed. "That's...nice of you."

Chris reached over and pushed my hair back behind my ear, causing me to flinch out of shock. He smiled.

"You're a beautiful thing, you know that," Anissa said, snapping my attention back to her. Her voice took on a seductive tone that I was sure made me feel violated.

Flustered, I cleared my throat and said, "Thanks, but—"

"We have a proposition for you," she smoothly interrupted.

Tilting my head to the side, the look on my face conveyed all the questions flowing through my mind. This sounded like a weird dream—one that I was ready to wake up from now!

"My husband and I have a certain...lifestyle that we really enjoy. Choosing a suitable guest takes time and patience. We've been watching you for a few months, and quite frankly, you've passed every test we've thrown at you."

Is this bitch crazy?

Really confused, I looked to Chris for some type of answers. He was busy staring at me like he was mesmerized. Totally creeped out, I tried to calm my racing heart so that I could think of a way to get the fuck out of here.

"We'll make it more than worth it if you oblige," Anissa stated. She stood from her chair and seemed to glide to my side.

My breath hitched as she took my chin in her fingers and lifted my face.

"I'd love to fuck you," she crooned. "I bet your pussy tastes just as good as you look."

Chris chuckled. "You're scaring her, Beal dear. Be a lil' less aggressive."

Ignoring her husband, Anissa continued. "My husband will watch, and then he can join us afterwards. He likes to watch me play in other women. I've been told I'm quite addictive." She seductively smiled. "How does that sound?" she asked, running her fingers across my partially open lips.

Wide-eyed, terrified, and fucking shaking, I started to panic when my phone rang. Anissa's fingers fell from my lips as I glanced down at the screen, not even caring who it was but was happy to see that it was Faith.

"Faith!" I answered. My voice trembled, but I held a fake smile on my face so that neither of these psychos realized that I was about to make my exit.

"Tiffany, what's wrong?"

"What!" I feigned shock.

"You're not due for three more months!" Abruptly standing, I snatched my purse and keys, then hurried towards the door. "I'm sorry, Chris, I have to go. We'll talk soon," I said to Chris who only nodded. Anissa's cool gaze said she knew exactly what I was doing, but I didn't give a fuck. I stayed in character.

"Tiffany!" Faith called, concerned.

"Oh my God! I'm on my way, Faith!" I fumbled with the stupid lock on the door, then damn near fainted when Chris came up behind me, rubbing his dick on my ass as he reached around to unlock the door.

"I'll see you in the morning," he said.

I didn't even look at him as I nodded and raced towards my car. Tears stung my eyes as they rushed forward.

"*Tiffany*!" Faith called again.

I slid behind my steering wheel and shook as I pressed the brake and start button.

"Faith!" I sobbed as I sped off the Dawsons' property. "I love you so much, girl!"

"What's wrong? Are you in trouble?" Faith questioned back to back.

"Oh my God!" My heart raced so fast that I had to pull over and gather myself.

"Tiffany, please tell me what's wrong. I'll come to you."

"No," I croaked out. "Can I come to your place?" I needed to go somewhere but it couldn't be my house, nor Grey's. There was no way I could tell anyone what just happened.

"Of course you can, boo, you know how to get here. I'll stay on the phone with you until you pull up."

Wiping the onslaught of tears from my face, I eased back on to the road and made the twenty-minute drive to Faith's apartment. She was waiting at the door for me, a concerned look marring her face. Feeling my stomach coming up, I ran past her and to the bathroom. As I cradled the toilet and cried, Faith rubbed my back.

"Shh…" she soothed. "Whatever it is, it's gonna be okay," she stated. It sounded like she was crying, too, as she whispered a prayer.

Thirty minutes passed until I was able to get cleaned up. Faith gave me a toothbrush, a sweatshirt, and sweatpants so that I could brush my teeth and shower. I spent too much time under the spray, trying to scrub away both Chris' and Anissa's grubby, nasty ass hands. My body felt raw by the time I turned the water off. When I came out of the bathroom, she was sitting in the living room with a bowl of soup, crackers, and ginger ale waiting for me on the coffee table.

Once again the tears started.

"I won't pry," Faith uttered. "But I'm here if you wanna talk. Eat what you can and then rest. I'll bring you a pillow and blanket."

Nodding, I sat down and grabbed the bowl. Hesitantly, I took one bite, then another. Going slow, I was able to finish half the bowl by the time Faith came back into the living room.

"You saved my life tonight, Faith." I sniffled.

She sat next to me and let me finish my soup without asking me one word. I finished eating and placed the empty bowl down, then sipped the ginger ale.

My phone vibrated, causing me to jump in fear.

"It's your brother," Faith stated.

Oh, God, I groaned.

GREY:

You good, baby? Lemme know when you make it home.

ME:

I'm staying with Faith tonight. I had a long day so I'm crashing early. I love you, Grey.

GREY:

... Aight and I love you, too.

Shit! Grey was suspicious.

BLU:

Love you, lil' mama.

VIOLET:

Love you *heart emoji*

EMERALD:

Love you, sis!

MA:

I love you, my sweet girl.

DAD:

I love you, sweetheart.

Messages went off back to back, each one expected, yet needed so much more now than ever before. Sometimes, I took these little messages for granted. Never again. There were many people in the world who didn't have the luxuries of being in a strong, loving family as I did.

I responded to each of them with an I love you, meaning it from the bottom of my heart. There was only one other message I missed. Kingston wasn't on this thread. Lord, I desperately needed him right now!

"I'll stay up with you until you fall asleep," Faith said once I'd placed my phone aside.

She took my hand in hers and firmly squeezed it.

What the hell had happened to me tonight?

In no devil's hell was I taking my ass back to work after what happened two nights ago. First thing the morning after, I called my OBGYN and asked for a work excuse due to me being exhausted. She didn't hesitate to provide me with one, keeping me off for two weeks.

I was home now, unable to sleep, halfway eating, and unable

to keep anything down. Every light in my house was on throughout the day and into the night. Fear gripped me as if someone was standing over my shoulder, waiting for me to close my eyes so that they could attack.

I'd never felt paranoia until now. I found myself showering with the curtain open and jumping at every sound I heard. The TV was on, but muted so that I could hear a bird pee if I needed to. The surveillance around my house was top tier, but I was still afraid.

Neither Chris nor Anissa tried reaching out to me. Either they were waiting for my next move, or they were strategizing theirs. No one would believe me if I told them what the hell they'd done. Sick bastards violated me! *Ugh*! It made me sick to my stomach. I could still feel that bitch's fingers on my chin, and the fucking lame ass dick that Chris pressed into my ass.

Growling out of both exhaustion and frustration, I wanted to go to both of them and put a bullet in their heads! I wasn't a fucking punk, and although I'd been frozen with fear *then*, now I was full of anger, malice, and rage. I paced the confines of my living room until the sun set. Normally, I'd go outside and watch the beautiful transition. However, I stood at my patio door, watching from the safety and confines of my house, afraid to step out of these four walls.

Faith offered me her couch, Grey and Gianna kept begging me to come see them or let them come by. My parents called every hour, and Blu and Jacoba were in my messages every thirty minutes. As much as I loved my family, this couldn't be something they knew about. My brothers were crazy, but *this* would drive them to do some crazy shit. So, I kept them at bay, requesting that they give me some space.

Faith was the only one I actually spoke to and assured that

I'd be okay, although I was over here losing my mind. She stayed on the phone with me however long I needed her to, just to listen to me breathe on the other end. Lord knows Faith had the heart of a saint for putting up with me, but she remained patient.

Once the sun set, I sighed and shuffled back to the sofa where I'd been resting. I wanted my bed so bad, but my anxiety wouldn't let me be in the closed in space. Picking up a Kleenex, I wiped my nose, which was sensitive because of all the crying, and laid down. As my eyes drifted shut, I stared at my gun, knowing just how fast I could reach for it in case I needed it. This wasn't the life.

Chapter Twenty-Five

KINGSTON

I floated through life like a zombie, missing the fuck out of my woman. Tiffany had no idea the amount of love I had for her. For her to think that I'd fuck up the bond we had and the bond she created with my granny, irritated me. One minute I'd be okay, and the next I was contemplating homicide.

I made a vow to Tiffany that I'd be the only nigga she ever knew, and I was standing flat-footed on that shit. If any nigga thought he was gon' slide in on my shawty, I had a long ass banana clip waiting for his ass. I wish the fuck she would try to be with another nigga. Smoke pooled around me as I blew a plume into the air. All I needed was one chance to make shit right with her. I was legit heartbroken like a muhfucka, and no matter what I did, I couldn't shake her.

My phone vibrated with me ignoring it. It wasn't Tiffany, nor was it work, and seeing as I was wallowing in despair, I wasn't about to answer that shit. It rang again, prompting me to check the screen. Seeing Grey's name had me both irate and concerned at the same time. If this nigga was on some bullshit, I he'd picked the wrong muhfuckin' time. I'd fuck him up just to blow off this anger inside of me.

On the other hand, nothing had better be wrong with Tiffany.

"The fuck you want?" I answered.

"I need a favor."

I chortled. Surely he had the wrong number.

"Ain't no favors over this way, nigga. 'Less you tryna run me one."

"Mane, shut the fuck up. As much as I hate to ask ya ass anything, I need you to go check on Tiff. I promised her I'd leave her alone, but some shit ain't sittin' right with me."

Ashing the cigar, I was already on my feet half-walking, half-rushing through the living room to grab my keys and slides.

"Yeah, I got her," I stated, already out of the door.

"Don't kick her shit in either, my nigga. Lemme know wassup."

"Bet," I growled.

I made it to her house in less than twenty minutes. Every light was on in her crib, including the porch light, but nothing seemed amidst. Cutting the engine, I stepped out of my car, then made my way up the pathway to the porch. The door opened before I rang the bell.

"What're you doing here?"

Tiffany not only looked afraid, but her eyes were puffy, and her hair was strewn all over her head. Baby looked like she hadn't slept in days.

"Can I come inside?" I asked calmly. Whatever she was

feeling, I wanted to remain calm so that I could figure out what the fuck was going on. This wasn't Tiffany standing before me.

Silently, she turned away from the door, leaving me to trail behind her. I locked the door, then followed her to the living room where she sat on the sofa. Two pillows and a comforter were on the sofa, as well as several books laid out in the middle of the floor. Both side lamps were on with the overhead light as well. The television was muted but adding more light to the brightly lit house.

Tiffany sat down then balled up under the cover. She wore a gray sweatshirt and sweatpants, and thick socks but huddled under the blanket like she was freezing cold. Discarded tissues littered the end table where a plate with a half-eaten slice of pizza on it, and cup of tea.

What caught my attention and held it for a minute, was the nine lying on the coffee table. I stooped down staring at the glazed expression upon Tiffany's face. Her nose was red from where she'd profusely wiped it. I waited to see if she'd talk, glancing around also to see if anything was out of place. Everything was in its place. My eyes turned back to her, now furious because she had tears in her eyes.

"What is it, baby?" I softly prompted although rage spawned inside of me for whatever or whoever had put those tears in her eyes. I peeped her gulping as if she had to muster up what she was going to say.

"He...uhm." She paused, nervously scratched her neck, and stuttered over her next words. "He...uhm, wanted me to...they, wanted me to sleep with them."

"Who, Princess?" I questioned but she continued to mumble like she didn't hear me.

Tears slid down her face. "They kept touching me before I realized what the hell they were doing."

I moved closer, trapping her in my arms that flanked her balled up frame. Darkness consumed my mind, poised to get at whoever fucked with the purest part of me.

"Who, baby?" I asked, gently wiping her tears. When she allowed me to touch her and didn't flinch, I wanted to shout.

"Chris...and his wife," she tearfully whispered.

Rage. That's all I felt.

"I was at their house for a business dinner. The whole time it felt awkward but I thought it was just me. Anissa kept offering me liquor, which I kept declining. I can only imagine what she'd put in that shit because she wouldn't stop offering me drinks. I wasn't feeling well, so I barely touched the food." She groaned at that. "She...uhm... She propositioned me like I was a piece of meat."

"Have you been back to work?"

She shook her head.

"Aight," I started. "Can you wait right here while I turn these lights off? You're comin' home with me, aight?"

She nodded again as her eyes darted around. Baby was paranoid as hell.

"Look at me, Sapphire." She hated when I called her that but it did the trick, snapping her attention to mine. "You trust me?"

Without thought, she confirmed softly, "Yes."

First I cleaned up the books, tissue, and discarded the plate. I took her gun, secured it, then stuffed it back where she told me she kept it. Next, I grabbed her purse, then scooped her off the couch, blanket, and all. I secured the house before carrying her to my car as she clung to me. I missed holding my lady but damn the muthafuckas that brought her back into my arms. All I heard was kill them.

I cleaned Tiffany up, fed her what she'd eat, then put her to bed. As soon as her head hit one of my pillows, she was out.

Granny's concerned face met me as I entered the kitchen to clean the dishes I'd used.

"She alright?" Granny asked.

"She's gon' be just fine," I answered.

"You?"

Smirking angrily, I shrugged.

"Someone's hurt her, I can tell. Are you feelin' vengeful?"

I washed the plates Tiffany and I'd used, not wanting to get my granny involved in my deadly thoughts.

"Nothing good will come outta vengeance, baby. Even if you never get caught or face consequences, a piece of you dies. Trust me. I've wanted to stab ya daddy through the heart on numerous occasions. But God assures me that Nate's time is comin'."

My attention snapped to her as I cut the water off.

She hunched a delicate shoulder.

"Doesn't always mean death. It can mean several things. Whatever it is, he will face more pain than death could give him."

Knowing what my dad went through weeks ago settled into the pit of my stomach.

"Just don't kill anyone, King. I wouldn't be able to take it."

I went to my granny and hugged her to my chest.

"You have my word," I told her.

Inside, a part of me warred with the other, for the first time wanting to go against the very vow I'd made. I trudged back upstairs to shower and lay next to Tiffany. She was out cold, with her mouth open.

Remembering I needed to hit up Grey, I shot him a text.

ME:

I got her. She's sleeping, so I'll have her hit you up in the morning.

GREY:

Bet. I owe u, big dawg.

Grunting, I placed my phone on the counter, stripped, then hopped into the shower.

Fifteen minutes later I turned everything off and slid into the bed, bringing Tiffany's body to mine. I inhaled the scent of her hair, closing my eyes at the familiar smell that had never been eradicated from my mind.

"Did you fuck her?"

Tiffany's quietly issued question had me both aggravated and coolly chuckling, yet I refrained from getting upset.

"I gave you my word that I haven't been with no one since me and you've been together. That includes the time we haven't been together."

"I don't want you to hurt me, Kingston. If you can't see us being together without you adding other women to the equation, then we should just be friends. And don't feed me that 'I'm a man' bullshit."

I turned until we were face to face, making sure she could see my eyes as we talked.

"Just like you trust me to protect you, trust me to love you,

Tiffany. Trust me to be faithful to you, trust me to carry you when you're down. Trust me to brighten up ya day. Trust me to make you laugh uncontrollably at the stupid shit I say or do, just to see ya beautiful smile and hear ya angelic laughter. That's what I want. I've never played games witchu. I've never hidden a single part of me from you. You know my words." I took her hand, shaking it like only we did. Her fingers gracefully followed the pattern I'd set for us, until our fingers locked into a fist. "Loyalty. Respect. Honor."

"Love," she whispered.

"Love." I smiled. She finally figured out the fourth code. "I love you."

"I love you, too. It's been hell without you. I'm sorry for doubting you and being stubborn when you tried to make things right."

I placed a kiss on her forehead and said, "All is well now. Close your eyes and rest."

While she drifted off, I laid there begging the night to go ahead and be over.

As soon as morning came, I slipped from the bed without stirring Tiffany. Quickly, I rushed through my morning routine, dressed, and was out the door praying this nigga was at work. It was Christmas Eve, and I shouldn't have been out for blood, but I was.

When I arrived at Chris' office, several vehicles were in the parking lot. Hoping one belonged to him, I parked and got out.

My long stride carried me through the parking lot and into the entrance. My eyes darted around the lobby, ignoring the woman asking me if I needed help. A hallway to the right had several doors, so I headed that way first.

"Sir!" the lady called.

"What're you doing here?"

Heavily mugging Vicki, I ignored her and kept stride to my destination. The name plate on the door confirmed I was at the right office. Turning the knob, it gave without any issues.

"Excuse me, I'm in a meeting."

"My fault," I apologized to the two men sitting opposite Chris. Absently, I noted that I recognized them but had other things on my mind at the moment. I rounded his desk with his eyes bucking as my fist caught him in his face, knocking him out of his chair. Shoving it to the side, I rushed Chris who tried to scramble from the floor.

"Aye, big dawg!" I heard, but dismissed, stomping Chris in his stomach.

"Ahhh!" he roared in pain.

Incensed, I punched him repeatedly, trying to break every bone in his face.

"I warned you, nigga! You wanna put ya fuckin' hands on my woman! Nigga, I will fuck you up! I'll kill you and ya bitch!" As if I needed to show him better than I could tell him, I snatched his ass off the floor and rammed him into the floor-to-ceiling glass window, wanting to put him clean through it.

While he tried to block my blows, it was no use. Blood spattered everywhere but the only thing that stopped me was someone pulling me off of him.

"I got you, bruh." One of Chris's guests held me back, while the other stood between me and a blood-soaked Chris who lay in the middle of the floor, dazed.

"Oh my God! Security!" That was Vicki's stupid ass screaming like I had a gun in my hand.

"Yo, you gotta dip, King," the other dude said just as security rushed the room.

I didn't give a fuck though and didn't resist when minutes later, the cops showed up to arrest me. I kept my eyes on Chris who was so dazed that he mumbled incoherent shit as he drifted in and out of consciousness. I needed to go back in time and take back the promise I made my Granny. I wanted this nigga in a box.

"He'll be sore for a while, but at least you ain't kill 'em," Granny quipped when I walked out of the booking area. Grey stood there, too, smirking.

"You told me I couldn't kill 'em," I reminded her, then placed my arm around her shoulders.

Begrudgingly, I dapped Grey. He came through for a nigga, so I was gon' try to remain cordial.

"You straight?" he asked.

"*You* straight?" I shot back.

All must've been well because he didn't reply and led us to his ride.

Twenty minutes later, as we neared my driveway, I grumbled at the two niggas propped up against a black Suburban holding up space on the curb in front of my house.

"Oh my, they're handsome," Granny commented as I helped her out of Grey's truck.

"Granny," I warned just as August came out of the front door.

She tooted her nose up. "I got eyes, King."

"Well, take ya eyes in the house, so I can see what they want."

Tsking, she shuffled towards the porch where August helped her make into the house. He stared after me, curiosity written all over his face.

Approaching Dallas and Houston, Grey and I dapped them, both of us wondering what they were doing here.

"You walked in that bitch like yeen know who we were, behbeh. I said, damn this nigga *big* mad."

"I was gon' let you do ol' boy in, but D soft ass stepped in tryna play save a bitch ass nigga," Houston, Dallas' younger brother, chimed in.

Dallas chuckled. "Nah, I couldn't let you dead his ass. I need him breathin'."

Confused, I questioned, "'Sup?"

Dallas and Houston owned their own sports agency firm where they managed some of pro sports most famous athletes. That's how most people knew them. However, Dallas and Houston had side careers dabbling in underground shit, meaning, they fucked with folks that were considered ghosts. Neither of them had a title, but most definitely worked for the law. Houston was local while Dallas resided in New Orleans, their hometown. I ran into Houston a little over a year ago when he helped bring down Beal's organization.

If a muhfucka wanted something done, these two niggas was who they'd call.

Something clicked for why they'd been at Chris' office.

"This involves Beal?"

Dallas nodded.

"Somethin' ain't sit right when I saw Chris at Smooth's crime scene. I pushed it to the back of my mind 'cause I was more pissed that he had my shawty there, too."

"Wait—what!" Grey barked.

Nodding, I said, "That ain't even the half, big dawg. The house Smooth was holed up in belonged to a ghost company owned by Chris."

Grey's face flared with anger. We'd been at odds for a while, but we had the same thing in common and that was our love for Tiffany.

"Smooth is dead, and he's the only one that could testify against Beal. This means Beal could walk."

Houston shook his head. "That's the thing. Beal is still free."

Confused, I cocked my head. "No muhfuckin' way!" I spat. "That nigga's been in lock up since we put him there." Beal was never even issued a bail.

"That's the *other* thing," Dallas added. "*Beal est une femme.*"

"A fuckin' woman?" I asked incredulously.

Their head nods confirmed what Dallas said.

"Wait a minute," Grey interjected. "Y'all mean to tell me the FBI and the DEA has the wrong muhfucka locked up?"

Again, they both nodded.

"Which is why I'm here," Dallas said. "One of Chris' clients came on my radar a few months ago. Derek Wilks raped two women who just so happened to be close to some folks I know. Me bein' me, I wanted to dead that nigga on sight. But when he lawyered up with Chris', I had to fall back."

"Why?" I prompted.

"Chris is on my radar, too. He has a habit of puttin' his hands whea they 'on belong."

Knowing firsthand that it was true, I sneered.

"Exactly," Houston quipped. "We had to come see ya."

"What're we talkin' about here?" Grey questioned. I hated to reveal what happened to Tiffany and was glad when Dallas spoke up.

"Chris is being investigated for rape allegations and so is his wife. While I'd love to say that was my sole reason for bein' here, it ain't. It's believed that Anissa, Chris' wife, is Beal."

I shook my head in denial. "No muthafuckin' way, dawg! How the fuck is that even possible?" I argued.

"She has one of the most powerful lawyers in the country as her husband," Houston said by way of explanation.

"Okay, so how y'all know it's her and really not a nigga?"

Dallas chuckled and looked at me like 'really nigga'. If he said some shit, it was law. So his receipts were A1. Still I wanted to know.

Dallas grinned. "You know how I get down," he stated.

In the underworld, Dallas' name was *Fantome,* or Phantom. He knew some shit that was top level secure. He was known for making things, *and people*, disappear. Questioning him was stupid.

"This is crazy as fuck," Grey grumbled.

I went to second what he said, when I caught Tiffany peeking through the curtains.

Chuckling, I waved. She hurried up and closed them like she didn't want me to catch her.

"We need a minute with her," Dallas said, prompting Grey to shake his head.

"Fuck no! She'on have shit to do with this," he responded. "All she did was work for that nigga 'cause I'll be damned if she goes back."

He didn't know the half. What happened to Tiffany was going to be between me and her until she said otherwise. My loyalty was to her.

Sensing that Grey didn't know the depth of the reason why I beat Chris' ass, Houston shrugged. "She may have heard some things that she doesn't realize she has. She's his assistant, and from what we could tell, he kept her close."

"Just five minutes," Dallas insisted.

Whether or not Grey agreed, Dallas wasn't going to take no for an answer.

"Five minutes," I replied, and led them towards the house, with Grey following.

Chapter Twenty-Six

TIFFANY

Kingston assured me that the men sitting across from us were good people, however, I begged to differ. The one he called Dallas, who sported long brown and blonde dreads, was devilishly handsome, possessed blue eyes and a New Orleans twang that could finesse anyone into giving him whatever information he sought. His blue eyes held a deadly undertone that made it difficult for me to maintain eye contact with him. His millions of tattoos didn't help.

Then there was Houston, the brother. Like Dallas, his eyes were blue. The same deadly undertone was in his keen gaze. Deep waves sat atop his head in the cleanest Caesar cut. They were both a part of the beard gang, but Houston's held a darker brown than Dallas'. Their light skin was deceiving, but the texture of their hair said it all.

"How ya feelin', lil' mama?" Dallas drawled.

"Depends on what you're talking about," I replied.

I hadn't yet recovered from the other night but being in Kingston's arms right now eased most of the fear I felt. This morning I woke up late, having slept like a baby in his protective arms. To find him not only gone, but in jail, I instantly panicked knowing he'd gone after Chris. Granny calmed me down and explained that nothing I could've done would've stopped Kingston from seeking his revenge.

"I made him promise me not to kill him," she'd said, like that was supposed to make me feel better.

What did make me feel better is when Grey showed up to pick Granny up, so that they could go bail Kingston out. He didn't ask me any questions, just rocked, and hugged me tightly before leaving.

"We're hea to talk about Chris and Anissa. Is that aight witcha?"

Gulping past the lump in my throat, I stuttered, "What about them?" I'd play stupid until they came right out and told me what they were here for.

"You flew outta thea like a bat outta hell, sug."

Eyes popping, I whispered, "You were there?"

He shook his head. "We've been watchin' them though."

Kingston's lips touched my cheek. I didn't realize that tears flowed from my eyes.

"Tell us what you can," Houston requested softly.

Gulping again, I closed my eyes and did my best to tell them what happened without breaking down. Anytime I thought about Chris' or Anissa's hands touching me, I shuddered. But Kingston was right here, assuring me that he wouldn't let anything happen to me. His support helped me through until I was done talking. I did, however, say one last thing.

"Chris had the audacity to laugh as though nothing was going on. He said, 'You're scaring her, Beal, dear. Be a lil' less aggressive'." My breath hitched on that last part and sent me jumping from Kingston's lap so that I could rush to the bathroom.

He was right behind me, practically catching me as I tumbled to the toilet, emptying the contents of my stomach.

"I got you, baby," he pledged, joining me on the floor and rocking me as I sobbed.

"Tiffany." Grey's worried tone made it to my ears, making the flood of emotions heavier.

"They didn't rape me," I whispered to Kingston. "But why does it feel like it?"

Kingston smoothed my hair back and placed kisses all over my face. "Shhh, love. We gon' get through this, and I swear on my life ain't another soul gon' hurt you."

He stayed there with me, until the tears stopped. Somewhere in that time, Grey left the doorway.

Although it wasn't evening yet, he drew me a bubble bath, lit some candles, undressed me, and deposited me in the tub. While I lay back and relaxed, he brushed my teeth and washed my face. He kneeled beside the tub and took his time washing me, as if he too was trying to wash away the stain of what took place. His eyes, heavy with both anger and love, focused on mine so intently, that it caused me to bare my soul.

"I'm pregnant," I whispered, hoping to God that he was okay with it.

Kingston's hand never slowed from washing me as his face drew closer to mine. I saw the water in his eyes, felt the emotions flowing from him as he licked his lips, then repeatedly kissed mine.

"It's forever gon' be me and you," he declared.

My hands went up to cup his jaw, wetting his beard, but he didn't care.

"You're makin' me a father, baby?" he questioned, although it was more of confirmation than doubt.

I nodded, smiling.

He was back to kissing me and promising me that everything was going to be okay. And truthfully, I trusted every word he said.

One month later...

With the new year came many changes. My holiday season had been so crazy that I barely remembered anything accept being surrounded by my family, Kingston, and Granny. Even the gifts didn't mean much to me. Not as much as having love surrounding me.

Kingston and I decided to announce that I was pregnant since everyone was gathered together. The amount of tears shed that day still made me smile. Grey and Blu, who I thought would hit the roof, did the total opposite. They felt like proud parents, giving their daughter to a man they could trust...and even like.

What happened with Chris and Anissa just so happened to be days before Christmas, threatening to spoil arguably the most joyful time of the year. I didn't want to have a single memory of that incident come this Christmas. Daily, I worked to eradicate the sheer fear I felt from being placed in such a scary situation.

With that being said, I hadn't been back into the law firm since the last day I was there. I didn't put a notice in or anything, not that I needed to. Chris and Anissa were both arrested for some shit that was even crazier than what I went through with them.

Turns out, Chris' wife was more than just a beautiful woman, who oozed elegance. Apparently, she was a queen pin out here in these streets. She had connections that touched far and wide, but ultimately, weren't far enough to keep her ways hidden.

Chris, on the other hand, was still a big thing in the news. Most of his cases were being reviewed, especially the ones that involved sexual abuse of any kind. Now it all made complete since why he got along so well with Derek Wilks, who by the way decided to plead guilty to his rape charges to avoid trial. Shit was just all around crazy, but thankfully, Kingston and I were pretty much back to normal—almost.

While Kingston and I shared a bed every night, we hadn't made love since the last time we did. It had nothing to do with Kingston and everything to do with me. After feeling violated by Chris and Anissa, I'd had the worst anxiety about having sex. Kingston was so patient with me that he never pressured me, no matter how much of a mood he was in. He'd still hold me close at night and assure me that I was safe and protected.

KINGSTON:

Leaving now, baby. Everything went well.

ME:

Okay, great boo! I ordered dinner.

KINGSTON:

Bet.

I was glad to know that the visit with his dad went well. Mr. Wells was healing nicely, and according to Kingston, in a better mood in the last few weeks. Being back in Georgia brought back good memories. Funny thing is, I didn't once have negative vibes about being back in Kingston's house. Quite the opposite. I remembered what he did to me the last time we were here together. For the first time in a while, my body heated.

Going with where my body was leading me, I threw all my fears to the side. Kingston wasn't the one who'd violated me. He was the one loving me through this awkward time in my life. He deserved his woman's touch, and I was going to give it to him.

I'd already soaked and rubbed my body down in body butter. My skin felt soft and smooth and smelled like coconuts. Rifling through my duffle bag, I found the box holding my necklace and placed it back around my neck. The familiar weight resting just above my breast wrapped me in the sweetest embrace.

The doorbell rang, signaling that the food was here. Kingston had another thirty minutes before he'd be here, so until then, I prepared the living room for our in-house picnic dinner. By the time I heard his pipes, everything was ready. I clicked the television onto the soft jazz station then turned it down low. The lights were dimmed and the drinks poured. The only thing missing was my man.

I went and stood by the front door, anxiously waiting for him to open it. His keys jiggled in the lock, making my heart skip a beat.

"I just made it in," he was saying. "Give Granny a kiss for me, and—" He looked up and saw me standing here, muting him.

"Uh... We'll be home tomorrow," he said, then hung up the phone. His eyes traveled the length of my body, taking in my naked frame from head to toe.

I loved that no matter how many times Kingston saw me butt ass naked, he acted like he'd never seen me this way before. He softly closed the front door, then locked it, the whole time keeping his eyes on me.

"I started the shower for you," I stated. "Why don't you go get cleaned up..."

My words trailed off as he headed for the master bedroom.

In the living room, I patiently waited until he made his return. Like I knew he would, he came back to the living room butt ass naked. He held his dick in his hand, forcing himself to be patient. When I held my hand out to him, he quietly took it. Turning, I led him to the large blanket I'd put down and told him to sit.

Once he did, I straddled his powerful thighs and got comfortable.

"You hungry?" I asked.

Speechless, he nodded. Hesitantly, he placed his hands on my thighs, waiting to see how I'd react. Smiling, I picked up the plate topped with roasted vegetables, mashed potatoes, and savory grilled chicken.

Piling up a fork full of food, I offered it to him. His lips wrapped around the silverware, licking it clean. I fed us both, enjoying how labored his breathing was and how his dick jumped in excitement anytime I stuck the fork into my mouth. The tip of his thick mushroom head glistened, while my pussy ached, throbbed, and moistened for him.

"You miss me, baby?" I asked him. Slowly, I slid the fork out of my mouth and watched his eyes glue to my tongue that stroked the tines.

"You know I do," he answered. His lids fell low as I handed him his drink and sat the empty plate aside.

Downing my drink in one gulp, I discarded the glass flute, then fisted Kingston's hard dick. Before he knew what was happening, I was sliding to base of him on an exultant groan. I hadn't felt this full, satisfying, painful yet sweet feeling in so long, I melted around him.

The half-empty flute tumbled from his fingers as he palmed my ass.

"Ssss... Oh shhiiii...." His head tilted back and rested against the sofa seat as his eyes snapped shut. He bit down on his back teeth, struggling to relax beneath me.

"I missed you, King," I whimpered as my hips took over.

Dipping my fingers in the whipped cream, I smeared it across his nipples, causing him to squeeze my ass so hard, it would've hurt had his dick not been inside of me touching every crevice of my walls.

I stuck my tongue out, and dragged it slowly over his pebbled left nipple, drawing a sexy ass moan from his gangsta lips. I did the same to his right nipple, toying with the ring, producing the same reaction. It's like he grew bigger inside of me, making me fill even more full than I ever had.

Once again I dipped my fingers in the cream, scooping up enough to apply to my nipples. The cold dessert chilled me to the bone. However, the second I told Kingston to come get his dessert, he inhaled my titties, his whole mouth encompassing one of my breasts at a time, licking, biting, and sucking them clean.

Screaming in ecstasy as my hips moved faster, I dug my

fingernails into his shoulders, loving how my pussy grabbed and sucked him, refusing to let him go. One of Kingston's hands pulled at my thick strands, while the other spanked my ass so hard, I came on a throaty scream.

"Fuucckk!" Kingston growled. Both of his hands were back on my ass, slamming me down his thick shaft. The cords in his tilted neck stood to attention while he bit savagely at his bottom lip. Sexily he moaned my name, before commanding, "Gimme another one, baby!"

"Kiiinnngg!" I panted as an orgasm seized me in its clutches.

"Shit, I'm cummin'!" he praised.

Leaning back, I placed my hands on his thighs, giving him a better angle as sought his release.

"Dammnn, baby!" he grunted as his body tensed and his breath shortened to quick intakes. His eyes rolled into the back of his head, and his mouth dropped open. Holding me in place, he stroked up until he was good and dry.

Spent, I draped across his chest and listened to his heart thud rapidly.

"I'ain hurt my baby, did I?" he questioned. I busted out laughing.

"No, King," I assured. "Your baby is good." We'd find out in a couple of more weeks what we were having, and neither of us could wait.

He ran his fingers across my barely rounded belly, tickling me. It was just enough there to notice I was pregnant. Kingston lifted my chin, then sweetly kissed me.

"Thank you for trusting what we have," he said. "You're strong as fuck and every day I watch you beat down your insecurities and fears, makes me love you even more. I'm happy that you're the woman carryin' my child. I pray you let me give you some more. All I wanna do is fill ya life with everything good. 'Cause that's what you do for me."

He dashed the tears away that escaped and sighed. "Sometimes my mama comes to me in my dreams. Usually it's reflecting on times past and how I remember everything she's ever said to me. It took me a while to realize that while my mama was always happy and smilin', inside she was hurtin'." He shook his head in sadness.

"Whenever I see you smile, I wanna know it's real, and from within, not 'cause you puttin' on a front for me or anyone else. If I'm slackin' in any way, say somethin', aight? Don't wait 'til you feel like you at the end of ya rope before you make ya feelings known. That ain't what I want for us. Aight?"

Nodding, I replied, "Alright. Thank you for being patient with me, Kingston. Thank you for not allowing my brothers to run you away. Most of all, thank you for coming to my rescue, when I gave you no reason to."

"One thing I want you to always know, I'ain goin' nowhere. And if you try and take ya ass anywhere, just know I'm comin' for you."

Leaning back, I giggled. "What if I get tired of you, Kingston?"

"Then you gon' take ya ass a nap, wake back up and realize you really wasn't tired of me, the fuck."

Again, I busted out laughing. "You're right, baby," I stated, squeezing his cheeks. "I could never get tired of you making me *genuinely* laugh and smile."

He was stuck with my ass.

Chapter Twenty-Seven

KINGSTON

A couple weeks later...

I was so proud of Tiffany for rising above the shit that happened with Chris. She'd been fighting the demons of that night for weeks, and finally, she'd come out of her shell. If it weren't for Dallas and Houston handling shit with Chris and Anissa, I swear I would've bodied them.

I'd made a promise to Granny not to kill anyone. However, over time, the shit just made me angrier that both of those muthafuckas were still breathing. Aside from that bullshit, cloud nine had nothing on the cloud I'd been on since learning Tiffany and I were having a boy. I'd never considered myself as an emotional person. I, more or less, bottled a lot of my feelings in —that is unless it came to Tiffany. She could reduce me to puddy in multiple ways, and I wasn't ashamed to say that it didn't bother me. I was sure in my masculinity and had no problems understanding that sometimes being a little emotional wasn't a bad thing. Which is how I found myself tearing up at the sound of my baby's heartbeat, and the doctor informing us that we'd be having a boy. I left the doctor's office in deep thought, reflecting on my relationship with Nate and even August.

With Nate, I loved him just as a son should love his father. Was I proud of him? No. Sounds harsh, but Nate made some fucked-up decisions that changed the dynamics of his entire household. Then there was August. Raising him alongside Granny made it feel at times like I was his father. Any time he rebelled against me, I took it just like a parent would. I'd feel disappointed, angry, but most of all lacking. The feeling that I wasn't doing enough as his brother is exactly how parents feel when their children go astray. I ended up questioning myself so many times, wondering where I was at fault.

Now, it was my turn to raise up a child, one that the love of my life and I had created. Clearing my throat to relieve the clog in it, I took a sip of my drink and observed the three gentlemen joining me for lunch.

"I hope you know how hard it was for us to sneak into the city," Blu drawled. He took a sip of his drink and assessed me with the eyes of a killa.

"Good thing you offered to pay for this lil' trip, 'cause I'm sure my wife is lookin' at the bank statements to try and figure out where the fuck I am," Mr. Summers added. He kept looking over his shoulder like he expected Mrs. Summers to pop up on his ass any minute.

"So, what's this about?" Grey questioned.

"I want to ask for Tiffany's hand," I answered.

"Nigga, she already pregnant, the fuck you thought?"

"Shiidd, where else was this shackin' shit leadin' to?"

"Hm! I knew I liked you!"

Grey's, Blu's, and Mr. Summer's responses were comical, yet I accepted them as if they'd all agreed that I could marry Tiffany.

"Wait," Grey said. "I know yeen 'bout to propose on Valentine's Day? That's corny as fuck, dawg."

The day in question was this weekend.

"It's not," Mr. Summers defended.

"Pops, that shit is whack as hell," Blu sided with Grey.

"Yeah, my lil' baby deserves more than that cliché shit. All females know when *that* day rolls around, some diamonds are bein' copped," Grey continued. "At least wait 'til the day after, so her ass can cry herself to sleep thinkin' you'on fuck with her like that."

Blu's face balled up. "Nah, don't do that shit. Soon as she call you, you gon' be ready to lay hands on him."

Grey grumbled and hunched his shoulders.

"You know what my daughter loves," Mr. Summers said. "These two knuckleheads want to control everything, however, this ain't their story to control. Do what's best for my baby, in the way that you see fit. All I want is for her to be happy.

I agreed with Mr. Summers and chuckled at the look on both of his sons faces as they mugged him.

"Any parent's dream is to have their daughter cared for by a man that they have no problems handing her over to. Same way with my sons, believe it or not. Gianna and Jacoba *had* to be exactly who they are, 'cause dealing with these two takes a lot of tolerance and patience. I love my daughters-in-law for how good they treat Grey and Blu. As a father, it makes me proud as fuck to see my sons being properly loved."

Neither of his sons made a peep.

"Now, on the other hand, if there's ever an issue with my baby girl, if you come to a time when you think it's somethin' or someone out there better than her, if you find yaself unable to sleep next to her at night, if you find yaself no longer courting her...call one of us so that we can politely take her off ya hands. 'Cause ain't gon' be no sometimin' with my angel. Either she's yours forever, or she ain't yours at all."

"Now *that*, we can agree on, Pops," Grey seconded.

"Fa sho," Blu acknowledged.

"Oh, Kingston!" Granny beamed. "It's beautiful!" she cried as she beheld the engagement ring.

"I'm proposing this evening, and for some reason, I'm nervous as hell," I confided.

Granny tsked as she wiped her tears. "Ain't no need for none of that. Tiffany loves you like a woman is supposed to love a man. When ya granddaddy was alive, we'd be in that garden all day. No matter how much I got on his nerves, he'd sit out there with me and talk about nothin' but as long as I was happy, he was happy. Tiffany is that way with you. She goes out of her way to make sure you're happy, King. And it's genuine. Her heart is so pure."

Nodding, I had to agree.

"You've become such a wonderful man, King. Continue to be what you are to her. Don't ever switch up what you've shown her all this time. Otherwise, ya granny is so proud of you, I couldn't ask for better."

Hugging Granny, I was thankful that she'd helped calm my nerves. I was tripping for nothing. Tiffany and I were made for each other.

Tiffany took my breath away. Our baby had her glowing more than she normally was, bringing adoration to my heart. She was barely showing, however, her hips had gently spread over the last few weeks. And that damn faucet she had between her succulent thighs… Her shit was already juicy, and now it felt like a water park —one that I played in non-stop. Whether it was my tongue, fingers, or my dick, I kept her knowing what the fuck I could do to her.

"You're gorgeous, baby." Mesmerized, I drew her into my arms and kissed her forehead, then her nose, and lips.

She shyly smiled. "Thank you, love."

She'd straightened her curly mane, causing the strands to touch her lower back. The black sheath draped over her sexy curves was gon' be in pieces by the end of the night. I had plans to rip that shit clean off of her before we even made it to the bed.

"Look at my man all fancy in his slacks and button down. Don't make me have to smack a bitch tonight," she quipped.

Chuckling, I pinched her chin. I rarely got a glimpse of Tiffany's attitude, but when I did, she cracked me up. Baby played that sweet and innocent shit but was a straight savage outchea in these streets. I thought she'd been playing about having a nine in her purse. From now on, I knew she meant that shit. I still found her attitude funny though.

"You ready?"

"Definitely."

I took Tiffany to the place where we watched our first sunset together. Like last time, everything was set up perfectly, and with the sun due to set in an hour, our waitress was sure to have our meals and drinks out in time for us to enjoy it before I made my move.

"Dinner was excellent," Tiffany gushed.

She fawned over her gifts—a diamond necklace and hoop earrings. Neither of those is what brought her to tears.

"King!" she exclaimed. She snatched my left hand and brought it back into her view. I'd be waiting for her to notice it for the past two days. My skin was richly, deeply brown, but that ink still popped.

"Is that?"

It was. Tucked on my left ring finger was her name in cursive script. Her hazel orbs, big as saucers, flicked to mine.

Grinning, I asked, "You like it?"

She glanced away and started fanning her eyes, causing me to chuckle.

"You're not about to make me cry like I'm soft or something, King. It's this baby, I swear," she fussed. She had to dab at her tears with a cloth to keep them from coming.

I busted out laughing. Standing, I took her hand and asked her for a dance. She was still a little emotional yet impressed that I wanted to do such a thing; she didn't hesitate to mold her body to mine.

As the soft notes of Tyrese's *Sweet Lady* made it to the deck, I placed my hand at the small of Tiffany's back and fit her perfectly to my front. We swayed perfectly together, the same way we did between the sheets. She laid her head on my chest and listened to my heartbeat instead of the melody of the music. She smiled because she felt my shit racing.

That's because I was about to take the biggest step of my life.

Did I doubt that it was the right decision? Hell nah. I wasn't 'round here calling her Mrs. Wells for nothing. I spoke this into existence and I was standing flat-footed on my decision. She had me in a chokehold, only I wasn't suffocating from the pressure—I lived for it.

"I questioned how I would propose to this amazing woman, thinking of all this elaborate shit I could do. Then I remembered who my woman is. She loves the simple things that many take for granted—like the sunset." Tiffany's head popped off my chest to stare at me.

Just as the sun begin to make its descent, I dropped to one knee.

"There's nothing fancy about this proposal, Princess, but there's more meaning to it than the mind can fathom. 'Cause just as God is painting the sky with all those beautiful colors right now, I pray that He paints our love just as beautifully, every day, for the rest of our lives. I'll never take anything about you for granted. Not even the simple things."

Shocked, mouth open, tears flowing, and hand over her racing heart, Tiffany blinked down at me, too stunned to speak. I produced the ring, opening the box so that she could see this was real.

"Will you marry me, Princess?"

Weak in the knees, she dropped down to my level, wrapped her arms around my neck, and proclaimed, "Yes!" she screamed it so loud the whole world could hear.

Laughing, I hugged her, then took her left hand to slide the custom rock on her finger.

"King!" She gasped in awe as she beheld her glistening ring finger.

"Yes, Mrs. Wells," I answered.

She screamed as she covered her face in excitement. Standing, I brought her with me and swooped her up into my arms. The kiss we shared was both sweet and sensual. Now that I'd made things officially official, there was nothing or no one that could come between us. I had my baby, who was having my baby. A nigga couldn't be happier.

GRANNY

That same night...

My night ended well. I could sleep well knowing Kingston was proposing to Tiffany tonight. He'd become such a good man. Nothing like his lame daddy. Only because I believed in forgiveness did I forgive Nate for the lifestyle he chose. Still, I didn't like him. How could losing his wife not change a man for the good? No, this fool went off and got himself arrested, leaving behind his boys.

In hindsight, I believe God gave me Kingston and August to get me through my own grief. Without them, I wouldn't have made it. A strange noise woke me from my sleep. Glancing around my darkened room, I was surprised to find Marie standing by my bedside. Waking up to an apparition could be a little crazy, but my daughter often visited me. I took it as her way of giving me some peace. Lately, she'd been away.

Smiling, I said, "Hey, daughter."

As always Marie smiled back. "Hey, Mama."

"It's been a while," I commented, leaning back into the plushness of my pillows.

Marie shrugged with a grin. "Been a little busy."

"Oh? Do tell." I grinned.

Marie chuckled. "In due time, Mom."

She was still as beautiful as she was the day I last saw her alive. Sadness gripped my heart in a way I couldn't explain. It had been so long, but the wound of losing my only daughter was still fresh. My sons did their best keeping in touch with me, but them being so far away and only seeing me every blue moon had really hurt a part of me.

Maybe them being away kept them from remembering the loss of their sister and father. That's what I chose to believe rather than believe they'd purposely stay away from the woman that bore them. And no, I never wanted to leave Pensacola although they tried every now and again to talk me into it.

My daughter had grown up in this city and was buried in this city. So was my husband. Leaving them behind would make my life of nothing. Kingston and August were my reasons for pressing forward on days when I wanted to give up.

Kingston... My dear grandson had the patience of Job and saw to it that I enjoyed every day of this old life I still possessed. My love for August was no different than it was for Kingston. I just prayed August would come to his senses.

Once or twice I caught August on the phone, talking to his dad. It wasn't like I was being nosey, but the way August responded to Nate made my skin crawl. He sounded like a little boy talking to his daddy, instead of a grown man talking to his father. It was the weirdest thing.

Another noise had me sitting up.

"Did you hear that?" I asked Marie. She was no longer in the room with me.

Sighing, I flipped back the covers grumbling. The least my daughter could've done was say goodbye. I chuckled to myself.

The thought brought tears to my eyes as I ambled into the kitchen.

"August!" I called. The wall clock showed a little past ten. He should've made it home from Georgia by now.

My attention was averted by the barking of that ol' mutt next door. Thinking he was in my tomatoes again, I opened the sliding glass door to go give him a piece of my mind.

"Rattla!" I fussed.

He barked again. I noticed the back light was out, making it difficult for me to see him, but I heard him shuffling through my garden.

"I'ma strangle yo' neck," I continued fussing, going towards the stairs. Kingston would be mad, but I was tired of this ol' fool tearing up my vegetables.

Sure enough, Rattla took off running his goofy ass through the yard.

"I'ma getcha!" I threatened.

I held on to the rail and slowly descended the stairs, grumbling as I slowly descended each step one by one.

"You ol' foo—"

My foot slipped. My hands and arms weren't strong enough to hold my weight up. I stumbled and tumbled, crying out in pain as my hip hit the wood stairs along with my back. Not a second later, my head made contact with the concrete at the bottom of the stairs.

Groaning in pain, I silently called for August as my eyes fluttered. Heavy dizziness coupled with the pain I was in had my heart racing from fear.

"Relax, Mama." Marie appeared and kneeled over me, smiling the sweetest smile I've ever seen her wear. "I've got you."

Chapter Twenty-Eight

KINGSTON

Tiffany and I left the restaurant, then headed towards her last surprise for the night. She was still in awe with the ring, and the fact that we were engaged. Every now and then she'd peek at me, as if she was scared I'd change my mind any minute.

Once I assured her with a smile, she'd go back to watching the passing scenery with a content smile upon her face. Securely, she held my right hand as I palmed the wheel with my left. If the tattoo wasn't proof that this shit was permanent, then where we were headed would definitely make her realize this was some forever shit.

The Bluetooth cut through our comfortable silence.

"Bruh!" August barked, sounding frantic. "You gotta get home! Granny fell down the fuckin' stairs!"

My heart nosedived as I made a U-turn on the busy highway,

prompting several people to blast their horns. The way August sounded, it wasn't good.

"Call an ambulance!" I ordered, fear gripping me too tight for me to breathe.

"I did, mane! Oh my God, Granny, please say somethin'," August begged. He was crying and that shit, instilling the worst kind of fear in me.

Tiffany's hand squeezed my thigh in support as I hauled ass back to my crib. Her eyes were just as worried as mine. In the background I heard sirens.

"The ambulance is here," August informed me. "Hurry up, bruh," he begged.

The line clicked the same time as my heart stopped. I had to get to my granny.

I made it to the house as Granny was being wheeled to the ambulance. I lost all my shit at the sight of her lifeless atop the gurney. Millions of questions ran through my head, but none of them stuck as I hopped back in the car to race behind the ambulance.

A couple hours later, I paced the lobby of the ER, afraid to even ask for an update. August was a mess, unable to stop crying, breaking my heart. I couldn't help him though. The amount of fear coursing through me was too great to do anything except pace. Tiffany rubbed August's back as she followed my movements, shedding her own tears.

About fifteen minutes later, a nurse entered the lobby, her eyes searching us out.

Shit! I knew right then whatever she had to say wasn't going to be good.

"Mr. Wells?"

I nodded, then felt both Tiffany and August at my side. Tiffany grabbed my hand, holding it tightly.

"Please come with me," the nurse requested. The second she led us to a small conference room just off the main lobby, August damn near lost it.

"I'ain goin' up in there," he protested.

"Sir, just have a seat." Security intervened, seeing how hostile August's demeanor was. Like me, he knew we were about to receive news we didn't want to hear.

We sat in the little room for what felt like several more hours when only minutes passed before a doctor walked in, followed by two nurses. The solemn expression on their faces had me hanging my head. Tiffany's arms were around me, sharing her strength with me.

"Your grandmother took a very nasty fall. She hit her head, causing severe swelling in her brain. We've attempted to alleviate the swelling by removing sections of her skull. We'll keep an eye on her throughout the night..." He sighed dejectedly. "However, I'd advise you and your loved ones to spend as much time with her as you're allowed. It's going to be an uphill battle, but we'll do all that we can to see her through this."

“What're her chances?” I had to know.

“Honestly, the prognosis isn't good. If she makes it through the night, we can discuss doing more testing. In cases like this, brain damage is most likely too great to survive.”

August flew off the handle, roaring as he damn near flipped the table.

"Fuck outta here!" he shouted.

I didn't even have the strength to stop him when he blasted out of the room. This man stood here telling me that my granny wasn't going to make it. I couldn't stop the threat of tears if I wanted to. Tiffany's sniffles did me in.

"Ain't nothin' else you can do for her?"

He shook his head. "We're sorry, sir."

I nodded, understanding.

"We'll take you to her," one of the nurses said.

I held tightly to Tiffany's hand as they led us down what seemed like Death Valley.

My heart raced, and my mind roared with anger and confusion. I entered my grandmother's room, shaken by the sight before me. As much as I wanted to turn and leave, I took the heaviest steps of my life and trudged to her bedside. The only part of her head exposed was her cheeks and lips. I kissed her cheek, leaving my tears there.

"Don't leave me," I pleaded. "But I understand if you have to."

No I wouldn't understand, but I needed her to know she didn't have to suffer on account of my feelings. Tiffany and I stayed by her side, praying because that's all we could do.

I did my best to field calls from my family. Uncle Todd took things hard but understood how independent and head-strong his mother was and took the accident as no more than that—an accident. Uncle Leon, on the other hand, ripped me a new one. So much so that I had to hang up on him or take my anger out on this whole hospital. I found it funny that between him and his sons, none of them called my line more than they were right now. I hated that family never considered themselves such until tragedy reared its ugly head.

Putting my uncles and their children to the back of my mind, I focused all my attention on Granny. I thought about every day I'd spent with her and how the years had been filled with many signs of her love for me and August. I'd never forget how she stepped in and became everything we needed.

For two and a half hours, Granny fought. She took her last breath with me holding her hand and beseeching God, and my mother to be at the gates waiting for her.

Chapter Twenty-Nine

TIFFANY

August's car was in the driveway when we pulled up. I put the car in park and cut the engine. Kingston didn't move, prompting me to get out and go to his side. I wiped my tears so that I could be strong for him. My baby was deeply hurt and broken. The man with that beautiful smile wasn't who sat in the passenger seat. In his place was a man, so broken that I had to help him out of the car.

Once inside the house, I saw evidence of August's fury. There were holes in the walls that hadn't been there before. His room door was shut, but the biting smell of weed permeated from it. Kingston didn't even flinch at the smell.

Instead, he stopped in front of August's door and turned the knob. When it gave, his arm slipped from around my shoulders. He entered August's room, then shut the door. I stood on the other side and clutched my chest as August's heart-wrenching sobs broke the atmosphere.

My feet didn't move. I stayed put until Kingston emerged several long minutes later. His downcast eyes held no life as his arm went back around my shoulders.

I helped him into our room and to the bed, where he heavily sat. While he stared into space, I removed his shoes, socks, and clothes until he was left in his boxers.

"Lay down, baby," I urged, assisting him. He stared at the ceiling then, his jaw set in a tight fixture as he repeatedly fought back his tears.

“I'm going to the kitchen for a second,” I informed him, with no response.

Deflated, I left him there to quickly change before making my way downstairs to make something to eat. He needed something to stave off the raging headache he'd have from crying. As I prepared leftovers from a casserole Granny had prepared last night, I thought about the conversation she and I had a while back.

She promised me she'd do as Kingston wished and stay off the stairs. Over the course of time I'd spent with Granny, I'd witnessed her stubborn streak often. But the look in her eyes that day was unforgettable. She'd made a promise, one that I knew she would keep. What drove her to break her promise?

While the food heated, I went to the sliding door and looked out over the illuminated backyard. Sliding the door back, I took a deep breath before stepping onto the deck. I swear it's like Granny's spirit surrounded me the closer I went towards the stairs. At the base of the stairs, Granny's blood stained some spots. Rattler's bark startled me and had me swiftly turning to the neighbor's gate.

"Did you do this?" Not that Rattler would answer but the evidence that he'd been in Granny's tomatoes was clear. He whined like that would make my, Kingston's, or August's tears cease.

Once I got Kingston situated, I'd look on the cameras to confirm if Rattler had indeed been the cause of Granny bringing her stubborn self out here. Poor Granny. Kingston and August would probably never recover from this. Rattler wasn't the only one my mind implored for answers. Where the hell had August been?

My phone vibrated, breaking my thoughts.

GREY:

Just checking on y'all, baby. You need me, I'm there.

I'd texted my family to let them know about Granny. Everyone was devastated.

ME:

Getting settled for the night. I'll text you if I need you.

GREY:

OK. Love you. Let my dawg know we got him for whatever.

Through these tears, I smiled at Grey calling Kingston his 'dawg'. The two of them were like oil and water, but somewhere along the way, they became tolerant of each other.

ME:

I will and I love you, too.

BLU:

We're heading that way in the morning.

ME:

OK. Be safe, and I love you.

I sighed.

BLU:

We love you, baby.

I replied to my parents' and sisters' texts, then went to check on the food. Granny had made such an impact on our lives in the months we'd known her. We were losing a piece of us, too.

Kingston's phone rang, which I debated answering or not. It was his Uncle Leon, who'd called a little while ago, but had somehow found himself blaming Kingston for what happened to Granny. Kingston hung up on him and had since been ignoring calls from both of his uncles and his cousins.

Deciding that they'd continue blowing up Kingston's phone, I answered it.

"Hello?"

"Where the fuck is my nephew?" Uncle Leon demanded to know. "He ain't got the balls to talk to me so he sent his bitch?" He was somewhere between crying and drunk. "Just like his muthafuckin' daddy," he continued. "Ain't shit been right since that muthafucka came into my family! First my sister, and now my mama, all at the hands of them bastard ass Wells muthafuckas!"

Incensed, I snapped. "Mr. Leon, I understand that you're upset, we're all upset, okay? But what you're not gon' do is, call my man's phone and disrespect him nor me. He took damn good care of Granny and I'd be damned if I let *anyone* imply otherwise. Don't bring ya ass to this house on no disrespectful shit, or I will *disrespectfully* have you removed from the premises. This is hard enough for my man as it is. Now I don't know what kinda family situation you got goin' on in North Carolina, but the family I come from...if I say so, it's so. Please don't make me have to get them involved."

The line was silent, but his breathing and sniffling broke through seconds later.

"Will you be here soon?" I asked.

"Yes," he answered, much calmer.

"Alright. Please feel free to relay this message to anyone else who feels the need to place blame where it doesn't belong."

"Okay, thank you..."

"Tiffany," I supplied.

"Oh, right," he replied. "Mama's mentioned you."

I only smiled.

"See you tomorrow."

"Have a safe trip," I stated, then hung up the phone.

Sitting it on the counter, I leaned over to catch my breath as tears clouded my eyes again. I hated to come across as a bitch, but Kingston was already hurting. I wouldn't dare let anyone compound on his grief.

I slid the phone into my sweatpants and finished fixing us a plate. It took two trips for the food and drinks. Kingston was still stretched out on the bed, staring at the ceiling. I retrieved some Tylenol from the bathroom medication cabinet, then offered it to him.

Without any words being spoken, he downed the pills, ate his food, then climbed under the covers.

Like he would me, I held Kingston and stroked his scruffy cheek. His eyes were puffy and his tears still flowed, breaking me into a million pieces. I kissed his closed eyes, letting him know that I was right here with him.

Before the sun rose, I left the bed and headed back out to the deck, bottle of bleach in hand. Fighting the urge to break down, I descended the stairs, bypassing the dried blood to get to the water hose. I poured bleach over the blood stains, then did my best to rinse away the remnants of an incident neither of us wanted to relive.

The next two weeks were a blur. Between keeping an eye on Kingston and fielding two families, I barely had time to think. My mom, Gianna, and Faith doted on me, making sure I took time to myself and reminding me that I that I had a baby boy to nurture. While I wanted to put myself to the side and see to Kingston, they stepped in and took watch while I'd rest.

As requested, Uncle Leon arrived like he had some sense. His sons were nice enough and stayed out of the way once they caught sight of Grey and Blu, who manned the house like it was theirs. I appreciated my brothers more than they knew.

Things had quieted down around the house once Kingston's family returned to North Carolina. Although they promised to do better at keeping in touch, Kingston didn't take it to heart. He knew them better than I did, so I didn't offer my two cents.

For the past few days, Kingston had kept himself secluded. He was going through every stage of grief and all I could do was be there to pick up the pieces whenever he crumbled. One night I woke up to him having a nightmare, one that involved his dad. It reminded me of something Uncle Leon had said about Nate and Nate's presence screwed up his family.

I had yet to pry into Kingston's nightmare, but he wore the signs of it in the way he dodged his father's phone calls. Whatever he had to do to gain some sense of peace, I'd support.

August and I hadn't been as close as Granny's death brought us. I looked after him, making sure he didn't fall between the cracks as he was grieving heavily, too. His friends came to see him from time to time trying to lift his spirits, but ultimately, he'd go back off in his own world, staying locked up in his room.

August confessed that he'd been upstairs at the time Granny fell. It was Rattler's barking that drew his attention and had him coming outside to investigate. He was full of remorse and guilt. However, Kingston didn't hold anything against him.

Faith confided that she wished she could be by his side but was compelled not to because of August's vulnerability. He'd take her support for something else, and at the stage of peace she was at, she couldn't have him ruining it. I didn't blame her for choosing self-preservation. Especially because their baby was due soon. She didn't need any more stress on her.

I stood at the deck, overlooking Granny's garden. Not being tended to in two weeks had it looking messy. Rattler's normal barking was gone as the neighbor's had erected another fence on their side, to keep him out of our yard. It was difficult watching the video of some of Granny's last moments. But I had to watch it for myself, Kingston, and August. Neither of them could muster the courage to view the grainy footage.

In the darkened night, I watched Granny amble over to the steps wondering why the flood lights didn't pick up her motions. Still, I was able to see Rattler running his goofy ass through the yard, with Granny hot on his heels.

Sighing, I pushed what happened next to the back of my mind. I wish I had been there. The wind picked up, surrounding me with February's cool air. I tucked my hair behind my ears and pulled my light cardigan shut. The motion had the sunlight bouncing off of my ring.

Granny's death superseded anything that came before and after it. Being without her was a devastating blow that would be felt many years to come. Swallowing the tears threatening to flow, I'd muster up the courage to clean up the garden another day. Today, I wasn't ready.

Chapter Thirty

AUGUST

"You're so handsome, baby boy," my mother beamed.

Smiling, I said, "I look like you, Mama."

She laughed. "The older you get, you're looking more like your dad."

I didn't understand why her voice faltered as if it bothered her that I looked like the man she loved.

"You were our blessing. After King, we struggled getting pregnant again. I guess God knew that King would need you, so He finally gave us you."

"King doesn't need me." I chuckled.

She tsked. "He's your brother, baby. He'll always need you."

"He'll hate me for this, Mama."

"King could never hate you."

"But Dad said—"

"What did I *say?" she interrupted. "One day you'll learn that*

your dad...isn't always right, baby. When that time comes, look around and see who's standing by your side."

I opened my eyes to the sound of my phone's alarm blaring. I had class in an hour, but I wouldn't make it today. Damn, before Granny passed, I'd been doing better at school, and was getting my act together.

One night, a few months ago, my mother visited me for the first time. At first I was scared as fuck, not knowing how to take the dream I'd had of her. She was so beautiful, more beautiful than I remembered.

She told me how proud of me she was, and that no matter what she'd always be by my side. Since then, I'd been putting in a lot of effort to continue to make her proud. I went to sleep every night, waiting for her to return. Some nights I'd be blessed with her sweet smile and glorious light, while other nights I was left bereft.

Either way, I'd been on the come up. My homeboys thought I was trippin' and these females really thought I'd lost my mind 'cause I wasn't fucking with them either. I'd even been trying to pry myself out of some shit that I had no business involving myself in.

Weak, I couldn't do anything except crawl out of the bed to make it to the toilet. After emptying my stomach, I brushed my teeth and washed my face. Staring at myself in the mirror, I barely recognized myself. On my body were the same clothes I'd worn three days straight. Even as I dried my face, tears came.

Pain shot through me. causing my knees to buckle. Hanging on to the counter, I used it for support as I cried. My fucking granny was gone. It's been three weeks since we buried her, and I still wasn't able to grasp the fact that she was no longer with me—the woman that loved me in spite of my bullshit. The woman who wouldn't turn her back on me for shit. She was gone.

Now I understood the pain Kingston felt when our mother died. Back then, I was too young to understand the finality of death. I wasn't capable of understanding that death meant I couldn't hug my mother anymore, that I wouldn't ever see her smile again, that I'd never get to tell her how much I loved her. Tears for both my mother and my granny fell heavy, ripping my soul in two.

My ringing cell phone drew me out of the bathroom. Stumbling back to the bed, I fell onto it and reached for the phone. Gathering myself, I answered on the third ring. The automated voice informed me that I had a collect call from my dad, which I accepted.

"Son," he stated by way of speaking. "You still comin' this weekend?"

"Yeah, I'ma make it," I answered, but was a little put off that he wanted me to come to Georgia while I was grieving Granny.

"Why it sounds like you been cryin', boy?" he questioned.

"Dad." I sighed, not giving a fuck about hearing any bullshit. Too much was already on my shoulders than to have to deal with him.

"Son, ain't nothin' you can do about the dead. Ya granny lived a long, good life. Be happy she made it to her age from how fucked up this world is."

My dad's half-assed attempt at uplifting me did the opposite. Shit didn't even sound genuine or compassionate.

"Look, don't tell me how to grieve the woman that raised me, aight? Where the fuck were you?"

Silence met me on the other end. I'd never spoken to my dad this way. In my eyes, he could do no wrong. But speaking on my granny was gon' get him a quick way to get the fuck out of my life.

"How you gon' say that to me?" My dad's tone was full of rebuke. "She never even liked my muhfuckin' ass. You'd come at me sideways over a woman that couldn't stand the ground I walked on."

War commenced within me. On the one hand, I loved my dad, despite of him being in prison. On the other hand, my granny was exceptional.

"You're not gon' sit on this phone and make me question my loyalty to you. You know what it is."

Hanging up the phone, I barely sat it down before it rang again. It would keep ringing, too. I loved Nate, but this wasn't the time to fucking try me. I'd done everything to prove my loyalty to him only for him to try and question my shit. At this point, I wasn't sure if Nate even knew the meaning of loyalty.

As if they never stopped, the tears started again. On my soul I wanted to be with my granny and would do anything to switch places with her. The nine sitting on my nightstand called to me, willing me to pick it up and end the pain I was going through and the guilt eating at me. For several days I'd been contemplating this very thing. Taking my life would make me weak in my dad's eyes. Yet, I had no strength to fight.

Reaching for the gun, when I slid it off the nightstand, a picture sitting underneath it sailed to the floor. Blinking at the picture, I picked it up to study the image on it. The distorted image was that of my unborn son. Faith crossed my mind. Kingston had given this picture to me a while ago. I'd never reached out to Faith, and she never tried to reach out to me.

In an instant it occurred to me that, had I kept shit right with Faith, she'd be the one consoling me, helping me get through this grief, just like Tiffany was doing for Kingston. Tiffany was a gem. Remembering how she sat next to me at the funeral, rubbing my back through the anguish I was feeling sent me standing to my feet.

Faith had been at my granny's funeral. Although she was in the company of Jericho, the fact that Faith came to pay her respects to Granny was proof enough that she was a good ass woman. One that I let get away because of my foolishness. Vaguely, I remember Jericho having his arm around Faith's shoulder. Still, that didn't deter me from going into the bathroom to shower and get myself together.

I had to make shit right with Faith. Kingston wasn't weak by a long shot, but he needed his woman and allowed Tiffany to help him through his grief.

I needed Faith. She'd be able to talk me off of this cliff that I dangled from.

"Can I come in?"

Faith peeked at me through the slit in the door, regarding me with skepticism.

"I just need to talk," I explained.

Mulling it over, she finally stepped back to open the door. Seeing her protruding belly brought an unmistakable softness to my heart. It looked like she was about to drop the baby any minute.

"Wooow!" I drawled.

She hid a smile, then placed her hand on her belly.

"He's gonna be big." She smiled.

We both fell quiet. She avoided my gaze while I kicked myself for fucking her over. Faith had that timeless beauty, and her spirit was even more beautiful. I couldn't see that shit because of my own selfishness. I felt like even greater shit when I remembered telling her to get an abortion. Standing before her, seeing her growing our child, there was nothing better than this moment. It's exactly what I needed after the season I'd just went through.

"I apologize, Faith. For everything."

Tears welled up in her eyes, which she quickly blinked away. She cleared her throat and shrugged.

"Thank you, but it's not needed. I've moved on from the past."

Shit, I hated how cold she was towards me. Faith came from a rough background, so I wasn't surprised that she could turn her feelings on and off. She'd been hanging with Tiffany a lot, and for some reason, I thought she'd opened up some. Not giving a fuck about a person was easy for her. Yet, she'd given a fuck about me at some point. So much so that she allowed me to put a baby in her.

"Can I get a hug?" I asked, stepping towards her. She quickly took a step back. "Wow, okay." I chuckled.

"You said you needed to talk. Is everything okay?" she asked, moving back towards the door. She didn't even let me leave the foyer.

"We can't sit down?"

She shook her head and peered at the tiled floor before glancing back at me.

"You and that nigga together?" Leaving her by the door, I walked into the living room anyway.

"Who, August? And anyway, I'm not your business."

Even if she didn't answer me, my answer hang big as day on the wall above the couch. Three of them to be exact.

"So, is the baby mine or his? You takin' pictures with this nigga like that's his fuckin' child you're carryin'." My initial reason for coming over here was shot to hell as I felt anger rising in me. First my pops was on bullshit, and now Faith was playing in my damn face.

"You know this is your baby, August." She hadn't moved from by the front door, and judging by her standoffish demeanor, she was ready for me to leave.

"If that's my fuckin' baby, why the hell he got his hands on ya stomach, rubbin' on my fuckin' baby like it's his?" I approached her, incensed that she would allow another man to disrespect me in such a way.

"A baby boy that you didn't want, August," she reminded me. Not an ounce of anger was in her voice.

Glaring at her, I stepped in her face.

"Back up," she warned, trying to move around me, but I blocked her.

"You just like all the rest of these bitches. First my mama, then my granny, and now you. All you muhfuckas good for is leavin' a nigga when he need you most."

"August." Eyeing me fearfully, she backed up even more until her back hit the wall. "You need to calm down."

"Shut the fuck up!" My voice thundered through her apartment. She jumped and whimpered, shielding her stomach with one hand and her face with the other.

"Now you think I'ma put my fuckin' hands on you?" I chuckled. "Yeen shit, Faith. I see why ya parents ain't fuck witchu."

"Get out!" she screamed.

I sent my fist through the wall, not an inch from her head, causing her to cry out in fear. As she slid to the floor, I stormed out of her apartment. Coming here hadn't been a good idea, even if my intentions were good. Suicidal thoughts had already been plaguing me. Homicidal thoughts joined them.

Hours later, I was cruising the city trying to rid myself of some of this anger when I received a message.

BAKE:

We're at the spot. Come through.

Groaning, I almost said fuck it to this text. How I let myself get caught up in some shit that had absolutely nothing to do with me pissed me the fuck off.

ME:

On my way.

BAKE:

Bet.

The spot was my daddy's old stomping grounds. Bake was a nigga that used to work for my pops back in the day. You see, all that time I'd been going to Georgia, is was for me to meet and get to know Bake, as my dad had requested of me.

According to Nate, Bake would teach me the game, so I could pick up right where my dad left off. King would flip if he knew what I was outchea doing, which is why I'd been doing my dirt in Georgia and laying low, but after my mom had been visiting me, my heart had changed. I no longer wanted the lifestyle that my dad lived. I no longer wanted anything except to be a better man. Which is why I'd been slowly pulling away from Bake and his crew. A part of me knew that he was on to me though, and feeling how I felt, I didn't give a fuck. If Bake and his crew wanted smoke with me, at this point they could have it. 'Cause I was ready to be up out this bitch anyway.

Fifteen minutes later, I pulled into the parking lot of a five-star restaurant where my pops used to stash his drugs. The owner was an old, Black dude who kept his mouth and allowed any type of shit to go on in his restaurant. He had friends in high places, which kept his restaurant off the map. Not even Kingston and his team suspected anything was going on at this place.

Bake and three of his crew were standing in the back parking lot, chiefin', waiting on me to get out the car. But as I put my car in park, a car rolled up beside me.

Chuckling, I wondered what Jericho was doing here until I remembered I'd been by Faith's place. Of course, she'd called him.

Jericho was Atlanta royalty so I wasn't surprised that he knew Bake and his crew. It was the fact that these niggas were on some setup type shit that had me climbing back into my car for my heat. I wasn't quick enough though. Jericho snatched my ass out the front seat like I wasn't seeing him in weight class.

"I told you to stay the fuck away from her!" He rocked my ass so damn hard, I stumbled back and hit the ground. My eye instantly swelled, blurring my vision. Scrambling to my car door, I dove into the front seat like it was a gang of niggas after me and snatched the heat from under my seat.

Turning, I aimed wherever I could and let that bitch fire. If I was going out today, I wasn't going out like no bitch.

Chapter Thirty-One

KINGSTON

Pure love. Deep love. True love.

I stared at her from my spot on the deck, memorizing her every move and every nuance her face made under the bright sun. As she fussed over my granny's tomatoes, I smiled at her perplexed expression. She'd spent countless hours out here with Granny, however, she'd still been learning her way around some of the vegetables. This was her first day venturing out to clean things up, and because I knew it would be tough for her, I sat on the deck keeping vigil.

Tiffany was my rock. On everything this woman had shown me a different type of love, one that I was afraid of ever losing. Last night I'd made love to her, needing her to understand that no matter what I was going through, she was my everything and the one person that I needed by my side. The amount of patience, care, and attention she'd shown me over this entire ordeal with losing Granny had me looking at her in a different light.

Sure I was in love with Tiffany. The bond we'd built in the last few weeks was even stronger, more solid than any time previous. Experiencing loss was one of the greatest tests a relationship could face. Grief wasn't something a significant other could magically make disappear with a kiss, hug, or an I love you. There was nothing that person could do to make the pain of losing someone go away. All they could do was patiently be by your side, wipe your tears, and pray that one day, you'd recover enough to be yourself again.

Losing my granny hurt like a muhfucka. However, having a woman like Tiffany beside me, made me have a reason to keep pushing and healing.

"Princess!" I called. She glanced up and smiled at me.

"I love you," I said.

Getting up from her position, she practically skipped her way to me, removing her gloves in the process. I didn't care that she had dirt all over her sweats. When she crawled into my lap, I let her snuggle me. I wrapped my arms around her and buried my nose in her neck, just as she did me.

For a minute we stayed this way, enjoying the simple, yet profound gesture of a hug. She kissed my neck, then my lips.

"I love you, King," she said.

"When is our weddin' day?" I asked, surprising her. "I'd rather it be sooner than later."

"Are you sure?" she whispered.

The day I proposed to her would forever be remembered as the day we lost Granny, but with our wedding, we'd make it our day and every day after.

"Very, sweetheart. So, when you gon' let me make you Mrs. Wells?"

Shyly, she smiled. "I'll ask Gianna how soon she can have me a dress ready."

"And I'll pay her whatever it costs."

Something else was on her mind, I could tell by how she quickly glanced away before sighing.

"What is it?" I asked.

"I've been thinking about what I want to do."

We'd discussed her plans of not returning to school to pursue her law degree. I was cool with it because I wanted whatever she wanted. As long as she was happy, I was happy. Bringing up the incident with Chris had me ready to bail that nigga outta jail so I could put a bullet in him. Granny was gone now so our agreement was null and void.

"Whatcha got for me?" I prompted when she hesitated. Smoothing a few stray curls from her forehead, I marveled at my beautiful woman. I didn't care if she wanted to tend to Granny's garden for the rest of her life, I was content with that.

"I used to work with Gianna before school got too hectic. I'd help her around the boutique. I'm not a seamstress or anything, but I love fashion, and I love being at her boutique when I'm not with you." She laughed then. "Which means I haven't been there much in months."

"I'ain apologizin' either," I joked. "I told you from the gate how I was comin', nie you ready to get rid of me."

She smacked her teeth. "I am not," she denied. "It's just... with me not working, and no longer tutoring, sitting in the house all day is..."

"Sapphire," I interrupted.

She balled her face up. "I'm starting to hate I told you that's my first name. You only get to call me that when—"

"I'm fuckin' ya brains out?" I finished.

Her cheeks reddened and her hazel eyes bugged.

"I was gon' say when you make love to me," she said with a roll of her neck.

Chuckling, I said, "Oops, my fault, baby. I do be fuckin' ya brains out though," I reiterated.

She busted out laughing this time. "Stop! I'm tryna be serious."

"Me too, shit," I countered. "Tell me I can't call you Sapphire less I'm knee deep, the fuck."

She laughed harder, making me join her.

"I miss that," I told her. I ran my fingers across her lips and watched her blush.

"Miss what?" she questioned.

"Ya laughter. I miss that shit more than you know, baby girl. It soothes my soul. We've been through a lot and I wish I could say we won't ever see rainy days. Regardless, don't ever forget that I love you, I'm in love with you, I adore you, I cherish you, and most of all I need you. I'll never stop protecting you, nor protecting what we have. Our children will know the value of loyalty and family, 'cause we will teach them that by example."

She sniffled and placed her hand on my jaw. "Thank you for loving me, King. I'm honored to be spending the rest of my life with a man that isn't afraid to love me deeply and openly. Whatever you feel, I feel. And I believe it's because we were created for each other. I'll never think otherwise. Until the death of me, I'll be in love with you."

"We got each other forever?"

"Forever," she confirmed.

“Bet. Now if my lady wants to go work with my sis-in-law, I’m cool with it.”

I was rewarded with a big white smile.

“If in the future you change ya mind, ain’t nothin’ to it for us to make some shit happen. I’m literally here to support you on whatever.”

She stared into my eyes and sweetly pecked my lips once more.

“Nie get ya ass up off my mans ‘cause in a second I’ma have you bent over this table.”

Her laughter continued until she was back in the garden, cleaning up the tomatoes.

Ten minutes later, I was responding to a message from my Uncle Leon when Tiffany uttered my name. The way she said it had me quickly glancing her way, to see what was wrong. She held bags in her hand, confusion lining her face.

“The fuck?” I bounded down the stairs and over to her where she sat in the same spot as ten minutes ago.

“I was pulling up the old vines, so that I can plant new ones,” she explained.

There was a gaping hole behind the tomato bed. Tiffany held two Ziploc bags full of money, while the hole was filled with other shit that I right off knew were packed drugs.

“The fuck!”

Screeching tires snapped my attention to the house. If this shit was August’s, I was about to beat his muthafuckin’ ass! Grabbing the bags from Tiffany, I didn’t make it two steps before August was in the backyard, eyes wide as he saw what was in my hands. He was bloody and had his gun tucked in his right hand. Forgetting that I was mad, I threw the money down and made my way towards him.

"What happened to you!" I demanded to know. A nigga put his hands on my brotha? I was going back to jail today!

My thoughts skid to a stop when August lifted his gun, pointing it at me.

"August—"

"The fuck you doin' in my shit!" he barked.

I peeked over my shoulder when I heard Tiffany gasp. The fear in her eyes had me backtracking and standing in front of her to shield her from him. August's face was set in a deep frown as he moved towards us.

"August, calm down," I ordered.

"No! I fucked up, mane!"

His eyes flittered to the stairs, where bleached spots now existed rather than Granny's blood.

"Whatchu mean?" My heart stalled.

"Why the fuck she had to die, mane?" His voice broke as he cried, but he didn't lower his gun.

August had already explained that he didn't hear Granny calling for him the night he died. I couldn't fault him for that. However, he was carrying a greater weight, one that had him reckless right now.

"Tell me," I urged.

He shook his head. "I can't, bruh."

"August—"

"Why y'all in my shit!" he demanded to know again as he took more steps towards us. I had my heat at my back because I always kept it on me, even in my house. I wasn't about to draw my weapon on my brother though.

"August, listen!" I snapped. "Tell me what the fuck is goin' on, aight? Let me fuckin' help you!" I eased back some more until I fully shielded Tiffany, who was stunned into silence.

"You can't help me! Dad was right about yo' ass, bruh! That's the fuckin' problem I got witcho ass! You willin' to lose everything over her and not ya own fuckin' family!"

"The fuck are you talkin' about? I'd do anything for you!" I countered, angry that he thought otherwise.

"Not me! Dad!"

Eyebrows snapping together, I questioned, "What? This is about dad?"

August sneered. "You'on deserve to call him that shit! You let him rot in a fuckin' cell and don't even give a damn!"

"I'ain lettin' him do shit!" I railed. "He made his fuckin' decision long before we were adults, August!"

He chuckled. "He said you'd eventually turn on him. But to hear you say it..."

"August," I reasoned, "listen to yaself!" Whatever he's told you is fuckin' bullshit!"

More tires screeching sent August running towards the deck and had me reaching for my gun. As car doors slammed, I quickly swooped Tiffany up and tucked her by the deck. We ducked down as footsteps bounded against the ground.

"Kill his muthafuckin' ass!" one of the niggas ordered.

"I'm sorry, bruh," August whispered.

"How many of 'em?" I asked, ignoring his apology as Tiffany whimpered. I shooshed her with a kiss.

"Two," August informed me. "I shot... Fuck I shot one of 'em!" His voice carried, bringing one of the niggas around the deck. He never had a chance to fire his gun as I sent one into his chest.

"Ahh!" Tiffany screamed as bullets bounced off the deck.

"Shit!" August exclaimed as a bullet ripped into his shoulder.

All-consuming anger pierced my soul. I started shooting back in the direction the other nigga was shooting from, not giving a fuck how many times I hit his ass.

When the shots ceased, I hurried and ushered Tiffany and August into the house.

"Stay right here," I commanded.

I heard Tiffany call my name, but I was already back out of the door. Snatching my phone from the table, I dialed for paramedics. Sirens blared in the distance, and I knew the police were already on the way here. We'd just turned our quiet neighborhood into a war zone. I checked both niggas, who were still breathing but clinging to life. The need to protect my brother had me rushing to his stash. I couldn't let the police find this shit. Fuck that I was DEA! My loyalty lie with my brother over anything!

"Here," Tiffany's sweet ass voice said. She appeared next to me with a trash bag already opened.

Without question, I hurriedly threw all the shit in there, then took the bag from her. She quickly covered the hole and concealed it with tomatoes. It was like nothing was ever discovered here. The sirens drew closer, prompting me to shuffle her back into the house.

Taking the stairs two at a time, I busted into my room and into the bathroom where my safe was located behind a hidden wall. I threw the bag in there then shut it back. Next, I erased all the footage from the surveillance system for as far back as it would let me. I wasn't sure how long August had been involved in this shit, but I be damned if I let him go down. Especially since I had a feeling that the real culprit behind this was the man that spawned us.

The two niggas in my yard, fighting for their lives...I knew. They were connected to Bake, a muhfucka that used to run with my pops. They were older now, but black don't crack and them niggas looked the same now as they did back then. I was willing to protect my brother, willing to lose everything for him. As far as what he had to do with my granny's death… I prayed to God I'd be able to handle it.

I never was the type to need a nigga to dead some shit for me. I'd been on the right side of the law my entire career. Not only had my loyalty to my family been tested but so had my honor and dignity to self. I never wanted to do the things I'd had to do today. But… At the end of the day, I couldn't turn my back on August. Those phone calls I said I could make and have shit disappear—I made them for my brother.

DALLAS:

Everything's handled.

It's good having niggas on your team who had just as much love and loyalty for family as you did. Dallas was my dawg, and I'd be forever indebted to him. That was the thing though. Dallas wasn't the type to make niggas repay a debt—not in this sense at least. If he fucked with you, he fucked with you no matter what.

ME:

Bet. Good lookin' out.

"You just gon' sit there?" August drawled.

I'd been sitting by his bedside for thirty minutes now. He'd woken up from surgery an hour ago and was still a little groggy.

The bullet he took tore through his arm and shoulder, requiring extensive surgery to fix the damage. His ass was lucky he'd be able to use that arm again with the right amount of therapy.

As for his swollen eye and the reason August showed up bloody in the first place, I couldn't even blame Jericho for beating his ass. I lit into August for five straight minutes about the amount of disrespect he'd caused Faith. Then the fact that he didn't even shoot Jericho, but shot Bake, who survived, but was not going to let this situation die. His homeboys who stormed my fuckin' yard were lucky too. Well, lucky to be alive. One of them was paralyzed from the waist down, while the other had to wear a shit bag for the rest of his life.

I'd been so heated with August that I almost kept myself from reaching out to Dallas. How was he going to learn from his mistakes if I'd just rescued him from every damn thing that he did? At the same time, he was my little brother, and I hated to see him caught up in this bullshit.

"I'ma sit here 'til you tell me what you meant about Granny," I answered. I wasn't letting it go. I allowed for no excuses even if I did rescue his ass. If he could be a man for one second and own up to his shit, then I would feel better about coming through for him. If he sat here and made excuses... I'd have to wear the price I'd paid for reaching out to Dallas.

"I've been under anesthesia, King," he uttered.

"I'on give a fuck. I'ain put you here and neither did Granny. The only person at fault is the one layin' in this fuckin' bed."

August gulped, then sighed as tears slid down his temples. I leaned forward and rested my elbows on my knees, preparing myself for whatever he had to say.

"I forgot to turn the fuckin' lights back on," he started. "That night I'd been in the yard... I always remember to switch the lights back on but I forgot. She wouldn't have fallen if..." His voice hitched as I fought the urge to get up and strangle him. "By the time I went to see why she'd called me, I was too late."

I dropped my head, disappointment raging through me.

"I'on know how I'ma live with myself," he said. Anguish filled his statement. He was already suffering from his mistakes. Me going in on him wouldn't change anything. August sounded hopeless and helpless, and the last thing I wanted to do was push him over the edge.

"I'on know either, August," I replied. Biting back the pain I felt, I said, "But you can start by gettin' ya muthafuckin' act together. We'll never know if things would've been different that night had the lights been on. Yes, you fucked up. But it's time for you to man the fuck up and get ya shit together."

He nodded. We were interrupted by a nurse who came in to check August's vitals and administer him so more medication. When she left, I regarded my brother and how I'd almost lost him.

"As angry as I am, you're my brother, and I love you. I've always told you that, and I'll never go against that. What you need to do is start realizing who has ya back and who doesn't. Arguments and disagreements should never come between blood. Even if I don't agree with everything you do, my job as ya big brotha is to protect you. But there's only so much I can do to save you, August. You gotta want to save yaself."

He reached over to me, and we shook hands; this code only we knew. I taught him this when he was twelve. We hadn't done it in a while, but neither of us had forgotten.

"I can't believe Dad got into my head the way he did," August groaned. "I didn't want to disappoint him..." His sentence trailed off as he started dozing in and out.

I stood, then leaned over and kissed my brother's forehead, before leaving his room. In the waiting room, Tiffany sat curled under a blanket, with her eyes closed. My baby was tired and although I had Grey come pick her up, she refused to leave.

Scooping her up, I sat down, then placed her in my lap.

"How is he?" she asked.

"He's gon' be aight," I replied.

"And you?"

I kissed her temple, and said, "I got you. I'm good."

Two days later...

"King!"

This was as much personality as I'd seen my father have since he was attacked.

"Mama's been warning me about you for years," I said by way of greeting. Every time my mother came to me in a dream, she'd always drop some type of seed about the man she'd loved. Looking back, she had been subtly showing me that Nate wasn't who I thought he was.

My dad's smile swiftly disappeared.

"She's been talkin' to me, reminding me of the man you really are."

He briefly glanced away and chuckled in shame.

"Just like great minds think alike, small minds think alike too. Ya problem is, Mama always thought big, while her nigga was always thinking small. She gave you a fucking family, made sure we were everything to you. She was everything for you, and you turned ya back on her for the streets. The same streets that put you where you at. The same niggas that went outchea and built something off of your suffering. But that ain't please you enough, nor did it teach you shit. You're so selfish that you were willing to bring ya own son down."

The smirk on my dad's face crushed me. This nigga really was a piece of shit.

"You turned ya back on us the day you put on a uniform. I don't know you, and I told August the same thing. He was reluctant to turn on you." He chuckled. "He thought ya ass was perfect. I changed his mind though. You know nothing about sacrifice and what it means to do what you have to, to give your family the life they deserve."

"Fuck you!" I sneered. "It was never about us! Everything you did was for you! My mother deserved to still be breathing! Your sons deserved to go through life with a father that actually cared about them!"

He laughed. "Whew, Son, if you ain't yo' mama. That's why you never gravitated to me like you did her. Sometimes I wonder if you're mine. No son of mine would dare talk that sappy shit in my face. That lil' woman you got has you soft as hell. Yet, you'll do for her what you're not even willin' to do for me."

"You know why, Pops? 'Cause she understands loyalty. My shawty loves the ground I walk on. However, when it came down to it, when it came between me and her brother, whose side you think she chose?" I wasn't really looking for an answer. Often, I thought about the day I kicked Tiffany's door in, dissecting the situation bit by bit until a revelation dawned on me.

"Was I heated? Hell yeah. But I had to suck that shit up, 'cause I realized she did what was right. In her mind, I was the enemy. In her eyes, I'd fucked up. But when the dust settled, and

I put that ring on her finger, not only did I get my woman back, but the same way she's willin' to ride for her blood, is the same way she's willin' to ride for me. So, yeah I'ma hold my shawty down. I'ma go to war for her. I'll lose everything for her. The type of woman she is, whatever I lose, she gon' add it back to me ten-fold. 'Cause that's how much she loves me. That's the type of love you had from Mama. She would've done anything for you. Only you wasn't willin' to do the same for her."

Nate sat on the other side of the glass glaring at me like he wanted to kill me, then he busted out laughing.

"I wonder what prison they'll send August to. This'll be his first time in the system, so I'm sure I'll need to have someone protectin' him."

Chuckling, I winked at my dad. "My brotha ain't goin' to jail, let alone prison, Pops. And he got me to protect him. As long as I have breath, ain't a soul gon' fuck with him. Not even you."

Nate growled and punched the partition between us, prompting the guards to come and detain him. Laughing, I stood, chucked him the deuces, and waited for the guard to let me out. As much as it hurt, I walked away from my pops without looking back.

Epilogue

TIFFANY

"I know damn well this man is not callin' me again." Grumbling, I answered Kingston's call. "Yes, boo?"

"What time you comin' home? I'm lonely as fuck," he responded.

"Babe, it's barely noon. Nobody told you to take a vacation in the middle of graduation time. Gianna and I are swamped, and you callin' me every ten minutes is putting us even more behind."

Gianna snickered and shook her head. She'd been here before with Grey, so she understood what the hell I was going through.

"Lemme come by and rub on ya stomach and that cat, then I'll leave you alone," he bartered.

I busted out laughing so hard, I felt a hitch in my side.

"King, stop! Ya son just kicked the hell outta me for laughing too hard."

"Nah, he kicked you 'cause he's on my side."

Smacking my teeth, I questioned, "And how the hell are you lonely if Grey's there? What happened to y'all putting together my garden benches?"

It has been almost three months since the ordeal with August. Kingston and I were closer than womb mates, which is why he was on my line now. The night of our engagement, he'd had a surprise for me that was lost in the shuffle of losing Granny.

Shortly after getting everything situated with August, he took me out into the country, where he showed me the house he'd purchased us. It was beautiful, one that looked just like the one we'd been living in, only this one had a yard big enough for a garden and for our children to play in.

We'd been living there since that time. There was no point in living in a house where pain met us at every turn. Healing required letting go sometimes, and even though Kingston loved the house that held so many good memories of Granny, it was time for us to move on.

I did what I could to preserve Granny's garden by bringing most of her plants to the new house and planting them in our new garden. If you asked me, it was coming along great. Granny had taught me a lot, and in her honor, I would continue to grow and love on plants just as she did.

Kingston and Grey were practically joined at the hip now. They still bickered like they hated each other, but truth is, I knew they had their own brother-in-law love. They were currently supposed to be putting my benches together.

"Princess, the benches were put together in five minutes.

Grey's on the couch snoring his fuckin' ass off, talmbout he ain't sleep last night," Kingston complained.

Dying laughing, I wouldn't tell him why Grey hadn't slept last night. My brother spent half the night on the couch because he called himself asking Gianna to help him cook after she'd been on her feet all day preparing graduation dresses.

By the time he begged her to let him come to bed, it was nearing morning.

"Well, you and Grey need to get some business and leave us be. I'll be home as soon as I can."

He growled, but said, "I love you."

"I love you, too, baby. Now get off the phone!" I hung up, laughing because Gianna was laughing.

"All for a man that you claimed was *difficult to look at,*" she jeered.

Smiling, I thought about that day. I thought about how fine Kingston looked perched atop his Charger, watching me walk towards him. I thought about how he went out of his way to make me laugh, how he loved on me, and how everyday he managed to steal my heart all over again.

I thought about how my man helped me through arguably the scariest time in my life. He'd been there to pick me up and not only nurture me back to wholeness but love me the process. Not that I ever thought of Chris anymore, I felt vindicated that he would be spending a hefty amount of time in prison for the crimes he'd committed against several women, including his former assistants. I shook my head at the bullet I'd dodged. Anissa, on the other hand, was never going to see the light of day. Such a beautiful woman, with such a filthy soul made me no longer look at my own kind the same. If I thought I didn't have female friends before, if you weren't my family, or Faith who I considered my family, then I wasn't letting yo' ass in. Women these days were straight up crazy.

Speaking of crazy... The door chimed, signaling someone coming inside of the boutique. In walked Vicki and two other women. I heard through the grapevine that her ass was getting married.

She took one look at me and turned her nose up at my protruding belly.

"Can I help you?" Gianna asked the women.

"I'm looking to have a dress made," Vicki said but didn't take her eyes off of me.

"Okay. Is there anything in particular you're looking for?" Gianna asked.

Vicki couldn't answer because she was too busy staring at the rock on my finger and the necklace nestled around my neck.

"I'm sorry, is there a problem?" Gianna asked Vicki.

I smiled. "She's tryna figure out how I was able to get a man like Kingston to fall in love with me," I quipped.

Vicki's eyes narrowed, and the two women with her sneered.

"Bitch, nobody is concerned about you nor Kingston."

"Keep my man's name outcha mouth," I retorted. She could call me whatever she wanted, but she could back up off of my king.

"Bitch?" Gianna shrieked. Her voice garnered the attention of Patrice, who came from the back with her eyebrows raised in concern.

"I didn't stutter," Vicki boldly said.

I chuckled. "You gon' be stutterin' if you'on get yo' ass outta here fuckin' with me. Don't let me being pregnant fool yo' ass."

Vicki thought it was smart to step in my face, prompting me

to smack the dog shit out of her. She gasped and held her cheek in shock as Gianna and Patrice hurried to get in between us.

"You ratchet hoe!" Vicki exclaimed.

I busted out laughing. "Chile, bye!" I waved as they were led out of the boutique.

Gianna walked up to me with her hands on her hips. "Now why did you do that?"

"Girl you know how long I've been waiting to two-piece that bitch? She better be glad all I could do is slap her ass." Shit! I wanted to dog walk her through the showroom.

Patrice died laughing while Gianna glared at me.

Shrugging, I turned back to the dress I was working on and put my mind back on my man.

I couldn't help it. I had to.

"You on ya way?" he answered on the first ring.

"No." I sighed. "I love you, King," I said.

The phone clicked in my ear, then a FaceTime came through.

Smiling, I picked up. My man's beautiful eyes stared back at me.

"I love ya beautiful ass," he replied, stretching my smile even more. "I was hopin' you was gon' two-piece her ass though," he quipped.

Gianna, Patrice, and I died laughing. Figures he and Grey were watching the damn cameras.

KINGSTON

I heard that slap all the way across town. It was funny how karma came back to bite Vicki. She tried to come in between me and my woman, and ultimately, didn't succeed. If anyone ever tried coming between me and Tiffany, I wouldn't be so nice this time. Vicki got off clean and really, I should've hit Dallas up to hide her ass. She'd almost fucked up my life.

Shaking the negativity from my mind, I focused on better things. Like the fact that I had the sexiest, smartest, baddest woman that I laid next to every night. She and I never failed to watch sunsets together. I never ceased making her laugh. I swear her hazel eyes still had the ability to weaken my knees. Damn…I just loved the fuck out of my woman.

"I swear ya sister is hard-headed as fuck," I complained.

Grey chuckled. "Ain't like you gon' do shit about it."

Grumbling, I shot him the bird.

"Hey, now!" Mrs. Valentina fussed. "Y'all behave."

"I try to be a gentleman, Mama, but ya son stay tryna test my kindness of heart," I said in my defense.

The living room rumbled with laughter. I peered around the room at all of Tiffany's family, smiling. This is what family is supposed to be like, coming together, being at peace with each other, even if it involved some level of pettiness. It was all love in this room.

My gaze caught August's attention, as he stared across the room at Faith, who held their baby boy in her arms. The look of longing in his eyes wasn't so bad to see. At least I knew my brother really did have a heart. He'd been doing better, and with counseling, I prayed he someday would forgive himself for the shit he'd caused. I'd forgiven him because who was I to condemn him?

I still stood on my decision to rescue him and give him a second chance at what the system wouldn't have given him. Dallas tidied everything up so nicely that neither Bake nor his camp thought about pressing charges, nor coming for my brother. August, in essence, really did have a second chance at doing better for himself.

August moved Faith's way, the play of emotions on her face went from skepticism to acceptance as he sat beside her. When he reached for June, Faith allowed him to take him. That was their moment, so I minded my business.

Leaving them to it, I focused on the picture hanging above the fireplace. Granny and my mother beamed down at the small gathering. I continued to hope that everything I did made them proud. The hole left in my heart from Granny's death was slowly healing.

Tiffany was still just as patient with me as ever. My baby hadn't switched up shit. Although she was working with Gianna now, I still came home to her having my bath ready and possibly dinner. If I got off before her, I did the same thing. We were each other's backbone, and one couldn't move without the other. I loved my shawty to death and made sure she knew it every minute of every day.

Two hours later, Tiffany informed me that she was on her way home. Everyone scrambled to get in place after getting complacent from waiting. Thirty minutes later, an exhausted Tiffany came through the front door with a confused look on her face.

"Why're all those cars outside?" She glanced around, looking for the owners of said rental vehicles. "And whatchu got that tux on for?"

Gianna came in the door behind her, further confusing her. Across Gianna's arm was a garment bag holding Tiffany's wedding dress.

I walked up to Tiffany and smiled down at the expression on her face.

"Can you please go put that dress on, so I can make you Mrs. Wells?"

With her mouth open, she let Gianna lead her upstairs to get ready.

In the backyard, amongst the beautiful garden my shawty had erected, I watched her cry tears of joy as her father waltzed her towards me. Her protruding belly brought tears to my eyes, as did her gorgeous face. Tiffany was the love of my life.

Just when I thought I'd lost everything there was to live for, Tiffany gave it back—ten-fold. In this moment, I was sure that my granny and my mama were both proud of me.

THE END

Catalog

A Thug Has Feelings Too
A Baller Has Feelings Too
A Hitta Has Feelings Too, Part 1&2
Heart of A Champion Soul of a Boss
The Illest: A Gangsta's Holiday Love
Anything Necessary for Her
Falling For His Savage Ways
Painlessly In Love
Healing A Gangsta's Heart
Friend U Can Keep
Whisper A Promise
Uncovering Love
Blu
A Goon For Christmas
Kingston
Sneakin' and Freakin' With My Professor
Shot Clock: Love Is A Beautiful Game 1-3

'Tis the Season For Passion

The Body Hunter

Steele Waters

A Widow's Scars

Kidnapped By The Snowman

Summers: A Holiday Novella

Steele Waters: The Finale

The Hood Flower Girl

The Unhinged Best Man

Follow Me On Social Media!

FB: M Monique TheAuthor
IG: m. monique_theauthor
TikTok: mmoniquetheauthor

Made in the USA
Columbia, SC
16 June 2025